THE SWEETEST WORDS

First edition. February 1, 2022.

Written by Laura Ann.

DEDICATION

Every first book is dedicated to my husband.
Without your support, I would never had put
pen to paper. Here's to eternity.

ACKNOWLEDGEMENTS

No author works alone. Thank you, Tami.
You make it Christmas every time
I get a new cover. And thank you to my Beta Team.
Truly, your help with my stories is immeasurable.

NEWSLETTER

You can get a FREE book by joining my Reading Family!
Every week we share stories, sales and good old fun.
Go to lauraannbooks.com to sign up!

PROLOGUE

Aspen Harrison wiped her brow with the back of her hand. Her hand was shaking, and she clenched it into a fist. "Okay," she breathed, observing the cake set up. "I think that does it."

Estelle, her older sister, wrapped an arm around Aspen's shoulders. "You're amazing," she cooed. "Mom and Dad are going to be so proud." Letting go of Aspen, Estelle pulled her phone out of her back pocket. "In fact, I need to get a bunch of pictures so we can show them to our customers." She began to click away, then paused and looked back to Aspen. "And so we can put them up as products of the new owner of the Harrison Bakery."

"You mean The Three Sisters Cafe," Aspen corrected. As happened every time she said the new name of the business she and her sisters were inheriting from their parents, Aspen's mouth moved into a wide smile.

Her parents, Antony and Emory Harrison, had been running a bakery in Seagull Cove, Oregon for almost thirty years. In fact, it was on the thirtieth anniversary of the shop that they were planning to hand the reins over to Aspen, Estelle and their younger sister Maeve. The only child not involved was their brother, who was currently away on a military tour.

The sisters had decided that in order to truly get a fresh start out from under the shadow of their well-loved parents, they wanted to rename and revamp the whole shop. It would still be a bakery, but they wanted it to be just a little bit more.

Maeve, who was an accountant, would be running the books. Estelle, who had majored in marketing, would run the front and work on building the business from the advertising side. While Aspen, who had followed in her parent's footsteps and gone to culinary school, would be baking and creating the masterpieces in the back.

And it all started with the wedding cake display in front of them right now.

Aspen knew she had more than likely gotten the gig for Jude and Ruth Lisbon's wedding because she had underbid every other cake decorator, but right now she needed to build her catalog if she was ever going to really show her parents that she could carry on the family tradition of excellence.

It was intimidating to be the daughter of two acclaimed bakers. They had chosen to stay in small town Oregon in order to raise their family, but their names and creations were well known throughout the world, thanks to the magic of social media.

Their father's chocolate creations were internationally award winning and it was an honor to be his daughter.

But more than anything, Aspen wanted to be known for herself, not for her lineage. Taking over the cafe was her chance to do that. Her parents had left to visit family in Italy and it was time for the girls to sink or swim.

Swim, she assured herself. "We're definitely going to swim."

"Who's swimming?" Maeve asked, coming up to Aspen's side. She tucked a curl behind her ear and studied the display. "It's perfect." She smiled at Aspen. "You're a miracle worker."

Aspen turned and hugged Maeve tightly, ignoring her less exuberant sister's complaints. "We're going to do this!" Aspen cried.

"I'm sure we will," Maeve said primly, backing up from any further touching. "But we're not going to do it by assaulting each other in full view of our patrons."

Aspen laughed and bounced on her toes. "I can feel it," she whispered. "This is just the beginning."

Estelle came back their way. "This is a great start," she agreed. "But I have something even better lined up."

Aspen frowned. "What're you talking about?"

Estelle looked around to make sure they were alone before leaning in and dropping her voice. "Who can make or break a restaurant just by posting a picture online?"

Maeve groaned. "Who cares?"

Aspen's eyes grew wide. "Oh my gosh, you're talking about Eat It Austin, aren't you?"

Estelle nodded, a small smirk on her face. "And guess who managed to get ahold of his boss and finagle an actual review?"

"You didn't," Aspen said flatly.

Estelle pumped her eyebrows. "I did."

"Estelle! He could ruin us!" Aspen hissed.

"Or..." Estelle said firmly, giving Aspen a look. "He could send us racing right out of the gate."

Maeve shook her head. "That guy seems like a jerk."

"That guy is the biggest food critic in the Pacific Northwest," Estelle pointed out. "He's based out of Portland. With his endorsement, we're a sure thing."

Aspen felt as if she might faint. She could barely breathe and her vision was dimming.

"Aspen!" Estelle gave her sister a shake. "Breathe!"

Aspen sucked in a breath, her mind clearing and quickly working through everything Estelle had just revealed. "He's going to have to like my stuff before he'd give us an endorsement," she said hoarsely.

Maeve sighed and made a face. "If that's all, then I don't see what you're freaking out about. No one can eat your desserts without raving that heaven fell onto their plate."

Aspen shook her head. "That won't be enough. He's tough."

Estelle put her hand on Aspen's shoulders. "And so are you." She tilted her chin and gave Aspen a motherly look. How did older sisters always manage to pull that off so well? "You're the best baker I know. It's time everyone knew it." She winked. "Just don't tell Dad and Mom I said that."

"You're just trying to make me feel better," Aspen said, shaking her head. She had never been so terrified in her life. Eat It Austin was the creme de la creme of food critics. He was young, handsome and knew how to pose for a camera, which meant his female followers gobbled up everything he said as if it were pure gold. But he was also manly, well educated, and knew how to throw down an insult if something didn't live up to his expectations, making men enjoy a good laugh while following him as well.

"OH MY GOSH!"

All three sisters spun to see Ruth, the bride rushing into the banquet room. She put her hands over her mouth, her short hair standing up in darling spikes on top of her head. Not many people could pull off such a bold look, but Ruth did it with unexpected elegance.

Ruth turned from the table and stared straight at Aspen. "It's perfect," she breathed.

Before Aspen could absorb the compliment, Ruth spun and grabbed one of the cheesecake bites from a tray, downing it in one bite.

"Oh my gosh," Ruth said again, this time with her mouth full. She closed her eyes as if in bliss and didn't open them for a few moments. When she finally looked at Aspen again, Ruth was smiling wide enough to give the Columbia River a run for its money.

Ruth walked over and took Aspen's hands. "Thank you so much," she gushed, "for making my wedding perfect. I'll be recommending your bakery until the day I die."

Aspen couldn't help the smile that tugged at her lips. Ruth was a little on the dramatic side, but it was easy to see she was completely sincere.

Estelle elbowed Aspen's side and gave her an *I told you so* look.

"Thank you," Aspen said to Ruth. "It was such an honor to be a part of this." She squeezed Ruth's hands. "You have an open table at our cafe any time."

Because they *would* have a cafe. This was exactly what Aspen lived for. Making people happy with food. Food critic or not, Aspen was determined to succeed. She didn't come from a family of quitters. She came from a family of achievers, and now it was her turn.

Eat it Austin could come take a bite of anything he wanted. Aspen knew what she was doing and she wouldn't let his fame intimidate her.

The Three Sisters Cafe was going to officially open for business in two months, and when it did, it would dazzle even the toughest of critics.

CHAPTER 1

"No..." Aspen tapped her bottom lip. "I think we definitely want the ginger pear cake. It's an unusual flavor and better suited for fall than lemon raspberry." Her dark brown, nearly black eyes continued to scan the menu she held in her hand. "I love the graphic details you put on here," she gushed to her sister, Estelle, who had designed the page featuring the baked goods for the grand opening.

Estelle preened slightly. "I thought the cupcake motif was fun as well."

"What did that cost you?" Maeve asked wryly from her seat across the table. She casually licked her fingers free of the frosting left after eating one of Aspen's donuts, her eyes on a spreadsheet as if it were the most interesting documentation in the world.

"Probably like three bucks," Aspen snapped. "Why are you always so uptight about it? Sometimes you have to spend money to make money."

"The problem comes when you don't have money to spend," Maeve retorted, finally turning away from her study. She peered at her two sisters over her fake glasses. Maeve was convinced they made people take her more seriously, though her eyes definitely didn't need them. At only five-foot-two, the thin, youngest sister had a hard time getting other adults to assume she was anything other than sixteen, with the brains to match.

Aspen, however, knew better. Maeve was brilliant with math, something that no one in their family could quite figure out. The Harrison family was one of passionate creatives, not studious number crunchers.

Aspen internally shrugged. She supposed it really didn't matter. Maeve was who she was, and the fact that she was the financial advisor for their little shop was a blessing...until they needed to purchase anything. "We have three dollars," Aspen argued.

"We do now," Maeve said coolly. "But we won't if you continue to spend it."

Estelle held up her hand when Aspen went to retort. "Ladies...this is a useless conversation." Ah...Estelle...always the peacemaker. As the oldest of all the Harrison children, she seemed to take great delight in being their mother while their real mom was across seas.

Aspen snorted quietly. Who was she kidding? Estelle had come out of the womb playing the mother figure. Sometimes it was comforting, and sometimes it drove Aspen insane. She and Maeve both hated being treated like children, but sometimes Estelle seemed to forget that they had grown up just as much as she had.

"Anyway..." Aspen drawled, turning back to the menu. "What do you think about the ginger pear cake? We could do a caramel drizzle around the edge, maybe some crumbled cookies on top and display it right on the corner." She pointed to the spot she meant. The shop was just about complete, but the extra large display counter was still there from when their parents ran it.

The renovations the women had made had mostly worked around that centerpiece. There was new paint on the walls, new flooring under their feet and the decor was partially put up. The kitchen area in the back had seen several appliances replaced, giving Aspen brand new, up to date machinery to work with. Including some fun new toys that Maeve had been less than pleased to write down in the expense book.

"That does sound nice," Estelle mused. She cocked her head, her artistic eyes narrowing. "If we put that on the corner, we need something lower around it. Perhaps a small pumpkin display? With a garland of leaves?"

"Yes," Aspen said excitedly. "That'll be perfect."

Maeve groaned and let her head fall back. "How much is that going to set me back?" she asked.

Estelle sighed. "Mae, we have some small pumpkins at home. I can use those. All I need is the garland, which will only cost a couple dollars."

Maeve huffed. "I suppose we can do that."

Aspen shook her head and stood up. "We open next week. I need to finalize my grocery order and make sure I have all the stuff I can bake early taken care of, or I'll be running around like a chicken with my head cut off come opening day."

Ignoring her sisters' conversation, Aspen went into the kitchen. She grabbed the clipboard she had hanging next to the walk-in freezer and headed inside. She shivered immediately. The weather in Seagull Cove, Oregon was already starting to cool off, but it was nothing compared to a sub zero freezer.

"Idiot," she muttered to herself. When she had worked with her father, she had kept a coat hanging next to the freezer for occasions just like this. When grabbing supplies, she was in and out quickly, but when doing inventory, it required staying in the cold much longer.

With the renovation happening, the coat had been taken home and now Aspen was severely regretting not bringing it back. She made a mental note to fix that tomorrow when she came back.

"Two hundred cupcakes," she muttered, double checking her list. "Eggs, milk, butter...check, check, check." She accounted for boxes of cream cheese and bottles of sprinkles. Bags loaded with fruit fillings and pudding were also noted.

Finally, she stepped out, goosebumps breaking out on her arms and neck as the heat brushed over her skin. "Brrr..." she muttered under her breath.

"One of these days you'll come out of there a popsicle," Maeve teased from her place at the sink. She was hand washing her mug of tea from the morning. She kept a dozen or so of her antique teacups at the shop, and Aspen did her best not to complain about the loss of space.

Maeve was an early riser, which made her especially helpful when opening for the day. And if the woman needed a cup of tea in order to feel ready to tackle the world? Who was Aspen to judge? At least...mostly.

"I don't know how you drink that stuff," Aspen said with a dramatic shiver that was only half fake. "It's hot water with almost no flavor."

"Better than consuming enough sugar to fill the Grand Canyon," Maeve said, obviously not the least bit concerned about her sister's dislike. "Besides, herbs are good for us. They help me stay healthy."

"If by healthy, you mean looking like you're still a teenager, then I would have to agree." Aspen grinned, knowing that was one of Maeve's sore spots.

At twenty-three years old, Maeve should have been old enough not to care, but getting asked if you were old enough to own a credit card when you were buying groceries would bend any woman out of shape.

Maeve sniffed. "Better than the other way around."

"True...but no one's going to think you're old enough to date until you're in your forties, and then—" Aspen laughed as she ducked the dish towel headed toward her head.

Maeve was smiling when Aspen straightened. She pushed her glasses up her nose. "It's good to see you laugh."

Aspen's smile immediately fell. "Sorry," she said softly. "I've just been stressed, I guess."

Maeve nodded sagely. Her large, quiet eyes often saw more than most. "You know that Dad's proud, right?"

Aspen shrugged, her eyes on the ground. "I hope so." The words were quiet and vulnerable, and anyone with an ounce of compassion would hear them for what they really were. A little girl who desperately wanted her father's blessing.

His little trip to Italy had a much deeper meaning than anyone outside of the family understood. She wanted...*needed*...his legacy to live on. Which meant there was far more riding on this grand reopening than just three sisters taking over a family bakery.

AUSTIN LACED HIS HANDS behind his head and kicked his heels up on the desk with a sigh.

"Dreaming of that tiramisu?" his brother and coworker Tye asked with a smirk.

Austin grinned. "Something like that." In actuality, Austin was enjoying a rare moment of peace. His latest review was finished several hours ahead of schedule and there was nothing on the schedule for several days. He hadn't had a day off in months and it was starting to wear on him. Ever since his online persona, Eat It Austin, became popular on social media, Austin's editor had been running Austin into the ground with appearances and reviews.

Fame was such a fickle thing. No one would have ever guessed that a man from western Washington with an appetite bigger than himself would have suddenly become viral overnight.

At first, the small press that Austin worked for had been thrilled to capitalize on a few days of extra advertising. But days had turned into weeks, weeks into months and now Eat It Austin had become a household name.

He groaned internally. *And not always for the better.*

The main reason Austin had become so popular was because of a particular post that had captured the attention of the ever elusive twenty-something crowd, who had enjoyed a line from one of Austin's not so favorable reviews, comparing a flame broiled burger to someone trying to turn coal into a diamond, but lacking the proper skill set.

The remark had been cutting and wasn't even Austin's words, but since it was his picture on the profile, all credit had come directly his way.

The burger had been badly charred, Austin reminded himself. But never in a million years would he have been so brash about it.

He sighed and pushed a hand through his hair. With that one comment, however, Austin's fame had started and now he was known for being snarky and difficult to please. If a chef managed to get a good review from Austin, it was a great boost for their business. If he didn't like it, however, the online community, all safely hidden anonymously behind computer screens, often tore the restaurant apart until there was nothing left to salvage.

There had even been rumors about a couple of small town cafes going out of business when Austin was completely underwhelmed by the flavor of their milkshakes, though he had never checked to see if it was true.

"And just what does the great Eat It Austin have to sigh about?" Tye asked wryly. "Plotting world domination? Or do you just want to rule over food?"

Austin chuckled as if the comment were funny, but the words hurt. He hadn't meant to become known for being rude. Heck, he didn't even write most of the posts. Austin had a closet full of secrets and one of them kept him from being able to write more than a few sentences comfortably. That, unfortunately, had fallen on his brother's shoulders. When the Eat It Austin name was still small and unknown, Austin's brother Tye had stepped in to help out one day, writing a review with a great deal more ease and snark than Austin ever could.

The problem was, no one knew it was Tye who had written the article. The name Eat It Austin had taken off and now they *couldn't* tell anyone the truth, other than their editor, of course. Tye hated the public eye, and struggled with crippling anxiety most days, which made him perfect for ghost writing while Austin, who was crowd friendly and charismatic, took credit for it.

Despite the public's view of his personality, Austin couldn't completely complain about his rising career. The money was far better than he'd ever made before, he was welcomed like a celebrity almost everywhere he went and he had access to free food at almost every restaurant this side of Utah.

"Edwards!"

Austin dropped his feet and hurriedly sat upright. "Yeah, boss?"

Mr. Stanley came storming into the front area of the office. "What the heck did you just send me?" he asked.

Austin groaned and threw his head back. "Stan..."

"Don't Stan me," Mr. Stanley snapped. He hated the nickname the workers at the office called him, but the man's bluster was much worse than his actual bite, so very few worried about using it. "I thought we'd talked about this."

Austin held his hands out to the side. "What's wrong with what I wrote?"

"It's nice," Stan argued.

Tye snorted, then tried to cover it with a cough. "Sorry," he said with a forced frown. When Stan didn't look amused, Tye put his head down, his cheeks bright red, and went back to work.

"The place was nice," Austin said. He leaned his elbows on his desk. "The steak was cooked well, the fries were crispy on the outside and soft on the inside." He paused and tilted his head. "I actually think they double fry them."

Tye's head came up from his work. "Spoiled," he muttered.

Austin raised his dark blond eyebrows and smirked. "Yeah. They were great."

"I don't want great," Stan growled, coming closer. "I want catchy. I want insults. I want things that your fans can share and react to. *Nice*," he said tightly, "doesn't do that."

Austin sighed and pinched the bridge of his nose. "Stan, I'm not going to say bad things about a restaurant just for your ratings. The place was good. They deserve to get credit for that." He snapped his eyes open. "Besides, the last couple of restaurants haven't been all that great. You got tons of movements from those. We're due for something a little sweeter."

Stan paused to consider Austin's argument and Austin held his breath. He really didn't like shredding people if they didn't deserve shredding. His rabid fans seemed to take great delight in taking even the smallest weakness and running with it until the people involved died a fiery death.

Letting out a harsh breath, Stan's shoulders deflated and Austin felt a slight hope that he had won. "Okay. I suppose we can't ruin lives every time."

Austin wanted to roll his eyes.

"No one would want to ask you for a review if you didn't have a hit once in a while." Stan nodded sagely. "I'll let this one go." He pointed at Austin. "But I'm expecting the next couple to be snappier."

Austin put his hands in the air. "I have no trouble calling it like it is, but only if they deserve it."

Stan clenched his jaw. "We'll see." He began to walk away, only to spin on his heel.

Austin had been starting to relax back into his chair, but all that was cut short when his boss spoke again.

"Speaking of..." Stan said with an evil grin. "I've got a new place for you to review."

Austin glanced over and caught Tye's eye before looking back at his boss. "Yeah? Where's this one?"

"Down in Seagull Cove."

Austin frowned. "Seagull Cove? Where's that?"

Stan waved his hand. "A tiny little place down south." One side of his mouth pulled up. "But here's the kicker. You heard of Antony Harrison?"

Austin jerked upright. "The chocolate sculptor?" He snapped his fingers. "His wife was also a baker...Em...something...Emma?" Austin shook his head. "That's not it."

"Emory," Stan supplied.

"That's it." Austin nodded. "Yeah. Those two are powerhouses in the bakery world." His green eyes lit up. "Did they open a restaurant?"

Stan shook his head and Austin felt a push of disappointment. That would have been a place to visit.

"Apparently, they passed their little bakery down to their daughters." Stan snorted. "Not sure why someone like him would do that, but whatever." He raised a single eyebrow. "The three daughters are having a grand reopening. They've remodeled and are creating a cafe instead of just a bakery."

Tye slumped in his seat. "Why do you get to eat all the good stuff?"

Austin smirked. "That's the job, my man." He looked at Stan. "When do I get to go?" He didn't feel too sorry for Tye. Austin always brought him food back to try. His brother was just being a baby.

"Next week," Stan said, walking back to his office. "And don't forget." He pinned Austin with a look from his doorway. "This next one needs to be a zinger." On that note, he disappeared and slammed his door shut.

"Geez," Tye said under his breath. "This roasting thing is getting out of control."

Austin sighed and nodded. He knew his brother wasn't brave enough in public to let out his sarcastic side, and writing with it had been sort of fun. But no one enjoyed being backed into a corner. "I know, but what am I supposed to do? It sells, and the people are always clamoring for more."

"Are we really going to take the Harrison girls down?" Tye shook his head. "That sounds dangerous, considering their background."

Austin pushed his hands through his hair. "Hopefully it'll be amazing enough I won't be able to say anything against them." He groaned. "I really hate what he's asking me to do."

Tye didn't say anything, just got back to work.

Austin knew there really wasn't anything to say. They had a job. It was a good job, but it required him to be something he didn't like. He could always quit, but that would put him right back where he'd been. Broken, unemployed and homeless. He had no desire to go back to that life...ever.

Taking in a fortifying breath, he gathered his things and decided to go home early. His review was in, and until his next review next week, he didn't need to be in the office to get any work done. Tye would be home when he finished his editing work.

Maybe putting a little distance between him and his boss would help Austin find the motivation he needed to keep doing his job.

CHAPTER 2

Aspen was sure that she was going to throw up. She had prepped for this day for months. Well...years, really. Years of learning at her mother and father's elbows, years of school and eventually college, years of hoping and praying for a chance to make a name for herself. Years of experimenting and working in the kitchen to find the niche she truly enjoyed, and it had all come down to a single moment.

"Two minutes," Maeve said circumspectly. She pushed her fake glasses up her nose.

"How can you be so calm?" Aspen asked. She felt as if her knees might give out at any moment. "Our futures come down to this."

Maeve snorted. "Don't be so dramatic. This is great, but it's not the end all."

"What?" Aspen whirled on her younger sister. "Do you have any idea how much work I've put into this?" She waved her arms around. "How much all of us have put into this?" She shook her head. "How much our parents are counting on us?"

Maeve's skin paled at the last question. "You're not being fair," she said softly, which was a normal reaction for her. Maeve didn't get mad. She hated confrontation and always, *always*, backed away before something became too heated. "Mom and Dad love us. Yes, they want to see us succeed, but they also want us to be happy." She gave Aspen a glare. "If this venture burned and failed, they'd still love us. And yes, to answer your question, I'm fully aware of everything that's gone into putting this together." She pushed her glasses up again. "And I want to see you get everything you deserve, but not at the cost of our relationship or your sanity." She glanced at the wall clock in the shape of the Eiffel Tower. "Looks like it's time."

Before Aspen could make good on her thought of throwing up, Estelle came breezing through the backroom door. "Here we go!" she shouted, raising her arms in the air. Her smile was a mile wide. "This is going to be epic."

Aspen swallowed hard and backed herself to the pastry counter as Estelle went to pull up the blinds and open the front door. Part of her was positive that there would be no one outside. Aspen wasn't sure if that would be a good thing or a bad thing.

"It's going to be okay," Maeve whispered before going to move to Estelle's side.

Aspen wrung her hands together. This was it. The moment of—

"Welcome to our Grand Opening!" Estelle shouted as she threw open the door.

A loud cry went up from outside and Aspen lost her breath.

Maeve worked to pull up the window coverings and suddenly a massive crowd was visible even from her spot behind the counter.

Her heart fluttered at all the smiles aimed her way and slowly, Aspen felt the color come back into her cheeks. People rushed through the door, shaking Estelle's hand and oohing and aahing as they entered the new atmosphere the women had put together.

They had decided on a French theme, which probably wasn't extremely unique in regards to cafes, but there wasn't anything like it in Seagull Cove, Oregon, that was for sure.

One side of the cafe had bistro tables with pink tablecloths and black chairs. The other side of the space held a conversation set in the same pink as the tablecloths. The pillows were a mixture of black and white with French words or silhouettes of famous landmarks on them.

The walls were bright white and held black and white pho-
tographs and wall art, with the occasional splash of pink to break up
the monotony.

Estelle had worked tirelessly to create the perfect mix of cozy and
feminine, and Aspen was sure her sister had done it. With her eye for
marketing, Estelle was the perfect designer, and even Aspen used her
sister's talents when designing wedding cakes at times.

"Oh my gosh," a teenage girl said as she and a few of her friends
rushed to the counter. They were all dressed alike in flip flops, jeans
with holes in them and sweatshirts. A pair of sunglasses held their
hair off their faces, but their youthful grins told Aspen they were
genuinely excited to be there.

That revelation helped Aspen relax even further. No one had
even tasted her creations yet, and already people were gushing about
it all.

"Did you make all these?" the teenager asked, her eyes wide.

Aspen forced herself into motion. "Yes," she said with a stiff nod.
"Would you like a free sample?"

The gaggle giggled and every single one of them nodded.

Aspen pulled the tray of petit fours from its place farther down
the counter. "This one is red velvet," Aspen pointed to a white petit
four with a small red flower on top. "This is chocolate. This is cinnamon apple."

After appeasing the girls, who continued to giggle and gape at
everything, Aspen put the tray on her shoulder and walked out from
behind the counter. The more she mingled, the more she relaxed.

"They all love it!" Estelle whispered loudly in Aspen's ear.

Aspen's smile was a permanent fixture at this point. "I think
you're right," she said in wonder.

Estelle laughed and tucked a piece of her black hair behind her
ear.

Aspen had to look up to see her sister's face. Estelle had gotten the strongest Italian genetics from their father's side of the family. Taller and statuesque, with curves to make men weep, Estelle drew all eyes in a room her way, but her confidence and ability to take charge had a tendency to make people think she was aloof or stuck up, which couldn't be farther from the truth.

Estelle was the most motherly of all the sisters and therefore the warmest personality. Anyone who was willing to spend any time in her company got to meet an absolutely amazing person, and it still surprised Aspen at times that her sister was still single.

Really, they were all single, even their brother, who was currently serving a tour of duty. *Actually, it's probably a good thing he's single,* Aspen thought wryly as she smiled at a group of kids grabbing from her tray. Nobody would want that kind of distance if they were in love.

With their parents gone for the foreseeable future, the sisters hoped their brother would come home soon. It had been a long time since they'd seen him and Aspen could use his strong shoulder to help ease some of the pressure she felt to make this cafe a success.

A loud squeal caught Aspen's attention and she barely held her feet and tray when her best friend grabbed her in a tight hug. "You're a total success!" Harper said in Aspen's ear.

Aspen pulled back, unable to keep from smiling. "You're such an optimist. We just barely opened the doors."

Harper shrugged and looked around. "Who cares? You three are so amazing." Her blue eyes came back to Aspen. "Oh!" She took a petit four. "Mmm...love it. How many can I have?"

"Uh, uh, uh..." Aspen pulled the tray away, then winked to soften the blow. "You get freebies all the time. Save some for the others."

Harper's pink lips turned into a darling pout, but she nodded. "True." She sighed. "I'd really like to stick around, but I'm in the middle of a project, so I just wanted to pop in and say hi."

Aspen sent an air kiss to her friend and started to walk away. "I heard you, and I appreciate it. Come see me when you're done with whatever painting has your attention at the moment."

"Will do." Harper wiggled her fingers and disappeared into the crowd.

Aspen shook her head. Harper was the best. Always supportive and always smiling. She helped keep Aspen's heads out of the cloud. "Hello, Mr. Tensen," Aspen said, recognizing her old high school English teacher. "Would you like a sample?"

Mr. Tensen scratched his chin. "I see you finally put that day-dreaming of yours to good use," he teased.

Aspen laughed. "I suppose so. Can I help it if coming up with cake flavors was more exciting than Shakespeare?"

He chuckled with her. "I suppose much of the world would agree with you." He leaned in as if imparting a secret. "Sometimes even I agree with you."

Mrs. Tensen stepped up to his side and lightly smacked his shoulder. "What nonsense are you talking about now?" She smiled over at Aspen. "Hello, Aspen." She purposefully looked around. "Your opening looks like a wonderful success."

Aspen blew out a long breath. "Thank you and I hope you're right." She held out the tray. "The samples seem to be disappearing fast enough."

The Tensens laughed as intended and both reached for one. "People will take anything if it's free," Mr. Tensen said before popping the treat in his mouth. His eyes widened and he reached for another. "But they come back when they're this amazing."

His wife smacked his hand before he could get another. "Don't be greedy."

Aspen's smile widened. "I'm thrilled you enjoyed it." She pushed the tray at him. "And don't worry. I made plenty."

Mr. Tensen gave his wife a look, took a treat, then winked at Aspen. "Good luck to you, ladies. We're all so excited to see the Harrison legacy live on."

"Thank you," Aspen said. The ache from thinking of her father came back for a moment. "We're going to do our best."

Mrs. Tensen patted Aspen's shoulder. "And that'll be enough."

AUSTIN TAPPED HIS FOOT and looked at his watch. This was getting ridiculous. The line to enter the tiny cafe was down the block. He didn't usually like to announce himself at restaurants because he wanted to experience them as they were, but right now he was sorely tempted to break that rule and tell everyone to get out of the way.

He had definitely not expected such a large turnout in such a small town, which he was starting to understand had been a massive mistake.

Why wouldn't there be a big reply to the Harrison family opening a cafe?

He grunted and pulled out his phone to play a game while he waited.

"Thank you for your patience," a feminine voice shouted, catching his attention.

Austin looked up to see a stunning woman standing in the doorway. She had a pink apron on that made him wince at its brightness, but otherwise, the woman was something to look at. She had black hair with olive skin that was definitely a gift from her father. Austin had done a little research before coming, and Antony Harrison's Italian heritage was very evident in his daughter.

But which daughter is she? he wondered.

She appeared to be his age, or at least close to it, but he couldn't be sure.

"Please know that we've prepared enough free samples for everyone and will work you inside as soon as we can." Her smile was bright and Austin noticed several men who couldn't seem to keep their eyes off her. "So just sit tight and we'll see you soon." She pressed her hands together. "And thank you so much for coming! We appreciate your support."

Austin grunted a small laugh when the crowd clapped at her little speech. It was amazing how people reacted to a pretty face. Well, beautiful or not, Austin was here for the food. What the daughters looked like had nothing to do with his taste buds.

Another fifteen minutes went by and he only moved a few feet. This was starting to wear on his nerves. Was it really going to be worth his time to wait around for this all day? He sighed. It wasn't as if he had anything else to do. He'd driven down from Portland with the express purpose of eating here today.

A shout went up and Austin once again turned away from his phone. A waitress, with a tray up near her head, was working her way through the crowd. It appeared that they were now bringing the samples to the people.

"Petit fours, anyone?" the voice called out.

Austin moved around, trying to see who the woman was. Her hair was just as dark as the daughter who had been out earlier and he wondered if this was another one of the sisters. Her hair was long, halfway down her back with thick waves that gave it a nice flow.

Austin found his eyes trailing down her shape, noting she was much shorter than the first daughter, but just as femininely built. Something stirred in his stomach and Austin frowned.

Probably low blood sugar at this point, he grumbled internally. He put his attention back on his phone and began to scroll through his most recent comments. Stan had been right. His latest review hadn't been received as well as the ones previous. Apparently, being rude was much more newsworthy than being nice.

He huffed and stuffed the phone back in his pocket. He wasn't going to worry about it. That restaurant had been amazing. He wasn't going to hurt their reputation for no good reason.

"Petit four?"

Austin jumped slightly, the woman having moved toward him when he wasn't looking. "Don't mind if I do," he said, his eyes caught on the small, colorful pieces of cake. He picked one up, then finally turned his eyes to the woman, and for the first time in years, found himself without words.

Dark, nearly black eyes stared at him, framed by thick lashes, enhanced by a touch of mascara. The woman's skin was slightly lighter than the first sister, but there was no mistaking the two were related. This one had a little more of her mother's looks, if Austin remembered the pictures correctly, but the full pink lips, large eyes and shape of her face was very much like her sister.

Without taking his eyes off the woman, Austin put the cake in his mouth. The dessert practically melted on his tongue and the enjoyment of it snapped him out of his staring contest. "Wow," he said. "That's really good."

A blush crept across the woman's cheek bones. "Thank you," she said with a small smile. "We're thrilled you enjoyed it."

Clearing this throat, Austin stepped back a little. "Thanks," he said a little sharper than he should. "That was worth waiting in line for." He needed to get a little distance from her. He wasn't usually one to be so caught up in a woman's gaze, but there was something about this Harrison girl that was messing with his head.

The woman blinked and stepped back. "Glad to hear it," she said in a professional tone. "If you'll wait just a little longer, there are more goodies inside." With a polite smile, she turned to the next person in line. "Petit four?"

Austin went back to his phone, but kept his peripheral vision on the woman. She was wearing the same bright pink apron as the first one and Austin began to worry going inside was going to be like step-ping inside a Pepto Bismol bottle. He should have asked her which sister she was. The middle one, Aspen, was supposed to be the one who did the most baking, though her sisters helped out some. According to what he had read, each sister had a different job, but each covered anywhere help was needed. Or at least they would for now. He was sure that if things went well, they would eventually hire more help.

It doesn't matter, he thought. *I'm here for a review, not to get to know anyone.*

He wasn't looking forward to the decor, having gotten a glimpse at their aprons, but he hadn't been lying when he said that petit four was amazing. It was delicious. More than delicious, and he was eager to see if the other treats were just as good or if they'd used their best offering to lure people in.

He got up on tiptoe and tried to gauge how much farther he had before getting inside. The line wasn't budging and it looked like he probably had a couple more hours before his assignment would be done.

He sighed and fired up his phone again. When movement caught his eye, he couldn't help but let his eyes wander toward the sister who was still handing out samples. It was hard not to linger. Everyone she spoke to was smiling and enjoying the treats on her tray, which was nearly empty at this point. If this small glimpse was any indication, Austin was sure that the Harrison daughters would do their parents proud. He needed to leave his mind open for more information, but his initial glimpse told him that this place was going to be completely wasted in this podunk town.

There. That's something Stan can use. Only time could tell, but Austin wasn't sure he'd have much of a critique of The Three Sister's Cafe. But the tiny town? Yeah, he could work with that. He owed Stan something zingy, and that just might be it.

CHAPTER 3

Aspen could barely keep her knees from knocking together. As soon as her tray was empty, she smiled at the crowd and hurried inside, heading straight for the kitchen. "He's here," she gushed once safely behind the kitchen door.

Maeve frowned over the top of her glasses. "Who's here?"

"Eat it Austin," Aspen said breathlessly. She put a hand to her chest. Man, he was even prettier in real life than his online pictures. How was that fair? Nobody should be allowed to be that attractive. She'd gaped at him like some fangirl. All she'd been lacking was a shirt with his picture on it and a squeal pouring out of her mouth.

When he'd stepped back from her so suddenly, it had finally snapped Aspen out of her trance and she had managed to make her feet move enough to start sharing the samples with other guests. Could she have been any more stupid? Luckily, she hadn't shared her name with him, so hopefully he didn't put anything in his review about the ridiculous woman who couldn't stop drooling when she looked at him.

"Oh," Maeve said, completely unconcerned. She went back to re-filling a tray. "Has he eaten anything yet?"

Aspen headed to another counter and set her tray on top. "Yep. I gave him a petit four sample."

"And?"

A smile crept across her face. "I believe his exact word was...wow."

Maeve grinned. "And you were worried."

Aspen gave her sister a glare. "A sample does not a good review make. What if he orders one of the cake slices and hates it?"

Maeve shrugged. "Then he'll have a split review. He already liked one thing. Who cares if he doesn't like the other?"

Aspen rolled her eyes. "I care! Haven't you ever read one of his reviews? When he doesn't like something..." She shivered. "It's not a good thing."

Maeve never even looked up. "I'm not worried. Your cakes are perfect. He'll have nothing to complain about."

"I hope so," Aspen muttered under her breath. "For all our sakes." Once her tray was full, she hefted it back up on her shoulder and took a deep breath. It wouldn't be very long before Austin was inside the cafe. Maybe she would pass off the samples to Estelle and serve Austin herself.

She snickered at herself. *You just want to see his handsome face again.* She was practically giddy with excitement. Yes, she did want to see him again, if only to soak in his handsome face one more time before he left and she went back to admiring him online.

His reaction to her petit four had her filled with high hopes that things would go well, despite the rational voice in her head that told her to be careful. She hadn't been lying when she told Maeve he could still find something not to like, or that his bad review could ruin them.

Eat It Austin was all too well known for roasting restaurants when they didn't perform up to snuff. But it was his fans that took it to a new level. Aspen rarely read the comments on his reviews, knowing she would only feel bad for the people being attacked. His fans were ruthless and were never afraid to say exactly what they wanted to.

She used her back to push the door open and stepped out behind the counter. "Estelle?"

"Hmm?" Estelle smiled and handed a package to a customer before turning. "Whatcha need?"

"Want to do samples and I'll run the counter for a while?"

Estelle blew out a breath and smiled. "That'd be great. Moving around would be good for my legs." She reached out and took the tray. "Anywhere in particular I should walk?"

"I was working my way down the line outside," Aspen said. "I figured they deserved something to keep them happy."

"Good idea." Estelle winked as she headed out. "Good luck. People are going to buy us out if we're not careful."

"Then maybe it's time we be reckless," Aspen said with a soft laugh.

Estelle snickered and walked away.

Aspen tightened her apron and walked up to the register. "Hello! Welcome to Three Sisters Cafe. What can I get you?"

The next forty five minutes was spent cutting cake and boxing pastries and cookies for customers. Some new, many locals, all of them excited for the new cafe.

Wiping her forehead with the back of her hand, Aspen then wiped her hands on her apron. She was hot, sweaty and had frosting smeared on nearly every surface of her body at this point, but she wouldn't trade it for anything.

"Welcome to Three Sisters Cafe," she said without looking up. "What can I get you today?"

"What do you recommend?"

The deep voice caught her attention and Aspen jerked her head up, only to stutter for the second time that day.

It's him.

She bit her tongue to keep from blurting those words out loud. He more than likely would not appreciate her shouting out who he was for the world to know. "You want my recommendation?" she asked stupidly.

One side of his mouth pulled up into a smile and it was adorably boyish. It was completely unfair that he had eyes the color of emeralds and blond hair that looked like it belonged on a surfer. Slightly longer on top while short on the sides, Aspen knew that with a little gel, the hairstyle could look pristine and business-like, or left alone to flop adorably over one eye like it was right now.

She clenched her fingers into a fist to keep from pushing it out of the way so she could see that bright eye again. They really were quite stunning.

"Are you one of the sisters?" he asked.

Aspen blinked several times before the words penetrated her brain. "What? Oh...yes."

He waited before saying. "And which one are you?"

Aspen wanted to smack herself. She was acting like that fan girl again. Time to wake up and be the businesswoman that she was. "I'm Aspen. Everything you see in this cafe was made by me."

His eyebrows went up. "You're the baker, huh? Then yes, I definitely want your recommendation." He leaned in. "I'm guessing you know what's best here."

She smiled, feeling herself warm up to his playful personality. "I do," she assured him. Without saying anything else, she walked away and pulled the cake stand with her latest creation in it over to the register. "This is what you want," she said.

"Are you going to tell me what it is?"

Aspen nodded as she was cutting him a thick slice. "This is my ginger cake with housemade pear jam. It's got a white chocolate buttercream and a cinnamon ganache drizzle." She boxed up the slice and handed it to him. "You'll love it."

"It sounds delicious," he said, setting the box on the counter and pulling out his wallet. "What do I owe you?"

Aspen shook her head, feeling more and more confident as they conversed. "This one's on the house." She leaned in. "For being so patient outside."

He gave her a look. "Are you giving everyone free cake for waiting? There were a lot of people."

She shook her head. "Nope. Just the ones who say nice things about my petit fours."

He chuckled. "I'm still guessing that's a lot of people."

Aspen shrugged. "We'll see."

His smile widened and he picked up the box. "Well, thank you. I'm excited to try it."

"Come back anytime," she said, waving as he disappeared into the crowd. Aspen took a deep breath, satisfaction going through her as he walked away. Things were going to be okay. She just knew it.

WITH THE CROWDS STILL overflowing the small building, Austin took his cake and headed out into the street. He blinked at the bright sunshine. The day was chilly, since it was fall, but the light was a welcome change from the inside of the cafe. The black, white and pink were far too girly for him and Austin found the Paris theme a little cliche. He'd nearly gagged when he saw the bright pink sofa. Who in their right mind bought a couch that color?

The cake, however, sounded like something right up his alley. He walked down the sidewalk until he found a bench and plopped himself down. Unboxing his cake, he brought it up to his nose. "Oooh." The smells were delectable. Ginger, cinnamon and sweet sugar. He could even smell the fruity hint of pear, though that was a light scent on the back end of the spices.

He pulled out the plastic fork provided and cut off a bite. Using the tines, he got a feel for the texture of the cake and found himself impressed. He picked up the bite and once again brought it to his nose before finally putting it in his mouth.

As the flavors melted on his tongue, the world shifted. This...this was exactly why he became a food reviewer. Every once in a while, a person was born with an ability to create magic.

Austin had not been given that particular talent, but he *did* have the talent to appreciate it in others. It appeared that Aspen Harrison, just like her father and mother, had been blessed with that gift.

It took less than five minutes for that slice of cake to disappear and Austin was too full to move afterwards. It was a three layer cake and Aspen hadn't been shy about the size she had cut.

He chuckled as he thought of her flirting with him, giving him the cake for free. He wondered if she knew who he was. It wouldn't be the first time a restaurant owner had given him free food, but Austin made sure that special treatment never influenced his feelings about the food.

Besides, who would turn down food from someone as beautiful as Aspen Harrison?

It had been almost as much of a treat to see the woman again as it had been to eat her dessert. If he lived closer, Austin knew he'd probably become a regular customer, both for her and for the food.

His phone buzzed in his pocket and Austin grabbed the device, bringing it to his ear. "Edwards," he said easily.

"How was it?" Tye asked with eagerness in his voice.

Austin chuckled. His brother was always jealous of Austin's eating adventures, especially since he had to write about them but didn't always get to participate in the eating. "Delicious," he said. "Scratch that, I'm not sure delicious is even a good enough word. It was the best cake I've ever eaten."

Tye groaned. "One of these days, I'm going to come with you to one of these things. It's so unfair that you get to eat all the good stuff."

"Don't forget, I also have to eat all the bad stuff," Austin reminded him. He scooched down on the bench and leaned back, lounging as best he could on a wooden seat.

"Maybe so, but I think it would be worth it."

"That's only because you eat like a starving hyena," Austin said with a laugh. "Nothing tastes bad to you."

"Better than nothing tasting good," Tye argued back. "Being too picky means you don't enjoy life as much."

"Hey, it takes work to cultivate taste buds like mine," Austin argued.

"And that's why you get paid the big bucks," Tye said wryly. "Yeah, yeah. I've heard this before."

Austin smiled, but didn't respond. His brother could complain all he wanted. Austin and Tye lived together and neither was starved for food or money.

"This is a problem, you know," Tye hedged.

"Why do you say that?"

"Stan wanted a zinger. Remember?"

Austin sighed and rubbed his forehead. "Yeah...well...I can't do anything about that. The cake really was amazing. I also had a petit four and it practically melted on my tongue. There's no way I can write something bad about it. It would be completely dishonest." He didn't bother to mention that he already felt like some of his reviews were bordering on dishonesty. He knew Tye was doing the best he could. Stan wanted fresh and catchy, and it was hard to keep that up. But when it came down to pushing the truth or losing his job? Austin shook his head. There wasn't a contest.

"Wasn't there anything you didn't like? Maybe one of the servers was rude? Or the customers were upset?"

Austin shook his head even though Tye couldn't see it. "No. Aspen Harrison herself served me, and she was..." He trailed off. He wasn't sure he wanted to speak about her personally. It almost felt like if he told Tye about her beauty and slight sass, it would be sacrilege.

He rolled his eyes at himself. It wasn't like she was some kind of deity or anything, but still...he couldn't bring himself to share his experience, or the pull he felt when she was around. It would just be his memory. One to savor when he was frustrated with his job.

"She was what?" Tye pressed.

"She was very professional and friendly," Austin finished. "I can't say I loved the decor of their little shop, but...that really had no bearing on the food itself. The cake was perfect."

"What was wrong with the decor?" Tye asked. "Old? Moldy? They inherited the place from their parents, right?"

"Yeah. But I think they redid the whole thing. They went with the Paris theme. You know... black and white with bright pink." Austin scrunched his nose. "There was a whole pink couch in there that made me feel like a bottle of Pepto had spilled."

Tye laughed. "Sounds girly."

"That's probably a good way to say it. A little too feminine for my tastes."

"Are you going to bring me back some cake?" Tye asked, changing the subject.

Austin sat up and glanced back down the street to the cafe. "Nope," he said. The line was still out to the street. "I don't have time to wait in line again."

"Come on." Tye groaned. "Help a guy out."

"Sorry, man," Austin said, forcing himself to stand up. He really did need to get in the car and head back. His full stomach, however, wanted to lie down and take a nap. It would be a long drive. "The whole town seems to be hanging around and it would take at least another hour to get you something."

Tye grumbled, but didn't press him. "Fine. Guess I'll see you tonight. You can describe everything and I'll get it written up."

"Yep. See ya then." Austin ended the call and stuffed the phone in his pocket. Taking a breath of salty sea air, he began to walk. It was nice here, right on the beach, and it was easier than he thought it would be to see why people stuck around.

Seagull Cove definitely didn't have all the amenities of Portland, but there was a slight charm to all the coastal shops and buildings.

And Austin would be lying if he didn't say he enjoyed seeing all the locals chat and celebrate while they waited in line at the new cafe. The sisters were obviously well loved and their cafe would be in good hands with this kind of community. Not to mention the decor didn't seem to put off anyone else other than Austin.

Stuffing his hands in his pockets, he headed back to his car. He still had work to do and he was eager to get home and do it. The Harrison women deserved something special, especially Aspen, and Austin was determined to give it to her.

CHAPTER 4

Aspen wiped her hands on her apron. She knew she was probably covered in flour and sugar, but she didn't care. This was her happy place. The grand opening had been wonderful and she finally relaxed and enjoyed her time with the crowds, but now it was time to get back to work.

Since their opening a week ago, the flow of customers hadn't slowed down at all. Most of them were locals, coming in for a sweet treat in the afternoons, but they also had their fair share of tourists who seemed to be enticed by the cake displays in the window.

Aspen could barely keep up with the display case and she loved it. She had been so worried about taking over her parents' business and letting her father down, but with each passing day, with each piece of cake sold, with each smile covered in frosting, Aspen grew more and more confident that she was going to make this work. Between her and her sisters, they could not only form their own reputation, but they could uphold the standard their parents had built many years ago.

Her jelly on the stove began to boil and Aspen rushed over to give it a good stir. She was creating yet another fall themed cake, and if the smells coming from her stove were any indication, she knew it would be another hit. Who didn't love apples and cinnamon with a hint of cloves? Only crazy people. That was who.

"But pairing it with bacon?" she murmured to herself. "Now that'll get their attention."

"Oh my gosh," Estelle said as she walked through the door. She stopped to take a deep sniff. "What in the world is that? It's heavenly."

"It's my apple filling," Aspen said without looking up.

"And you're pairing it with?"

"Cinnamon cake and bacon crumbles."

Estelle's footsteps stuttered. "Bacon? Really?"

Aspen looked up and grinned. "Yep."

Estelle shrugged and made a face. "I'd say you're the boss, but...we're all the bosses." She smiled.

"How about, I'm the baker?"

"There is that." Estelle threw a pile of mail down on the counter. "I heard a rumor."

"Yeah? What's that?" Aspen's attention had gone back to her cooking. The apples looked like they were almost where she wanted them. She needed to pull them just before they were soft enough, because the filling would continue to cook while it cooled.

"I heard our review is here."

"What?" Aspen was having trouble pulling herself away from watching the apples. Timing was everything.

"Aspen!"

"What?"

"Look at me."

Aspen held up one finger. "Hang...on...one..." She gave the pan one more stir, then picked up the handle and removed the filling from the heat. "There. Just right." She wiped her hands together and finally gave her sister her attention. "What did you need?"

Estelle was looking at her with resigned, but warm eyes. "Our review is live."

"Review?" Memories of bright green eyes and messy blond hair came to mind. "Oh my gosh! Eat It Austin put it up?"

Estelle nodded.

"Yes!" Aspen clapped her hands. "Can this day get any better?"

Estelle laughed softly. "I guess we'll see. Maybe we need to see what he has to say first."

Aspen waved a hand through the air in a dismissive move. "He loved the cake. I know it."

One black eyebrow rose high. "You're so sure?"

Aspen glared. "Do you really doubt my cake?"

Estelle shook her head. "No. But sometimes I feel like his reviews are mean just to get a reaction, not because the food is actually bad. I was taking a risk by asking him here, I know, but it seemed like a good idea at the time."

Aspen sighed. "There is that. But I personally handed him a slice of my pear ginger cake. I also saw him swallow a petit four and say 'wow'. So, I'm feeling pretty good about it."

"Well. Why don't we go see if your prediction is right?"

"Now?" Aspen looked to the clock. "Don't we have... Oh." She hadn't realized how much time had passed. That was a common thing for her when baking. "Looks like I'm putting the filling in the fridge for the night."

Estelle walked toward the offices. "Well, I'm anxious to hear what he said, so let's read that first. Then you can clean up."

"Or you could help me clean up?" Aspen pressed.

Estelle laughed. "You wish!"

Aspen stuck her tongue out, but she knew in the end her sister would help. Estelle always helped. "Where's Maeve?"

Estelle turned back around to Aspen, gripping the door behind her before pushing it open.

Maeve looked up at the opening from her computer. "Did you ladies need something?"

Aspen laughed softly under her breath. She might get lost in cooking, but Maeve was even worse when it came to spreadsheets. And Aspen was pretty sure that the result of her concentration brought about something far sweeter than punching a calculator all day. She walked across the room. "You want to look up our review? Estelle says it's up."

Maeve's skin paled. "Oh... Yyeah, well..."

Aspen frowned and looked at Estelle's similar expression. "Have you read it?" she asked Maeve. "Is there a problem with it?"

Maeve's cheeks turned red, the color coming back. "Maybe."

Aspen stormed to the office. "What did he say?"

Maeve bit her lip but didn't respond.

Aspen slumped against the door frame. "What did he say?" she asked weakly.

Hanging her head and sighing, Maeve clicked on her laptop, then spun it around.

Estelle stepped forward and began to read.

"The grand opening of the Three Sisters Cafe should have been a wondrous occasion, especially considering the heritage of the new owners. And while the cake was enough to bring me to the drooling point, it was overshadowed by the cheap and cliche decor. Who wants to sit on a couch that blinds you with its brightness until you need a swig of the Pepto bottle it was designed from?'

Aspen's breathing had stopped, along with Estelle's reading. The world was spinning. How could that handsome man have said something so horrible? He even admitted the food was good, but instead of praising them, he still tore them apart. She knew from past experience his insane fans would be in a frenzy over this.

Only moments before, she had been happier than ever. Now she felt as if all her hopes and dreams were seizing like chocolate in water.

Estelle coughed and Aspen looked over to see her sister holding back tears. "Aspen," Estelle said hoarsely. "I'm so sorry. This is my fault. I designed the..." She couldn't even finish her sentence.

"Don't you dare," Aspen said with a hard shake of her head. She rushed over and wrapped her older sister in a tight hug and was surprised when Maeve joined them. "The cafe is beautiful," Aspen said tightly. Her shock was slowly turning to anger. How dare she be attracted to someone so cruel? He was never allowed inside their shop again. "This is nothing. *He* is nothing. We're still going to thrive. People love us, and they love the redecorating job." She leaned back enough to wipe Estelle's cheek free of tears. "Don't you dare apologize. We, and especially you, did nothing wrong. This won't hurt us. Eat It Austin is just a jerk who can't see a good thing when it slaps him across the face."

"But what if people stop coming?" Estelle asked, her normal confidence completely gone in the wake of the harsh review.

"We won't let them," Aspen said firmly. She looked at Maeve for support, who appeared sympathetic, but didn't offer any advice. "We're still going to be the best cake shop along the Pacific coastline and nothing will stop people from coming. Especially not beautiful custom couches that add just the right touch of color to our space."

Estelle sniffed and wiped her face. "We can switch them out."

"Not yet," Maeve said. "Not enough funds."

"We're not switching them out," Aspen argued. "We're sticking to what we've got. It's beautiful. We all love it and that's what matters. Eat It Austin can stick his nose in someone else's business. He's blackballed from ours."

AUSTIN KNOCKED ON HIS boss's door.

"Enter!"

"What is this?" Austin shouted as he shoved the door open, holding his phone out. The screen was open to his latest review. He and Tye had worked hard on that review, giving the sisters credit where it was due, but trying to give it a little edginess that would keep Stan happy as well. What was printed was *not* what they had agreed on.

Stan smirked from behind his desk. He splayed his hands to the side. "Your review is a hit. What can I say?"

"This isn't what I wrote!" Austin said tightly. "Shifting my words and taking them out of context to suit your needs is wrong."

Stan waved him off. "We left in the fact that you liked the cake. It'll be fine."

"Have you seen the comments!" Austin shouted. "Something like this could ruin them! They're brand new!"

Stan blew out a raspberry. "So we critiqued their decorations. Who cares?"

"I care," Austin said, feeling slightly sick to his stomach. This whole thing was getting out of control. Stan was obviously going behind his back to work directly with Tye. And Austin knew Tye wouldn't put up a fight. He struggled with his anxiety too much. If Stan asked for it, Tye would give it to him.

Austin could just imagine Aspen's beautiful dark eyes looking at him with something much different than the warmth he'd received last week. She had been so sweet and so confident in her cake baking skills. Did it really matter that Austin didn't like the pink? And why had he bothered to mention it at all? He should have just given his boss another nice review and put his foot down about it.

Stan leaned forward onto his desk, his fingers folded together. "Online fame is fickle," he said in a lecturing tone. It was a lecture Austin had heard before and could almost recite by heart. "One day they like you, the next day you're old news. The trick is to capitalize on it when you can. For some reason, you've captured the attention of a demographic with the shortest attention spans known to man. As long as you keep them happy, you'll also keep your bank account and this company and its investors happy." Stan's eyes narrowed. "But if you go soft, they'll chew you up and spit you out before you figure out what day it is."

Fear filled Austin's stomach and it began to churn. It was a feeling he was familiar with and had far too much power over him. Flashes of living in his mom's car and eating scraps came back to mind and he felt himself step down from his soapbox. He didn't like what his boss and brother had done, but he also couldn't go back to being homeless and poor. He just couldn't. The hunger pangs and being so cold he was sure he would never be warm were feelings he could still feel if he closed his eyes.

"Do we still have a problem?" Stan's question was entirely too smug. He knew he had Austin. He might not understand why Austin always gave in, but the man was no dummy. He had recognized long ago that threatening Austin with unemployment was the way to keep him in line.

"No," Austin said softly. Scowling, he closed the door and stomped back to his desk. Once there, he dropped into his seat and buried his face in his hands.

"You okay?" Tye asked.

Austin growled and dropped his hands, glaring at his brother. "Those women didn't deserve that. The cake was amazing. I can't believe he used you behind my back. Have you seen the reaction?"

Tye nodded, his eyes dropping to the desk. His cheeks were flaming red and it was clear he didn't know what to say. "Looks like it's going viral...again."

Austin shook his head. "Who cares? If the comments continue the way they're going, those poor girls are going to feel the hit against their business, and that would be tragic."

Tye shrugged and made a face. "Maybe it'll be one of those situations where people come just to see how bad it is." He winced at Austin's glare. "You know how it is. People are weird. Sometimes they build something up just because they don't like it."

Austin shook his head and rolled his eyes. "It wasn't even that bad. So there was a pink couch. I didn't have to sit on it, and it had nothing to do with the taste of the cake." He fell back against his chair. "And now I'll probably never get to eat any more of that cake again. They'll likely burn me alive before letting me step foot inside."

Tye snorted. "That's what you're worried about? And here I thought you were being all noble and worried about the women."

"I am," Austin insisted. "But that doesn't mean I can't lament my own situation as well." His smile fell. "But seriously. You shouldn't have done it." Eyebrows pulling together, Austin leaned forward. "We've been together in this for a long time, Tye. But this was low."

Tye shrunk back, then grabbed a handful of papers. "I need to go shred these," he mumbled before dashing away from his seat.

Austin pinched his lips together. The guilt was gnawing at Austin and he wasn't sure what to do. He couldn't go back to before, but he also didn't like the way his name and image were hurting people. He could talk to Tye again when they got home, but it wasn't going to do much good. His younger brother was more messed up from their childhood than Austin was. Tye gave in under the slightest pressure, where Austin usually put up a fight. *Unless it involves your job,* a far too logical voice said in the back of his mind.

A bad review once in a while happened. Not every restaurant was good or had good service. But to be rude just for the sake of ratings? It didn't settle well with him.

Tye slowly came back to his seat. "Sorry. I know I shouldn't have, but I was trying to keep us employed. Plus, with the way Stan was shouting, I was worried Izzy was going to find out about everything," he mumbled.

Austin sighed and scrubbed his face. Izzy would love getting her hands on the knowledge that Austin didn't do his own writing. More than likely because she was the office gossip and she took her job seriously. No water cooler required. Simply stand next to her for a few minutes.

"I *do* know everything...don't I," Izzy said with a grin as she walked by. Her laptop was held against her chest. She leaned her hip against Austin's desk. "Just what is it I need to know now?"

Austin pinched his lips together.

Izzy gave him a smirk. She was a single woman, closing in on forty, though she would never admit to it. But he had the distinct feeling that if he gave her a sign, the age difference wouldn't mean anything to her. "Come on, Austin. Tell me." She widened her blue eyes in anticipation.

He leaned back away from her. "I'm just trying to figure out where I should review next."

She tapped a green fingernail against her red lips. "You don't have a schedule? I thought Stan kept that all up."

Austin gave a curt nod. "He does, usually."

Izzy looked at him from under thick lashes. "Well, you could always come review my cooking." She smiled, but it looked more predatory than inviting. "I don't mind sharing my secrets."

Austin gave her a look. "I have work to get back to." No way was he taking that road. It appeared his hands were tied. At this point, there was nothing he could do. He would never see the Harrison women again, so it was time to just let it go. Eventually, the media frenzy would die down and their business would be fine. It would. He was sure of it.

I hope.

CHAPTER 5

"Let it go," Aspen murmured to herself as she spun her latest cake and smoothed the frosting. "Let it go..." The words turned into a song from one of her favorite cartoons. She smiled at the song until her phone buzzed again.

Yet another notification that her business had been tagged on social media. Aspen erased the notice without bothering to read the comment. Ever since Jerk-Face Austin had slammed her shop in his online review, his rabid fans had taken his comments and run with it.

Three Sisters Cafe had become the laughingstock of the internet. According to the news, they were one of the highest trending topics online. Customers had dwindled to a trickle and several times, Estelle said groups of teenagers had come in, only to take pictures and laugh before going back outside. Their antics only served to disrupt the few customers who still showed up. It was embarrassing and frustrating, and Aspen knew it was only a matter of time before her parents caught wind of what was going on. Something this big wouldn't remain only in the United States for long.

She felt her cheeks heat up at the idea of her dad seeing the laughingstock they had become. She cursed under her breath when her anger came out in her frosting and she pushed too hard, making the line uneven.

Dumping her scraper back in the bowl, she walked away, blowing out a long breath. There had to be something they could do to combat the situation. Aspen knew as well as anyone that going viral never lasted very long. When another scandal hit the internet, she and her shop would be old news. But she wasn't sure they would escape unscathed before that happened. Maeve was looking more and more upset each day when their numbers stayed down.

The kitchen door opened. "Hey, Aspen. We're down to two slices of the red velvet."

Aspen nodded. "I've got one in the oven."

"You okay?" Estelle's voice was wary and Aspen ached for how much her sister had been affected by the situation. Estelle had taken it as a personal attack. She had been the one to set up the review and it was her decorating job that Austin the Grinch had taken offense to.

"As good as I can be," Aspen said, forcing a smile for her sister. None of this was Estelle's fault and Aspen took it personally that someone would hurt her sister in such a way. The shop was beautiful. Maybe the pink was a little bright and not every man would enjoy the Paris theme, but they weren't the first, nor would they be the last, to use those colors. There was absolutely nothing wrong with having a feminine touch to things and it ticked her off that Dog Breath Austin thought his opinion was so important that he could say such horrible things about it.

He was a food critic, not an interior designer. Just who did he think he was to make fun of their shop that way? And especially to imply that their father would be upset by the change? Their dad would love it. His chocolate sculptures were bold and always broke the mold in the food art world. He believed in making your own path, and that's exactly what the girls were doing.

Estelle's eyes filled with tears as she nodded. "I need to get back," she said, jabbing a thumb over her shoulder.

"Wait," Aspen said, walking quickly to her sister. She grabbed Estelle in a hug. There had been a lot of those lately. "Stop blaming yourself," Aspen said softly in her sister's ear. "No one could have predicted that Ugly Austin would decide he was an expert in decor. None of this is your fault. We're in this together. Always."

Estelle sniffed and wiped at her eyes. "Thanks," she said in response. "I have the best sisters."

Aspen nodded. "Darn right, you do. And none of us are going to sit down and take Stupid Austin's criticism lying down."

Estelle frowned. "What do you mean?" Her eyes opened wide. "What are you planning?"

Aspen pinched her lips together. An idea was forming in her brain and she wasn't sure if she should say it. It was risky. If it went badly, she might hurt their business more than she helped it. "You know what they say," she said carefully. "Any attention is good attention."

"Aspen," Estelle warned. "What are you thinking?"

"I'm thinking that I'm not going to wait for the online community to get tired of making fun of us," Aspen said, sticking her chin in the air. "I'm going to use their attention to get back at Nightmare-Inducing Austin."

Estelle rolled her eyes. "How many adjectives do you have stored in that head of yours?"

Aspen smirked. "As many as I need. Idiot Austin might have tried to turn his fans against us, but with a little work, I think we can turn the tide."

The office door opened. "What are you two talking about?" Maeve asked, leaning her shoulder against the door frame. "I can hear bits and pieces in the office and I'm starting to get concerned."

"You should be," Estelle said, folding her arms over her chest. "Aspen is talking about getting some kind of revenge."

Aspen shook her head. "No. Not revenge." She pumped her eyebrows. "I'm talking redemption."

Maeve walked up, her glasses sitting in her hair looking sweetly academic. "Are you going to share your idea with us?"

Aspen paused. "Maybe."

"The fact that you're afraid to tell us, tells us everything," Estelle said, her mother voice coming through. "Obviously, it's not a good idea."

"On the contrary, it's a great idea," Aspen argued. "You just aren't going to like it."

Estelle rolled her eyes and looked over her shoulder when the bell over the door rang. She pointed a finger at her sisters. "Don't you dare make any decisions without me. Capiche?"

Aspen nodded and waited until her older sister was out of earshot.

"Spill it," Maeve said, her golden eyes sparkling. "What's your idea?"

Aspen tried to act cool as she headed back to the cake. "You heard Estelle. No decisions without her."

"I'm not saying we vote. I'm saying you share." Maeve pulled up a stool and sat down, watching her sister work. "Come on," she whined. "Tell me."

Aspen looked up from her work. "I think we should use his fans against him."

"How?" Maeve frowned and tucked a piece of hair behind her ear. "His fans love him."

Aspen nodded. "Right. Which means they won't want to see him embarrassed."

"You want to do something to embarrass him?" Maeve asked. "Again, I ask...how?"

Aspen shrugged. "Not embarrass him, exactly. But I think we should try to pull him down off his foodie pedestal. Frog-Face Austin thinks he's all that and a side of cheesecake, but he doesn't ever seem to consider the fact that he could be wrong."

"Who would in his position?" Maeve asked. "His fans reaffirm their love for his opinions all the time."

"Right. But how would they feel if someone challenged that opinion?"

"You want to put up a post that you think Austin was wrong?"

Aspen shook her head. "No. I want more. I don't just want to say he's wrong...I want Horse-Nose Austin to apologize."

AUSTIN WINCED AS HE read more comments about The Three Sisters Cafe. Of all the ridiculous posts to have stick around for days on end, why did it have to be this one? If Austin ever saw Aspen or her sisters again, he was sure he'd end up with a black eye.

If not worse.

"Dude, let it go," Tye said with a yawn. He picked up his mug and took a long sip. "All this publicity is a good thing." He had apparently gotten over his dirty deed in this case, convinced that the girls were lapping up all the attention.

Austin shook his head and shut off his phone. "I can't seem to let it go," he complained. "I really don't like that Stan went behind my back or that you willingly helped. This is wrong."

Tye choked on his drink and covered his mouth, wiping his desk from the sprays that had come out of his mouth. "I thought you said you forgave me."

Austin chuckled. "I do. You're my brother, but still..."

Tye rolled his eyes. "You really need to just walk away. What's done is done. Any time now some celebrity scandal will pull the public's attention away from that stupid shop and it'll all be over. Business as usual." He went back to typing on his computer, religiously editing whatever piece he was working on for the day.

Austin sighed. "You're right. I know you're right, but I still don't like it."

Tye raised an eyebrow. "Every time this happens, you freak. Are you sure this is really the job we want? Maybe we should do something else."

Panic hit Austin in the gut and he squeezed his eyes shut. "No," he said, his voice softer than before. "I need this job."

"We all do," Tye grumbled, sipping his drink again. "It's why we deal with the stress."

Austin forced his eyes open and nodded. "True. The life of a journalist is far from easy, right?"

Tye shrugged. "Yeah."

"You still working on that book?" Austin asked, desperately trying to change the subject. He needed to get the smell of the street out of his nose and the image of sleeping in the car out of his head. Otherwise, he would end up setting off Tye as well as himself.

Tye nodded, then looked around conspiratorially and leaned in. "I'm halfway through," he whispered. "When I'm not editing for Stan the Man, I slip in a few paragraphs here and there."

"And it's a space story?"

"Space opera," Tye explained. "You know, like Battlestar Galactica? Star Wars?"

Austin nodded and rubbed the top of his head. "Sure, sure."

Tye sighed and gave him a look.

Austin made a face. "What? I read. Don't cookbooks count?" They both knew that Austin didn't crack a book open if he didn't have to, though not from a lack of interest. It was the exact reason Tye had become the writer in the first place.

Tye laughed. "You are more obsessed with food than anyone I know," he said.

That's because I remember what it's like to be hungry. Tye had been so little when they were homeless and half the time Austin had given what little they had to help his brother. He'd been taking care of Tye for a long time. "I suppose so."

"And yet you don't cook." Tye shook his head teasingly.

Austin scratched the edge of his jaw. "I cook," he defended himself. "But we both know I'm not really good at it." He picked up a pencil and twirled it through his fingers. "I understand all the concepts, but somehow it doesn't translate very well when I try to create something." He glanced up with a grin. "The only creative part of me is my tastebuds."

"The public would say otherwise," Tye offered.

Austin groaned. They were right back where they began. "I don't like having things up that aren't even close to my words," he said softly.

"That's not true," Tye said. "They're your words. They're just...your words expanded." His face had flushed again, letting Austin know Tye hadn't let go of the guilt any more than he had.

"Yeah, well, I could go without the credit," Austin muttered to himself. He needed to stop fighting with his brother about it. It was over and done with. He sat upright. "But enough. You're right. I need to let it go. This review wasn't any different than any other review. Time to move on. The public will eventually do the same."

He wasn't quite sure why the reaction to this review bothered him so much. Stan had done this on more than one occasion, taking the tiniest flaw and exploiting it in order to get social media behind it. It had worked enough times that Austin knew he should know better than to expect anything different, but somehow he just kept hoping that what Tye wrote would be left as it was.

Austin tried to be honest and unbiased, he really did. As for Aspen's place, he loved the food, but disliked the decor. It was the truth. But that didn't mean he wanted her and her sisters reamed for it.

Dark, nearly black eyes came to his mind and he paused in his work. She really had been a very lovely woman. He ticked his head to the side as he pictured her more fully. Lovely didn't quite cover it.

She was beautiful. Stunning. Slightly exotic, if he was being truthful. Feminine and friendly, and she could bake like an angel.

If they lived in the same city, Austin would be all over taking her out to dinner. He knew just the right place to take her too. Somewhere quiet, where he could get to know her, yet had food that could make a grown man weep. There were very few places in Portland that he hadn't tried out, whether for work or not. If given the opportunity, he knew he could show Aspen Harrison the time of her life.

She probably has a boyfriend.

The unwelcome thought stopped him cold in his tracks. He shook his head. Boyfriend or not, daydreaming was not helping him at all. She was there, he was here and as of right now, she probably hated him.

"Any luck?" Izzy's ample hip rested against the side of his desk as she dropped a pile of mail in front of him.

"On what?" Austin didn't bother to look up at her. He didn't want to send her the message he was interested in the conversation.

"On figuring out where to go next?" she asked with an exasperated note to her voice.

"Oh." He shook his head. "Nope." He thumbed through the letters, dismissing most of them as junk...until his attention was caught on one that was postmarked from Seagull Cove, bringing Aspen right back to his thoughts.

"Maybe we could work on figuring it out together," Tye hedged, his eyes on Izzy as if she were the last drink of water in a hot desert. "I'm sure if we put our heads together, it wouldn't take long to—"

Izzy gave him a look. "Nice try, kid." She stood and bent over to get down at his level. "But I don't think so." With a huff, she turned and sashayed away.

Austin held back a snicker and gave Tye a commiserating look. "It was a nice try, man."

Tye shrugged and went back to his computer. "She'll come around...eventually."

Austin nodded. He wasn't quite so sure, but whatever. Austin had no claim on Izzy and didn't want one. Tye was welcome to her. But a woman with soulful eyes, who hated his guts? Well...that was one Austin couldn't seem to let go of quite so easily.

CHAPTER 6

"Okay, you ready?" Maeve asked, pushing her glasses up her nose. She fiddled with her phone a little more, then glanced over the screen, her eyebrows high in question.

Aspen fluffed her hair, straightened her shoulders and nodded. "Oh...wait." Using her finger, she rubbed her front teeth, double checking that none of her lipstick was on her teeth. "Okay. Ready."

Maeve pressed a button, counted down with her fingers from three and nodded.

"Hello," Aspen began, trying to make herself appear as pleasant as possible. "As many of you may know, my name is Aspen Harrison." She smiled gently. "Recently, my sisters and I opened a bakery called The Three Sisters Cafe." Her small laugh was planned, but she felt like she pulled it off fairly well. "The reason that should sound familiar is because Eat It Austin came to review our shop and I'm sure all of you know who that is." She kept the smile in place, though it was getting harder now. "While he was quite complimentary about the cake, he had some rather unflattering things to say about the decorations of our little cafe and apparently, that was enough to ruin his appetite." Her smile was so tight at this point she felt as if her face would break. "And while many of you may agree with him, I'm afraid that my sisters and I decided we had something we wanted to offer in return." She clapped her hands. "An invitation to apologize."

Aspen tried to be flirty with the camera, but she was sure people would just think she was ridiculous. Still... "Mr. Eat it Austin was asked to come review our food, not make rude comments about our decor. Truthfully, I've never heard of someone who had such a delicate derriere that it affected the way food tasted to them, but to each

55

their own, I suppose." She tilted her head, her smile far from friendly. "We formally request an apology from Eat It Austin, as an act of good faith, for a man who was called for one job, but so rudely did another instead. When we want help with our decorating, we'll call the Home Improvement Channel." She waved. "We'll be waiting!"

Maeve snorted as she pressed buttons on the phone. "You're a beast," she murmured as she worked.

"No, I'm Beauty." Aspen laughed. "Poop Head Austin is the beast."

Maeve snorted again and shook her head. She glanced up. "Do you really think this is a good idea? What if all of his crazy fans turn on us? It might be worse than before."

Aspen shook her head. "No way. They love drama and this gives them exactly that. I don't really think they love Big-Eared Austin as much as they enjoy having something scandalous to follow." Aspen huffed. "Have you looked at his demographics? It's all young people. Mostly singles at that. They're just looking for a juicy bit of gossip."

Maeve raised an eyebrow. "They're probably mostly women. I didn't see him when he was here, but his picture is...what's the word?"

"Ugly? Pathetic? Stupid?" Aspen supplied.

Maeve sighed and pushed her glasses up to the top of her head. "I think I was going for hot, or handsome or maybe even sexy. Definitely not what you're offering."

Aspen rolled her eyes. "All the more reason to fight back. No one that good looking should make a living at tearing others down."

"So you admit he's good looking?" Maeve teased.

"I admit nothing," Aspen said with a sniff. "Except that I'm ready for you to upload that video."

"You did it already?" Estelle asked, coming back into the kitchen. "I missed it?" She poked her lips out in a pout. "I was hoping to watch."

"You can watch now," Maeve said, holding out her phone.

Aspen chewed her bottom lip as she listened to herself recite the speech she had memorized. She really had done pretty well. All the right inflections and intonations were in place. Maybe the actress thing wasn't such a bad idea.

"Wow," Estelle said, handing the phone back. She tucked a piece of hair behind her ear. "That's bold. Really bold."

"And kinda mean," Maeve said through a fake cough.

Normally, Aspen would have agreed with her younger sister, but right now she was too caught up in her self righteous anger. "It's nothing compared to what he did to us or what he's done to other businesses in the past." She put her hands on her hips. "Now are you going to post that or do I need to handle things?"

"I'm on it, I'm on it," Maeve said, waving her hand through the air.

Secretly, Aspen was glad Maeve was handling it. She was all big talk right now, but Aspen knew that if given the opportunity, she was just as likely to erase the video as she was to upload it. She didn't know how Fish Lips Austin did it. He must have a heart made from granite, because even standing up for herself and her sisters made Aspen sick to her stomach.

She put a hand over said body part and took several deep breaths. This needed to be done. Their numbers were abysmal except for the few older locals who didn't bother to follow social media at all. Memes still ran rampant, and even after ten days, no other scandal had been able to replace the trending review.

"Done," Maeve said, finally looking up to meet her sister's eyes. "I sure hope you know what you're doing."

Me too, Aspen thought. "Publicity is publicity," she said out loud, in a much more confident voice than she felt. "This will turn the tide, I'm sure of it."

Maeve nodded and Estelle sighed. "Okay. Well, I'm back on duty." She pinned Aspen with a look. "Don't do anything else for a while, okay? I don't want to have to be the one to tell Dad that we ruined his business within our first month of being open."

Icy fear hit the already churning dread in Aspen's stomach and she almost doubled over from the sensation. It was because she was worried that she'd done this. Had she gone too far? Had she been meaner than she needed to be? She had pushed her kindness levels down in order to catch attention, but maybe she just ended up looking like a bitter shrew. Would her parents be mad about it? Would they understand that she was trying to fight fire with fire?

Aspen rubbed her temples. Why were all these questions coming up now? Why hadn't they appeared when she'd spent almost all night writing the script for the video? Or what about *before* she had Maeve post it?

"Here."

Aspen looked up to see Maeve holding a bottle of headache medicine. "How did you know?" she asked.

Maeve shrugged. "Because I know you well enough to know that guilt and shame are eating you alive." She shook the bottle. "You're gonna need this."

Aspen took it gratefully. "Did I do the wrong thing?" she asked in a small voice.

Maeve paused. "It's a little late for that, don't you think?"

Aspen gave her a look and Maeve laughed softly.

"I think if you wanted his attention, you're gonna get it," Maeve explained. "I don't know what will come of it, but I don't think this will ruin us. If something does, it won't be because you picked a fight with a celebrity." She held up crossed fingers. "Here's hoping the masses swing our way."

Aspen gave a small smile. That hadn't exactly made her feel confident, but it was nice to know her little sister wasn't putting the blame on her shoulders. Come what may, they were in this together.

"WHAT NOW?" AUSTIN GROWLED, grabbing his phone. It had been blowing up all morning, which normally would be fine, except that he actually had a piece he was working on today. He was already a slow writer and it wasn't easy to get anything done when your phone wouldn't stop buzzing.

Instead of the notifications he had been seeing, Austin realized with alarm that it was his boss calling. "Stan?" he asked, answering the phone.

"What in the world have you been doing?" Stan snapped. "I've been calling for the past half hour."

"Sorry," Austin muttered, pushing his hand through his hair. "I've been trying to write the review on that new restaurant in Vancouver. But my phone kept going off, so I silenced it."

"Just get down here now," Stan barked.

"Why?" Austin asked. "I've worked from home before."

"Now!" The phone line went dead and Austin blew out a breath.

This was ridiculous. Stan had never cared before if Austin worked from home. Although, with all the buzzing his phone was doing, Ausitn began to wonder if something else was going on. Grabbing his wallet, keys and computer, he hopped in the car and took off.

Lunchtime traffic made his commute a little longer than normal and by the time Austin arrived at the office, there was a deep pit in his stomach. Something was wrong, he just knew it.

He entered the doors warily, unsure how Stan was going to react. The two of them were already at each other's throat about the social media issue. What more could be happening?

"Austin!" Tye called out. The entire office hushed at the sound, and all eyes turned to Austin.

He jerked to a stop. "Uh...what's going on?" He quickly went over the date in his head. It wasn't his birthday. It wasn't a major holiday. He couldn't think of anything that should cause this.

Just then, Stan burst through his office doors. "The hero has arrived!" The older man's skin was bright red with excitement and the smile on his face could only be described as giddy.

"Hero?" Austin mouthed to Tye.

Tye made a face and nodded slowly.

"I don't understand," Austin tried to say to Stan, but his boss wasn't listening.

"In all my years in this business, I've never had such a reaction," Stan muttered under his breath. His eyes were wide and wild, and it terrified Austin. What plan did the old man have in mind now?

"Stan, what are you talking about?" Austin stepped back as Stan approached, clapping him on the shoulder so hard Austin nearly fell over.

"It's trending so fast they can't keep the numbers up to date." Stan chortled.

"What?"

A phone was thrust in his face. "Watch this," Izzy's annoyed voice said from behind his shoulder.

Austin glanced back and gave Izzy a grateful look, then took the device. Instantly, his attention was caught. It was Aspen Harrison. She looked just as beautiful as he remembered. Her hair was styled, and her lipstick? Perfection. Dang, it stunk that he'd never be able to show his face in her shop again.

"Ouch." Austin held his side when Izzy jabbed her elbow into his ribs.

"Listen, chump. She's talking to you."

Austin frowned and finally started paying attention to what Aspen was saying. Slowly, his eyebrows crept higher and higher on his forehead until he was sure they had reached his hairline. "What?" He gasped. He looked up when the video was done, his cheeks burning with humiliation. "Is she serious?"

"As a heart attack," Izzy said, snatching the phone back. "It's gone viral."

"You've got to be kidding." Austin rubbed his forehead. "She wants a public apology? What am I supposed to do with that?"

"Did you hear the subtle zingers she sent back your way?" Stan laughed. "Maybe I should hire her to do our media posts."

Oh, Austin had heard all right. Each one had been like a dagger to his chest. Even though he knew he couldn't exactly blame her for feeling that way, heck, he'd hate himself too, if he'd opened a business only to have some jerk come in and shred it apart. But the words hurt all the same.

"What're you going to do?" Tye asked, sidling up to the group. He drew close to Izzy's side, who rolled her eyes and stalked away.

The rejection didn't even faze Austin. Usually, he felt bad for his brother, but not this time. His mind was too caught up in Aspen's demands. And they were demands. There was no mistaking her tone of voice, or her anger. She was out for blood. His. Or at least his humiliation.

"Maybe we should just admit the truth—"

"What!" Stan roared. "Are you joking?" He shook his head. "You have to be joking." His thick finger jabbed at Austin's chest. "This is the best thing to happen to us since you started. Hits on our website have tripled today and your page is getting thousands of comments."

Austin groaned and moved across the room to sink into a chair. "I don't even want to know what people are saying."

"Actually, it's a bit of a mix," Tye offered. "Some people are calling for your head, and others are ready to defend you to the death." He ducked his head when Stan glared at him, obviously upset at having his thunder stolen.

"Don't worry about the comments," Stan said hurriedly. "The important thing is that we take advantage of this." He rubbed his hands together. "This kind of publicity costs millions, and we're getting it for almost nothing. It'll double our revenue this month alone."

Austin held up his hand. "What exactly are you wanting me to do?" he asked, feeling sick to his stomach. "I'm not getting into some kind of internet fight with her. She's right. I don't know anything about decor and how I felt about the pink couches had nothing to do with how good her cake was." He slapped his knees. "In fact, I should just offer her the apology. It's not worth arguing about when she's right." Austin made to get up, but Stan began shouting again.

"Sit your butt down," he demanded. "You're not apologizing to anyone."

"What?" Austin argued.

Stan shook his head, glaring at the whole group standing around, watching the display. "Backing down now would only mean that any restaurant that didn't like their review could come running with a few sniffles and tears and we'd have to change what we're doing. Absolutely not!" he shouted. "We stand by our work here, and we won't give in. We have to make a strong showing." He smirked. "The media will eat it up and eventually, that ridiculous woman will go back into her hidey hole. You're absolutely responding back." He gave Austin a significant look, then pointedly looked at Tye, who wouldn't meet their eyes.

Austin opened his mouth to argue. He didn't like Stan talking about Aspen that way, and he didn't like the idea of waging war any more than he wanted his younger brother used as a weapon.. None of this was her fault. Austin had made the comment about the couches, and Stan and Tye had taken the comment and run with it. Now Austin alone was suffering the consequences. This wasn't fair on so many levels, and he wanted to say just that, but Stan's look had him closing his mouth.

"Do I make myself clear?" Stan asked, the threat clear in his voice.

As if to remind Austin what it was like if he didn't keep his job, his stomach rumbled...loudly, causing snickers through several in the crowd. "Yeah," Austin finally responded. He hated himself in that moment. Probably more than Aspen did. He was a coward. A genuine coward. But how to fix it without losing everything he'd fought for?

CHAPTER 7

"Oh my gosh, oh my gosh," Estelle said, rushing into the kitchen, her phone in hand. "It's here."

Aspen frowned and pushed her hair net a little farther back on her forehead. "What's here?"

"His response."

Aspen froze. "What? Already? We only posted yesterday." And during that time, life had flipped upside down...again. The response had been insane. Her video had quickly gone viral. The phone had been ringing off the hook with calls from influencers and news stations who wanted the inside scoop on the story. The sisters had pretty much turned them all away. The person they were trying to get a hold of had yet to call, and they were holding out for Eat It Austin to make the next move.

Aspen had assumed, however, that it would take a few days for him to formulate a response. It appeared that wasn't the case. Her heart rate picked up and she felt slightly nauseated. "What did he say?"

Estelle cleared her throat and gave Aspen a significant look. "I want to thank Ms. Harrison for her clarifying remarks in regards to my recent review of her restaurant, The Three Sisters Cafe. I have to admit that I was shocked to find that she was unhappy with my services. While I'm not an expert in restaurant decor, I have been in enough food establishments to know what pleases the eye and what does not."

Aspen scoffed. "Really? *Really?*" She folded her arms over her chest. "This guy is asking for it."

Estelle's motherly look came over the top of her phone. "Aspen," she scolded. "Maybe it's time to turn the other cheek."

Aspen waved her sister on. "Just tell me what else he said."

Estelle cleared her throat. "And I can assure Ms. Harrison that neon pink in large quantities is not something that pleases anybody, especially those trying to consume food close by."

"Oooh!" Aspen growled.

Estelle shook her head and continued. "Nonetheless, if Ms. Harrison insists, I would be happy to come back to The Three Sisters Cafe and do a re-review. In fact, I look forward to seeing if her thoughts are correct about being guided by my...how did she put it? My delicate derriere?"

Aspen slammed her fist down on the counter top, shaking the cake stand she was working with. "Someone needs to punch that man in the nose."

Estelle chuckled and put her phone away.

"What are you laughing at?" Aspen demanded. "He's still insulting your work."

Estelle shrugged. "It's just all so ridiculous. You two are the hottest thing on the internet. If I'd known that getting into a fight was the way to increase business, I would have suggested it a long time ago."

Aspen paused. "Business is up?"

Estelle nodded with an amused look on her face. "The afternoon has been solid."

"Then what the heck are you doing in here?"

"Maeve is running the counter to let me get a break." Estelle stretched her back. "Plus, she saw the answer come through, so I had to come back and share it with you."

Aspen fiddled with a scraper. "And what are people saying as they come into the shop?"

Estelle smirked. "We've still got a crowd coming to get pictures on the pink couch, but a lot of people are actually ordering the cake. Oh!" She slapped her forehead. "I was supposed to tell you that we're almost out of the ricotta cake. That one has been a big hit today." She shrugged. "Sorry. I was too eager to share with you what Austin said."

Aspen tapped her fingers on the stainless steel counter. "I'm almost done with this one. I'll bring it out soon." She frowned, thinking hard.

"What are you planning?" Estelle asked.

Aspen looked up at her sister. "What do you mean?"

"I know that look," Estelle said wryly. "It means you're brainstorming. I want to know what you've got up your sleeve."

Aspen gave her a sarcastic smile. "You said yourself that the fight had caused business to pick up today."

"Aspen, I really don't think we should continue to argue back. Besides, he offered to come again. He's agreed to re-review. Let's just get rid of the pink couch and move ahead as planned."

"Don't you dare," Aspen ordered. "That couch is beautiful and we're not getting rid of it just because some jerk didn't like it. He doesn't live here. He's not a regular customer. He has no right to talk about our shop that way."

Estelle rolled her eyes and headed back to the front room. "Whatever. Just don't do anything that's gonna get you thrown in jail, alright?"

"Okay," Aspen quickly replied.

Estelle paused and turned around to glare. "Promise?"

It was Aspen's turn to roll her eyes. "I promise. Bickering on the internet isn't illegal, just annoying."

Estelle pointed at her sister. "Let's keep it that way."

Once her sister was gone, Aspen went back to work. She did her best thinking while she was frosting, so this was a perfect situation.

What do I say?

She needed to respond and she didn't want to wait too long. If they were already seeing an uptick in sales, then this fight of theirs just might turn into something helpful, especially after Frog Tongue Austin drove away their business only last week.

Aspen went through a thousand responses in her head, but none of them were quite right. She had no plans to take him up on his offer to re-review their cafe. He had liked the cake. That was undisputed and she wasn't going to give him the chance to take that back. His problem had been the setting of where he ate the cake.

Aspen paused. A thought was forming and she let it percolate for a moment before a slow smile crossed her lips. *Yesssss...*

She knew exactly how she wanted to get back at Color-Hating Austin. And if it went according to plan, Aspen knew she could drum up even more business for her cafe. She and her sisters would be set for good and their parents would have nothing to worry about.

A lot of planning was going to go into making this happen, but in the end...Aspen was sure it would be worth it.

She hummed a little ditty while she finished the cake, then proudly carried it out to the front room. A decent sized group of patrons met her gaze and Aspen smiled widely. "Fresh from the oven!" she called, holding the cake up before placing it among the other stands on the counter. "Maeve?"

Maeve pushed up her glasses and looked toward Aspen.

"I need you," Aspen said, crooking her finger as she headed back to the kitchens.

"Oh, thank heavens," Maeve muttered as she slipped through the door. "Thank you for saving me from working with crowds."

"Those crowds keep our business running and your heater on during the winter," Aspen pointed out.

Maeve gave her sister a look. "I'm aware. But that doesn't mean I want to be the one dealing with them."

Aspen waved a hand in the air. "Forget the crowds. I need you to do something for me."

"Does this involve your little fight with Eat It Austin?"

Aspen grinned.

Maeve sighed and pushed her glasses up into her hair. "What now?"

"Just wait until you hear what I've got planned..."

"SHE WANTS ME TO WHAT?" Austin cried. He closed his eyes and shook one finger in his ear. "Say that again, because I had to have heard you wrong."

Stan grinned, looking a little maniacal in how excited he was. "She wants you to come do another taste test, but this time she's throwing out a challenge for people to find you the right chair." He chuckled. "You've gotta hand it to her. She certainly knows how to get the public involved."

"Let me see if I understand this," Austin said, finally sitting in the chair across from Stan. "I'm supposed to go back down to Seagull Cove and eat her cake, but I have to do it over and over again in different chairs until I find one I like?"

Stan glanced at his computer. "She compared you to Goldilocks, and said that if you required a chair that was 'just right' before your taste buds actually functioned, then she would make sure you got what you needed." He laughed again. "The winner gets free cake for a year."

Austin whistled low. "That's a decent prize," he admitted before shaking his head to rid it of the thought. "But this is ridiculous. Can't you see she's just trying to make a mockery out of us?"

"You mean a mockery out of you," Stan said, pointing a finger at Austin. "She hasn't attacked the paper at all."

"But I'm part of the magazine," Austin said. "What happens to me reflects on it. I can't believe you're okay with this."

Stan leaned back in his seat, looking perfectly comfortable with himself. "It's publicity. Any publicity—"

"Is good publicity," Austin finished for his boss. "Yeah, I've heard that before." He growled. "If that's the case, then why wasn't The Three Sisters Cafe grateful for everything you and Tye offered in their review?" Austin slammed his hand down on the desk. "This is mockery. Pure and simple." He hoped the words would fire up Stan. That his bossly pride would take over and he would refuse to play the game that Aspen was setting up.

It sounded innocent enough. Eat cake in different chairs. But Austin knew better. He'd seen the intelligence in those eyes. He'd tasted the talent of her fingers. He'd read the snap of her sarcasm. There was no way he was getting out of this little competition with his self respect intact.

Instead of being upset like Austin wanted, Stan just laughed. "That's the beauty of it. The public loves to see people make a fool of themselves." He leaned forward, his manner still too eager. "And with someone as big as you being made the fool?" Instead of finishing the line, Stan just leaned back again, still laughing.

Austin jumped to his feet. "I won't do it," he said tightly. "I'm not playing this game." He turned to leave, hoping he'd made his point. He couldn't go through with this sick game. They wanted to play? Fine. Let Stan and Tye go down and have their names dragged through the mud. Let them lose everything they'd been working to build for the last five years. Let them lose their reputations and their shirts. Yet, even as Austin thought it, he knew he could never say that. He'd been protecting his brother for too long to suddenly throw him to the wolves.

"Austin," Stan said, his tone smug even though Austin wasn't looking at him. "You know my rules."

Austin closed his eyes and counted to ten.

"You do your job or you have no job."

Austin took in a deep breath. He could do it. He could tell Stan to stuff it and walk out the door with his head held high. He could find another job, find another way to make a living...

"Fine." The words felt like acid on his tongue. But even that pain wasn't enough to take away the memories of back alleys, cold nights and hunger pangs so sharp he was sure he would die before the morning.

Austin shook his head to rid himself of the memories. He really should be over them by now. Life wasn't like that anymore. He was safe. He had a home and clothes and food. So much food he didn't have to go to the grocery store for another week if he didn't want to.

But it's never enough.

Stan's laughter grew. "That's my boy. Now...go get ready for a trip. I'll have one of the writers send out your acceptance."

Austin hung his head. The coward had struck again. That ten year old child who was terrified of being hungry and hated being cold. How was he still directing Austin's life? Why couldn't adult Austin be stronger? The one who knew they wouldn't run out of food? The one who knew they could get another job? The one who knew they had a better life now?

Yet somehow, every time Austin thought of trying to go against those feelings, his heart sped up and he broke out in a cold sweat. The what if's were almost paralyzing. Even almost twenty years later, he still struggled with the nightmare.

His hand clenched as he walked back to his desk and he wanted to punch something. He needed a physical release for his brewing emotions, but what could he do? Causing damage at work wasn't the way to handle it, but Austin felt as if he were going to explode.

Grabbing his computer, he didn't even bother to sit down at his desk. He wasn't working here. Stan could do what he wanted, but

Austin needed to be at home. If he was going to play this stupid game, then he needed to have time to burn off energy, and he needed to pack. Who knew how long he'd be down in Seagull Cove.

"Where are you going?" Tye called after him.

"Home," Austin ground out.

"Wait up!" Tye grabbed his jacket and rushed to the door. "I'll buy you dinner," he said breathlessly.

"I don't need dinner," Austin growled. "I need the gym."

Tye rolled his eyes and walked confidently outside after catching his breath. "I'm not a kid anymore," he drawled. "You want dinner."

Austin wanted to laugh, but his anger kept it in check. He did love his food...a little too much. It was part of the reason he went to the gym so often. But right now, he really was upset. Not that he would dump it all on Tye. The kid would fold into a depression.

"Come on, man," Tye said, slapping Austin on the shoulder. "You can vent all you want."

Austin sighed and unlocked his car. "Hop in," he said.

Tye grinned and clambered into the passenger seat. They had been on the road for a few minutes before he broke the silence. "So...what did Stan want?"

Austin glanced over. "Are you really telling me that you don't know?"

Tye shook his head. "Nope. The whole office was watching Ms. Harrison's response. But Stan refused to share his plans."

Austin clenched his jaw and put his focus on the road. "It appears," he finally said through gritted teeth, "that I'm heading back to Seagull Cove."

CHAPTER 8

"I can't believe we're doing this," Maeve muttered as she set out another tray of cookies.

Aspen snickered. "I can't believe he agreed to it."

Estelle sighed. "Are you really sure about this? You don't think it's going to backfire?"

"Come on." Aspen groaned. "We've been through this. How can it go wrong?" She waved toward the front door of the shop where a crowd was waiting. "People have come from all over for day one of this thing. They're going to buy our goods, they're going to get a good laugh at Weirdo Austin's expense, and we'll all come out happier for it."

"Did you get a couple of teenagers to bring in the chairs?" Estelle asked Maeve.

Maeve pushed her glasses up her nose. "Yeah. Ethan said he'd get a couple."

Aspen glanced at her sister. Ethan was their next door neighbor. He was the exact opposite of studious, serious Maeve and in recent years, the youngest Harrison daughter had made it clear that he drove her crazy. He owned a surf shop and did lessons and rentals during the summer season. During the winter, he often got involved in construction projects in the area. It was odd that Maeve would turn to him for help since they bickered like little children.

"How many chairs have arrived?" Estelle asked, seemingly oblivious to Aspen's thoughts.

"I think there were close to twenty by my last count," Maeve offered. She didn't mention Ethan again and Aspen decided to let it go.

It wasn't worth causing another fight when they were all stressed as it was.

There was a banging on the front door and Aspen glanced at it.

"Can you get it?" Estelle asked. "I'm kinda full here."

"Me too," Maeve murmured, her attention elsewhere.

Aspen grumbled, but headed to the door. Who would be knocking at this time? They still had an hour before they opened. She unlocked the deadbolt and peered out. "Can I help..." She trailed off when she saw who it was. With a squeak, Aspen slammed the door shut.

Putting her back against it, she held a hand over her chest as she sucked in oxygen like a dying person.

"What in the world?" Estelle asked, her eyes wide and round. "Who was it?"

The door rattled again as the knocking came back.

"Aspen! Let me in!" Austin shouted.

Aspen felt the blood drain from her face.

"Aspen," Estelle scolded. She waved to the door. "Let him in."

Aspen shook her head, her words completely gone.

Estelle sighed. "Did you really think you wouldn't have to deal with him? You *invited* him for heaven's sake."

"Yeah, but I thought I'd only see him from a distance," Aspen whispered.

"Aspen!" The door rattled against her back.

"You've got to be kidding." Estelle groaned, storming over and pushing her sister out of the way. She unlocked the deadbolt and pulled the door open. "Austin. Hi. Thanks for coming." Estelle stepped aside and ushered Austin, along with a lanky man and a woman holding a camera, inside. "We'll be open in just a little bit!" Estelle called to the waiting crowd. "And then the fun will begin!"

The crowd roared and Estelle shut the door before turning to give her sister a scathing look.

Aspen had backed across the room and found she was struggling to hold Austin's intense gaze. She hadn't been lying when she said she hadn't planned to interact with him. He was supposed to show up, sit down, eat cake and leave. Nowhere in that scenario did he get to come inside and make Aspen uncomfortable, or force her to speak to him.

A snort caught her attention and she looked up...right into those green eyes.

He smirked at her and spread his arms. "Well, Ms. Harrison. Your sacrifice has arrived."

Aspen jerked back. "Excuse me?" Her desire to be hands off was gone in the wake of his condescending attitude.

He chuckled and turned fully toward her. "Isn't that what I am?" He sauntered her way. "It really was kind of a brilliant move," he pressed. "Turning my own public against me. Making me into a fool in order to get rid of the bad publicity that you'd been struggling with."

Aspen stiffened her spine. "Bad publicity that we've been dealing with? Do you have any idea what your little stunt did to our business?" She stormed right up to him, hating the fact that she had to look up in order to see his face. Sometimes being petite stunk.

"I'm sure you're going to tell me," Austin drawled, looking unimpressed.

Aspen could feel her face heating up. This guy was going down. She had planned to just take it easy during the chair competition, have a little fun, but now? No way. She wanted to make it into the most ridiculous and obscene showdown she could. Aspen put a smile on her face. "Actually, I'm not."

His eyebrows went up.

"I think I'll just enjoy the fact that I'm going to have a paying crowd for the next few days while you have to sit that," she curled two fingers from each hand in the air, "'delicate derriere' of yours on as many weird and crazy chairs as possible." Aspen patted his chest, choosing to ignore how hard his muscles were. "Good luck, Goldilocks."

"Okay..." Estelle burst up on them, giving her sister a significant look. "I think that's enough of that." She shoved her hand toward Austin. "Estelle Harrison. The oldest sister and the one responsible for the pink monstrosity you have a problem with."

Aspen couldn't hold back her snicker when Austin blushed.

"Nice to meet you, Estelle. And I'm sorry about how things turned out. It was never my intention to hurt you."

Aspen rolled her eyes and put her hands on her hips. *Never his intention to hurt her? Is he kidding? His whole job revolves around hurting people. Jerk.*

"That's alright," Estelle said coolly. "We've worked past it." She turned to the other man. "I'm Estelle."

"Tye," he said, his face blushing a deep red.

And just like that, Estelle, the mother of the clan, worked her magic and had the room calmed down. She didn't excuse Austin's behavior, but acknowledged it, said she'd moved on and then did exactly as she said.

Her abilities always awed Aspen, and now was no different. How did a person just let go of hurt feelings so easily? Austin had *hurt* them. In a personal way, and Aspen couldn't bring herself to just let it go. Acknowledging it was easy enough, but letting it go? No way.

Aspen was working her tail off to make this place a success and something her father could be proud of. She didn't want there to be the slightest bit of doubt that he regretted turning over his life's work to Aspen and her sisters, especially since it had happened before he was ready to retire.

No...she couldn't forgive Austin so easily. But that's what today was for, right? To give him back just a little of the humiliation he had heaped on the Three Sisters Cafe.

She found herself smirking as she thought of the chairs that had already been delivered. Yes...today was going to be a good day. And Austin had no idea what he was in for.

THE EVIL GRIN ON ASPEN'S face did nothing to help Austin calm his ire. He didn't want to be here. He didn't want to keep pretending that the horrible words in that review post had been his. He didn't want to have to pose for the camera and pretend that he thought it was funny to jump from chair to chair like a complete idiot.

He could only imagine the type of furniture that people had sent in. Just walking through the crowd to get to the door had been enough to have him rolling his eyes. He'd seen blocks of wood and camping stools in abundance, while one young man had gone far enough to tape a whoopie cushion to a dining room chair.

That was going to be fun.

Austin grumbled to himself as his team got to know the women. He wasn't feeling particularly charitable at the moment. He was here. He'd gotten a few words in edgewise with the lovely Aspen. And now he would finish his time and be done with it.

"Looks like it's time," Estelle said, clapping her hands. She looked directly at Aspen. "I trust that everyone is willing to play nice?"

Austin started to laugh, but then Estelle's gaze hit him and he felt like a little kid in the principal's office. Man, Estelle was definitely the one in charge here.

"Then let's go." She led the way to the door and swung it open. "Welcome, everyone!" Estelle called out as she walked into the sunshine. The day had turned out beautifully for their little publicity stunt.

Camera flashes surrounded the group as they stepped outside. Austin shielded his eyes from the glare.

"It's Eat It Austin!" a voice yelled. A young woman from the sound of it.

Austin tried to smile, but he was having a hard time getting excited about this situation. He could feel humiliation already riding his back. He was going to come out of

this situation with no self respect left. Still...by the sounds of the people, many of them came to see him and this was all his own fault.

"Hello," Austin said, waving and smiling as widely as he could manage. "Nice to see you. Hello." He nodded and worked his way through the crowd, shaking hands and posing for pictures.

An elderly woman was next, but she didn't look very excited to see him.

"Hello," Austin said, nodding respectfully.

She glared for a moment, then swung her purse and whacked him in the arm. "That's for being rude to the Harrison girls." She leaned back to whack him again, but Austin stepped back.

"Point taken," he said, putting his hands in the air.

"Are you gonna apologize?" she demanded. "Like Aspen asked?"

"Uh..." Austin looked around for help, but Aspen was standing to the side, laughing at his predicament. Estelle was schmoozing her way through the crowd. Tye looked even more uncomfortable than Austin was. And his photographer, Sue, was busy snapping pictures. *Who can control the crazy lady?* he wanted to ask, but no one came to his rescue. "Look, I'm sure we can..."

"Hi, Mrs. Stalin," the last of the Harrison women said as she jumped to his side.

The older woman softened considerably. "Sweet Maeve," she said, placing her purse back on her arm. "How are you three doing?"

Maeve nodded and pushed a set of large glasses up her nose. "Great. Isn't it a beautiful day for our celebration?"

Mrs. Stalin huffed. "It would be if *someone* would learn some manners," she grumbled before shuffling off.

"Be sure to try the mint cookies," Maeve called after her. "They're my favorite."

Austin cleared his throat when the woman was gone and Maeve turned to him. "Thanks," he said, giving her a sheepish grin. He rubbed his arm. "I'm pretty sure she left a bruise."

Maeve laughed. "Yeah, well, no one can verify just what she carries in her purse, but it's been keeping boys and men in line for ages."

Austin chuckled. "Sounds about right. I think there's one in every small town."

"Probably." She pushed her glasses up again. "But she's not the one you need to worry about."

"Oh? More weapon wielding ladies in the crowd?"

Maeve shook her head, the high bun she wore shaking dangerously. "Nope." She leaned in. "It's Aspen. She took your review as a personal insult to our family and she's out to not only prove you wrong, but to make you pay in the process."

He paused. The news wasn't a revelation to him. Between her insults online and the contest, he had guessed exactly what she was doing. Problem was, she was doing it to the wrong person. Austin hadn't written those words. But he couldn't tell her that either. He smiled tightly. "I guessed as much." After a moment, he asked, "Is she always so...passionate about your family?"

Maeve took off her glasses and cleaned them on her shirt, nodding as she worked. "Yep. She's always been big into family reputation and history. Since she was the only one of us to truly follow in our parents' footsteps, she feels like she has to prove herself, and the weight of that responsibility is making her...grumpy."

Austin laughed without humor. "Grumpy? Is that what we're calling it?"

Maeve gave him an unimpressed look as she put her glasses back on. "You might be used to people deferring to your opinion, Eat It Austin, but make no mistake. Aspen isn't afraid of you. She waged war, fully confident she could win." Maeve stepped a little closer. "But you also need to understand that there never was, nor will there ever be, a person who is more loyal and more apt to watch your back than Aspen. She holds those she loves so tightly we can't breathe sometimes, but we'll never doubt her feelings for us."

Austin was taken aback by the fierce little speech. He wouldn't have expected that from Maeve, who appeared a little more quiet than her siblings. And he had to admit he was even more intrigued by the beautiful Aspen now. What would it be like to be part of that inner circle?

"Being part of her circle is one of the greatest honors you could have in this life," Maeve said, a secretive smile playing on her lips, letting Austin know he'd spoken his thoughts out loud.

Before he could argue, she continued. "Why? Are you interested?"

"Me?" Austin scoffed, but even he didn't believe his words. "I'm just...curious about her."

"Uh-huh." Maeve's golden brown eyes seemed to twinkle behind her glasses. She glanced over her shoulder. "I think they're ready for you."

Austin turned in the direction she was pointing. He swallowed. A line of utterly abominable chairs was lined up down the sidewalk and Aspen was standing by with a slightly maniacal grin on her face. She held up a tray of cake bites, as if taunting him to come start.

"Word to the wise?"

Austin glanced down at Maeve again.

"Show no fear," Maeve whispered. "That way she'll at least respect you." With a nod to some of the people standing around, Maeve walked away as if their conversation had never happened.

Austin took a deep breath. The words were wise ones. Aspen had proven herself to be intelligent, quick witted and with a definite sense of humor. He just hated being the object of that sense of humor.

Throwing back his shoulders, he walked her way, strutting a little more than usual.

"Ready to see if you can find something less...offensive to your backside?" Aspen taunted.

He leaned into her personal space, doing his best to ignore the fact that his first chair was made entirely from antlers. "Are you ready to see that I was right?"

The crowd oohed and Austin grinned. It was time to stop being a baby. Two could play this game, and if he stood his ground, he just might come out of this a little less unscathed than he'd expected. Besides...eating Aspen's cake and spending time with the sharp tongued beauty really shouldn't be that big of a hardship.

At least...he hoped it wasn't.

CHAPTER 9

Laughter carried through the crowd as Austin walked up to his first chair. The thing was a complete eyesore, but Aspen had to admire the contestant's ingenuity.

Horns and branches wove together to create what must be the most uncomfortable chair in the universe. Aspen was half afraid that when Austin sat, he would end up with a splinter of some kind in a very uncomfortable spot.

She felt torn between snickering at the thought and feeling bad about creating the situation.

Austin carefully sat down, as if afraid the entire thing would collapse underneath him. Once he determined it would hold, he relaxed, but only slightly.

"Our first chair comes from David in Vancouver, Washington," Estelle said loudly. "Thank you, David!" She turned to Aspen, giving her her cue.

Aspen brought over the tray of cake bites. "Care to see if that chair makes it...just right?"

Austin's grin showed none of his earlier anger or frustration. Instead, he smiled widely for the crowd, showing off his pearly whites and making Aspen grit her teeth against how handsome he was. It really wasn't fair that someone that good looking was such a jerk. It felt like false advertising.

"Let's see..." Austin looked at the tray and tapped his chin. "Are you sure these are up to snuff?" he pressed.

The crowd reacted instantly. Now it was Aspen's turn to pretend to be happy when all she wanted to do was haul off and smack him like dear old Mrs. Stalin had. "The one directly in front of you is my cake flavor of the month," Aspen said, making sure the crowd could hear her. "It's a vanilla bean cake with ricotta filling and fresh cherry compote." Her smile was more genuine when people began to react to her description. "I think you'll find it to your liking."

Austin never lost eye contact as he took the plate. The intensity of his gaze was enough to have Aspen gasping quietly. She straightened and backed away.

"Who told you cherries were my favorite?" Austin asked, a definite flirting tone in his voice.

Aspen raised an eyebrow and put a hand on her hip. "Lucky guess, I suppose."

He picked up the plastic fork and took a bite.

Aspen watched closely and couldn't help but feel slightly smug when his eyes widened ever so slightly. She had to bite back a curse, however, when he quickly schooled his face.

Austin lazily took another bite and leaned back in the seat, cameras flashing like crazy. "Hmm..." He drew out the moment, as if contemplating the mysteries of the universe. "I think...yes...no..." Austin shook his head and put the plate back on the tray. "Nope. This doesn't feel *just right*."

The crowd groaned and Austin stood, stepping over to the next chair.

Aspen knew he wouldn't pick the first chair. They had dozens to get through. But she couldn't help feeling a little frustrated at how well he was playing the crowd to his side. This was supposed to be a moment where she got back a little of her own. Instead, he was lapping up the attention and had the people eating out of his hand.

"Whoa," Austin said with a laugh as he settled into the next chair. Where the first one had been all hard angles and lines, this was the complete opposite. The chair could only be described as having...fur.

It looked like something in a teenage girl's room and the bright yellow color was enough to make a person wince. Still...it looked more comfortable than the first one.

Austin settled himself in, grinned and held out a hand for the next bite of cake.

"Dark chocolate cake with a whipped peanut butter filling," she explained. "Peanut butter cup crumbles on top and a dark chocolate ganache drip."

Once again, the crowd reacted to her description and Aspen held back a triumphant giggle that she was capturing their attention. Every cake she was offering today was one of her specialties, and she was confident that each and every one would be sold out by the time the day was over.

Then my work here will be done...almost.

The only other thing she could ask for would be to embarrass Austin the same way he had embarrassed her family.

"Nope. It's not *just right.*"

Aspen made a show out of groaning with the rest of the crowd and they went to the next chair.

Time slowly began to tick faster. Austin went from wild chair to wild chair, setting a few aside as "possibly just right" in order to allow himself to get through them all. Some of the chairs surprised Aspen and she was positive Austin chose a few outrageous ones just to be funny, but even more surprising was that as they went along and Austin continued to work the crowd, she found herself enjoying the event.

"I have to agree with Goldilocks on this one," Austin said. "It's too small." He stood from the doll chair, where he'd been perching his weight just above it, and Aspen found herself chuckling with the crowd.

More than one person had thought to send toy furniture and Austin had had a witty quip for each of them.

People's creativity astounded Aspen as they continued on. Some of the chairs were obviously homemade. There was a beautiful rocking chair that had been put in the "maybe" pile, while others had gone for funny by sending buckets with toilet seats on them.

"At least this one is soft," Austin said with a sigh as yet another five gallon bucket arrived. This time the sender had wrapped a pool noodle around the edge.

Aspen grinned, then realized her mistake and dropped the smile. She wasn't supposed to be enjoying anything except seeing the arrogant man brought down off his pedestal. And so far, she hadn't seen it happen. He was too good. Too well loved, and as long as he kept a good attitude, the crowd was enjoying every second of the competition.

But he's a jerk. Why can't everybody see that?

The words held a little less venom than they did before she'd spent time with him. Right now, Icky Austin wasn't being a jerk. He was being friendly, kind, good natured and funny. It was making it harder and harder for Aspen to remember that he was there because he insulted her family.

"I think this one needs to go in the 'maybe' pile," Austin said with a wink.

Aspen could hear several young women giggle at his flirting and a hot flash of jealousy hit her straight in the gut. *What the—?* Aspen shook away the feeling. That was ridiculous. She barely knew Austin and what she did know wasn't completely flattering.

"You like the bucket?" a little boy shouted over the noise of the crowd.

"Well, now," Austin replied, not missing a beat. "Who wouldn't want a chair that has extra padding?" He motioned to his seat, making the little boy laugh. "Sometimes we all need a little help down there, ya know?"

The boy buried his face in his mom's leg, but was still smiling.

Great. Now I have to add good with kids to Creepy Austin's resume? Why can't he just be the meanie he's supposed to be?

AUSTIN WAS TRYING TO ignore Aspen. Right now she had the weirdest look on her face, like she was trying to decide if he was a piece of cake himself, or a bug to be squished under her shoe.

Cake. I'm definitely cake.

The day had been torturous, thus far. Every time Aspen came close enough to hand him a new plate of cake, Austin felt his heart rate speed up. She was beautiful, she was handing him delicious desserts and she smelled like sugar and cinnamon. With his affinity for all things food, that held the ultimate appeal.

The little boy who used to spend his time with his nose pressed against bakery windows was crowing in delight and it was getting harder and harder to hold him at bay. It didn't help that the man in Austin was delighted to be around Aspen for very different reasons than the fact that she smelled sweet. Maeve had been right. Aspen was a fighter, but a loyalist. In other words...she was amazing.

He handed the stupid bucket seat to a man around his age. The guy had been hanging around all morning with a couple of teenage boys. Apparently, they'd been hired for their muscle since they were the ones moving the chairs around.

"Thanks." Austin held out his hand. "Austin Edwards. I've appreciated your help today."

"Ethan Markle," the man said with a lazy smile. He leaned in. "I'm the Harrisons' next door neighbor and resident surfing expert."

Austin chuckled. "Do any of them surf?"

Ethan shook his head. "No. Though I once convinced Maeve to give it a try." His lips twitched, but he didn't elaborate.

Austin's eyebrows shot up. There was a story there, but he didn't have time to hear it. "Well...thanks for helping out today."

Ethan gave a quick nod and walked away with the bucket.

"We're almost there, folks!" Estelle hollered. "Only six chairs left!" She swept the crowd with her smile. "Which one will win?" Estelle did a decent Vanna White impression as she waved to the next chair.

Austin held back a groan. People had certainly had a lot of fun coming up with these seats, though he had to wonder... What furniture company made such weird stuff? The neon rainbow colored leopard print couch made Three Sisters Cafe pink one appear tame by comparison.

"Ooh," Estelle said smoothly. "This one's a *love* seat."

Austin tripped a little before walking over. Why was she making such a big deal out of it?

"Love seats are meant for two people, aren't they?" Estelle hollered.

"YES!" the crowd shouted. Laughter rang out and they all began calling out suggestions for who should sit with him.

Austin tried to appear unaffected. These people really were trying to humiliate him. Was sitting on a toilet bucket not enough?

"What do you think, folks? Should our resident baker join him on the couch?"

"What?" Aspen screeched.

Austin bit his lips between his teeth. He had to admit...that made things a little more interesting.

Aspen waved her arm and shook her head. It was clear she had no intention of getting on the couch with him. But when the crowd began chanting her name, Austin knew it was only a matter of time.

"But I'm handing out the cake," she argued lamely.

Austin let himself fall backward, pretending he didn't notice the springs poking through the cushions. "Ahhh..." He spread his arms across the back. "I have a good feeling about this," he said loudly with a wink in Aspen's direction.

Oooh, she was mad now. He chuckled under his breath. When her brown eyes flashed, it was mesmerizing. He imagined that they were the color of the dark chocolate she seemed so fond of putting in her cakes.

He raised his eyebrows in challenge. "Are you scared?" When a snarl started to curl her lip, Austin knew he had her. She was definitely a feisty one. If only he could tell her that the review she hated so much hadn't been written by him at all. That he was strictly the name, face and tastebuds of the much loved and hated Eat It Austin review column.

Schooling her face quickly, Aspen sauntered toward him, the sway in her hips a little more than it had been before. "Nothing scares me," she told him coolly. With all the elegance of a queen at court, she sat beside him, mostly on one of her hips, and held the tray out in front. "We're back to the peanut butter," she said in a low tone.

Austin's heart skipped a beat. This game had just gotten dangerous. Why couldn't she be like some old grandma or something? Someone who sent maternal feelings through him, not pictures of kissing those lush lips or holding her close while they shared a slice of cake right out of the oven?

Unable to look away, he held out his hand. Aspen had managed to have twelve different cakes to serve him, but since there were far more than twelve chairs, they had simply re-eaten the flavors over and over again.

He was so full of sugar, Austin was sure he'd have a hangover tomorrow, but he couldn't bring himself to stop eating. The flavors were extraordinary and everything he had ever wanted in a dessert. Moist but dense cake, unique flavor combinations that gave him everything he was looking for. Sour, sweet, and savory were combined in a way he'd never experienced before and he was coming to understand more and more why she'd been so offended by the first review. No one with this kind of talent could sit by and let that go.

He held out his hand for the plate, but Aspen smirked. Setting the tray in her lap, she picked up the plate herself. "May I?"

The tension between them had to have been visible to everyone in attendance as the crowd broke into a frenzy. Austin's heart beat in rhythm with the screams of delight and encouragement as he opened his mouth and let her put a bite inside.

The blush on his cheeks was so hot he was sure he could bake his own cake with his internal temperature alone. Curse his lighter skin. Her darker, Italian complexion didn't seem to struggle as much as his. It definitely did not help the confident, manly persona he wished for others to see.

He chewed, keeping eye contact despite the intense desire to look away. It was almost too much. No woman had ever challenged him so fiercely. Austin didn't want to lose, but also could barely keep up. He was afraid if he let her win now, he'd never have the upper hand again.

Her dark eyes finally turned away and she delicately cleared her throat.

A massive weight was lifted from Austin's shoulders and he barely kept back the sigh of relief. "I think we found our winner," he murmured just loud enough for her to hear.

Aspen's head jerked back his way, her mouth gaping.

One side of his mouth pulled up in amusement and her eyes darted to the movement. Ah-ha! So he wasn't the only one affected by their proximity. Her little flirtatious display hadn't solely been for the public.

Before he could do something stupid, like kiss a woman he barely knew, Ausitn jumped to his feet. "This one definitely goes in the 'maybe' pile." He already knew the answer. This chair would be the winner, despite how abhorrent it was colored. He knew it made no sense, after the kerfuffle about the pink couch, but he had no choice.

The experience of sitting next to Aspen and being fed by her would stick in his mind forever. And with each remembrance of that moment, he would also remember the ugliest couch he'd ever seen in his life.

CHAPTER 10

"Are you really going to put that in the shop?" Harper whispered in Aspen's ear. Both women looked at the couch and grimaced.

"He picked it as the winner," Aspen said softly with a shrug. "There's not much I can do. Which seems contradictory after making fun of the pink one we already have."

Harper sighed. She made her living as a local artist and Aspen could only imagine how that monstrosity must offend her senses. Probably even more than the pink couch did for Austin the first time around.

"I think he did it just to get back at you guys," Jayden said as he walked up to the women.

Aspen punched her cousin in the arm. "Why aren't you back at the inn?" she asked, referring to the Gingerbread Inn her great-great grandmother had started ages ago. Aspen's Aunt Hope and Uncle Enoch now ran it, with Jayden, another nephew, helping at the desk during his spare time from his photography business. Hope and Enoch's own children had gone on to other jobs.

Michael was the only one still in town and he was a local high school teacher. He helped out at the inn during Christmas and summer break, but otherwise was too busy to do much.

Jayden held up his camera. "I was taking pictures for the newspaper."

Aspen rolled her eyes. "Of course you were."

He grinned, looking very much like his mother, Aunt Bella, at the moment. She also had that sparkle of mischief in her bright blue eyes. "I *might* have caught a really intimate one of you and Mr. Eat It Austin."

Aspen's cheeks flamed and she was grateful for her slightly darker skin. Estelle was the luckiest one in that category, but at least Aspen's blushes weren't usually visible. "There was nothing intimate about what happened today," she argued. When Harper snickered, Aspen threw a glare her way.

Harper put her hands in the air. "No romantic tension there...nope. None whatsoever."

Jayden laughed outright. "I think the old ladies were swooning with how stifling it was."

"You two are ridiculous," Aspen continued, though arguing with family and her best friend was somewhat difficult. Harper knew her better than anyone else. They shared the same creative brains and often were found daydreaming when they were supposed to be focusing. The only difference was, one was dreaming of color and the other of flavor combinations. "When's your next show?" Aspen asked Harper, trying to redirect the topic.

Harper bit her bottom lip and thought. "I have some pictures in a gallery over in Eugene. They said they might have an open house night closer to the holidays."

Aspen nodded, ignoring Jayden as he elbowed her and walked away to mingle some more. With the competition over, people were walking around eating cake and talking about the five hours it took to do the Goldilocks Game.

Once everyone left, Aspen and her sisters would have to rework the inside of the cafe to make room for their new addition. A woman out of California had won with the neon rainbow leopard print love seat. It was atrocious, but Aspen hoped the notoriety of it would make it all worth it. Besides...what did it say about Austin that he'd picked something so ugly?

"Hello, ladies," The deep, smooth voice of the very person Aspen had been thinking of came brushing against her neck.

She held back a shiver. Why the heck did this guy affect her like this? He was horrible. Plain and simple. No matter what she saw today, no matter how he treated the public, no matter what kind of indulgent attitude he had about being made a fool of, he was still a jerk. She turned to him with a tight smile, refusing to let him know that she felt anything but disdain for him. "Hello, Mr. Edwards. How are you feeling?"

His eyebrows went up. "Feeling? Are you referring to the fact that I ate my weight in cake?" He rubbed his flat stomach. "I have to admit I might crash from a sugar high some time tonight, but otherwise, I'm alright at the moment."

"Actually, I was referring to all those chairs you had to sit on." Aspen made her best sympathetic face. "Are you sore? Need a cushion, maybe? Anti-inflammatory?"

His smug smile should have warned her. "Actually, now that you mention it, I could use a little extra attention. Are you offering your services?" He leaned in. "If you wanted to spend time together, all you had to do was say so."

If her blush got any hotter, Aspen knew it would probably burn their new couch to tiny bits. *Wait...that might not be so bad.* "Actually, I was going to give you the name of my favorite masseuse." Aspen pointed to her friend, Mason. At six-foot-four, he was a massive man and his arms were every bit as big as his body. If he were really a masseuse, he'd more than likely crush his customers with his pinky finger. Between his build and his thick, dark beard, he was more than a little intimidating to those who didn't know a teddy bear resided inside that huge chest. Austin, however, didn't need to know that Mason was a lumberjack and wood carver. It could be Aspen's little secret.

Austin raised an eyebrow. "Wow. What does he do? Scare the tension out with his growl?"

Aspen glared at him. "Must not need as much help as you were implying." She sniffed. "Oh well." She turned to walk away. "Have a nice drive back to Portland."

The sooner this bozo left, the better...for Aspen's peace of mind as well as the town's.

"Actually..." Austin caught up with her and leaned into her ear. "I'm sticking around for a few days." A slightly lopsided grin overtook his mouth when she stuttered to a stop and gaped up at him. "I thought it might look good if I got a few shots of the finished project. You know...for publicity and all." He bent forward slightly. "Besides, I believe I was given an open invitation to enjoy your bakery whenever I wanted."

"Yeah, but...you live in Portland. I didn't expect—" Aspen snapped her mouth shut. She was saying too much. All day she'd been working to make sure he didn't know how he affected her, and she'd given it away in two short sentences. "Fine," she said, raising her chin into the air. "We'll be redecorating after we close for the day. You're welcome to come by in the morning." She walked away again.

Austin, as intelligent as he seemed, wasn't catching the hint and kept up with her. "I wouldn't dream of asking you three to do it all on your own. Tye and I will stick around and help out."

"We have help, thank you," Aspen replied, trying to walk faster. The crowds, however, weren't very helpful in letting her get away.

"Then it sounds like we'll get done faster." His voice dropped. "And then I can take you to dinner."

Aspen squeaked and spun on her heel, knocking into the person next to her. "I'm so sorry," she gushed, making sure the young boy was alright. When he glared and ran off, Aspen sighed. "See what you made me do?"

Austin put his hand on his chest. "Me? What did I do?"

"You...you..." Aspen clenched her fists and pinched her lips together. "You asked me on a date," she ground out, glancing around to make sure no one was paying attention to her.

"And that caused you to assault a young child?"

She closed her eyes, praying for patience.

"Say cheese!"

Snapping her eyes open, Aspen looked over to see Jayden grinning wildly at her and indicating she should stand next to Austin.

"For the paper?" Jayden asked, looking at Austin.

When Austin's arm came around Aspen, she had to swallow a gasp. The jolt in her body was enough to have her cousin laughing for days. "Of course," Austin said easily. He tucked a very stiff Aspen into his side, leaned his head down and smiled.

AUSTIN WAS SURE THAT at any moment, Aspen was going to reach up and claw his eyes out. He 'd never met a more prickly woman. She was an intriguing mix of fierce and kind, intelligent and sweet, loyal and protective. Her baking skills were out of this world, but so was her determination to keep him at bay.

He hadn't originally planned to stick around, but the longer the Goldilocks Game went on, the less Austin could convince himself he wanted to drive back to Portland.

Aspen was a puzzle. A delicious, feisty, amazing puzzle, and Austin wanted to figure her out.

The dinner invitation had been spur of the moment, but the shock she portrayed was enough to give him hope. He had felt a pull to her that had only grown all afternoon, but there were moments when he wasn't sure she felt the same. If she was truly immune to him, an invitation like that would have made her laugh, not gape like a codfish.

"Thanks," the man with the camera said. He winked at Aspen before disappearing into the crowd, and Austin stiffened.

"Stupid cousins," Aspen muttered under her breath as she pulled away from him.

Finding out the man was Aspen's cousin helped calm the green eyed monster inside, but it was the fact that Aspen hesitated the slightest amount before pulling out of his arms that had Austin really wanting to push his luck. "So..." He stuffed his hands in his pockets and rocked back on his heels. "Dinner?"

Her eyes went wide again, but she didn't respond.

"What if I promise not to critique the food?" he said with a grin.

Her lips twitched. "I...don't know."

"Why not?"

Aspen frowned. "Are you always this blunt?"

His eyebrows furrowed. "Have you read my reviews?" It was the wrong thing to say, and Austin knew it as soon as the words were out of his mouth. His review, or Tye's review, was the whole reason he'd gotten into this mess in the first place.

"Thank you for the invite," she said politely. "But I think I'll have to decline."

Austin nodded, trying not to show how much that stung. Despite the rejection, he wasn't ready to give up yet. Aspen was worth getting to know. He'd just have to work a little harder. He couldn't reveal that Tye was the writer in their little two man gig, but he could help her see past the online persona. "You don't plan to eat tonight?"

"Of course, I...what?" She was adorable when confused.

"It's just..." He made a thoughtful face. "Everyone in this town keeps telling me how nice you are. How sweet and kind." He tilted his head. "It seems to me that someone with that kind of reputation would want to make sure her guests ate dinner. Unless she didn't eat dinner. Then I could understand the rejection. But if a hostess *is* eating dinner, wouldn't it make sense for her to provide dinner for her guests as well?"

Aspen closed her eyes and shook her head. "You're not making any sense. What in the world makes you think I'm your hostess?"

"I just happen to be staying at the Gingerbread Inn," Austin said with a smile, pulling out a little tidbit he'd found online. "Isn't that your family place?"

"Well, yes, but—"

"Don't you provide food for the kitchens?"

"Yeah...I mean, sometimes—"

"And you're planning to eat dinner tonight?"

"At some point," she said, speaking faster as if trying to get in more words between his interruptions.

Austin though was prepared for her. "Then that means you're hosting me." He winked. "I'll look forward to sitting together." Without giving her a chance at a rebuttal, he spun and walked away, whistling softly and hoping he came across as carefree. He'd spun a tale to build a victory, but Aspen was tough enough she might just call him on it.

When he'd made it ten steps without being mauled, he relaxed and began to chuckle in his triumph. Aspen had no idea who she was fighting against. He'd made it from the streets to the front page. Austin definitely knew when to stand his ground and when to back off. With Aspen, he'd have to be creative, but he had every intention of getting closer to her.

No one had ever challenged him like this before and he wasn't going to let that go. He'd played her little game. He'd come and let people laugh at him and make a fool out of him. But now it was his turn to be in charge.

He looked over the sea of heads, trying to find Tye. When he spotted his lanky brother, Austin worked that direction, stopping every once in a while for a photograph or to speak to someone who wanted to ask him a question.

"Tye," Austin said as he got closer.

Tye spun, a plate of cake in his hand. "Hm?"

Austin smirked. "Enjoying yourself?"

Tye held up the plate. "Why should you get to have all the fun?"

"True." Austin put his hand on Tye's back and pulled him closer. "We're staying the night."

Tye jerked back. "What?"

"I have some...unfinished business," Austin said. "And I need you to do something for me."

Tye raised a single eyebrow. "Does it have anything to do with the fact that you and that baker could have given us all a sun tan with your chemistry?"

Austin cleared his throat and tugged at the collar of his shirt. It was that obvious, huh? "Uh...actually, I need you to call the Gingerbread Inn and make us a reservation."

"The Gingerbread Inn?" Tye frowned. "Never heard of it."

"It's a bed and breakfast run by the Dunlap family."

"Ooookay..."

Austin sighed. "That's Aspen's family. The inn was opened by her great something grandmother."

Tye chuckled. "I see. And how many nights am I asking for?"

Austin squished his lips to the side. "Let's start with a week and see where that gets us."

Tye choked on his cake. "Excuse me?" he asked between coughs. "Stan is gonna kill us."

Austin slapped his brother on the back. "You handle the reservations. I'll handle the boss." He turned to walk away. "Oh...and I won't be available for dinner tonight." Ignoring Tye's groan, Austin walked around, determined to mingle in order to pass the time. Aspen thought she could get rid of him, but he wasn't about to disappear into the night. They'd started something with this little internet show and he was going to keep it going.

Of course, he planned for his involvement to be strictly off cam-era, but nonetheless, what started with a fight was hopefully going to lead to something much more enjoyable.

CHAPTER 11

Aspen's hands shook as she dropped off a tray of baked goods in the kitchen of the Gingerbread Inn. *Not a date, it's definitely NOT a date.*

Ever since Austin had used his messed up logic to get her to admit she would be at the inn and that meant they could have dinner together, Aspen had been a mess of butterflies. She had struggled to argue back when he kept coming at her, and then he'd disappeared before she could formulate an intelligent rebuttal at all.

Now she was in the kitchens, dropping off dessert and hoping that he somehow forgot that he'd declared she was hosting him tonight.

"Hey, Aspen," Jayden called out, jogging through the kitchen to her side. "Your boy toy from earlier is waiting in the dining room for you."

"Excuse me?" she shouted, putting her hands on her hips. "What did you call him?"

Jayden's grin was so smug that Aspen wanted to wipe it from his face. Good thing she wasn't some wild cavewoman with no control over her emotions...most days anyway.

"You heard me," Jayden said with a chuckle. He flared his eyes. "I can only hope I have that kind of reaction to someone someday."

"The guy is my mortal enemy," Aspen lied through gritted teeth. "I don't know where you and everybody else are getting these insane ideas."

"Maybe the rest of us are choosing not to be blind," Jayden retorted. He jabbed a thumb over his shoulder. "Better not keep Fancy Pants Austin waiting. He might write you up in that blog of his."

Aspen pinched the bridge of her nose and counted to ten. How could one man throw her life into such upheaval? All she wanted was to open her shop, feed people cake and make her dad proud. Was that too much to ask?

Persistent media personnel who wrote rude posts and refused to listen to the word "no" were not necessary or welcome.

Not knowing what else to say, Aspen stuck her tongue out at her cousin and then headed out of the kitchen. Those dang butterflies started up again and she couldn't seem to help stopping for just a moment to fix her hair.

It's not for him, she assured herself. *Anyone feels more confident when they look good. It's just a fact of life.*

After repeating the lie to herself several times, she marched forward. Determined to get this over with.

"Aspen!" Austin stood from his seat and walked around to her, holding out his hands.

Aspen frowned and looked at his palms. They were nice palms. Large, with long fingers. Just right for holding another's.

She shook herself. *Get it together!* "Hello, Austin," she said curtly, not responding to his warm welcome.

If his smirk was anything to go by, he found her resistance amusing. Stuffing his hands in his pockets, he rocked back on his heels, looking adorably boyish. "I wasn't sure you would show."

She raised her eyebrows. "I didn't know I was given much of a choice."

He stepped a little closer, breaking the barrier of what would have been considered polite. "You always have a choice," he said in a low tone. "I'm just glad you used it to be here."

This guy was not only dangerous to Aspen's peace of mind and her business, but the more he flirted, the more she knew he was also going to be dangerous to her heart. As someone who was known for being stubborn and who dug in their heels when things got tough, she could totally appreciate a guy who pushed the boundaries a little. Someone who pushed the adrenaline level without going too far.

Fearing she would say something stupid, Aspen forced her legs into action and walked around him, planning to make sure she sat across the table from him. She wasn't sure she could handle bumping elbows and still manage to get food into her mouth. She came to a halt, however, at the table.

There were only two place settings...and they were next to each other.

"Your aunt allowed me to reserve the room for just us," Austin whispered in her ear.

His proximity sent a shiver down her spine and she spun, nearly falling when she tried to back up and put a little room between them.

"Careful," he warned, reaching out to grab her upper arms.

She'd been right. His hands were perfect. His grip was steady but not too tight, and his palms were warm. The heat of his touch traveled up her neck and into her face. *What am I? Twelve?* she cried mentally. But no matter how much she scolded herself, her traitorous body just didn't seem in a hurry to move away from the food critique.

"May I escort you to your seat?" he asked, his voice low and husky.

Aspen blinked. Maybe she wasn't the only one affected by their nearness. That could prove to be helpful later, if she ever got herself under control. "Why are you doing this?"

Wait...what? What was *not* the question she had intended to ask. She was supposed to tell him to get lost. That he'd hurt her family and she didn't suffer fools. That he wasn't welcome in her little haven of Seagull Cove. Anything but try to pick apart the reaction they were having to each other.

Austin took a deep breath and let go of her to shove a hand through his hair. "Truthfully?" he barked out a laugh. "I'm not quite sure."

Why those words stung, Aspen wasn't sure. It wasn't like she wanted there to be anything between them. But stung they did. Enough that she was able to jerk herself away from him.

"But," he said hurriedly, as if to stop her retreat, "I'd like to find out."

Aspen stood frozen as he closed the distance between them again. Her eyes couldn't seem to leave his. The green was mesmerizing and she felt trapped, but instead of fear, there was...anticipation.

"I know we didn't get off on the right foot," he said carefully.

"That's an understatement," Aspen muttered without thought.

He grinned. "True. But when I came down for my first review, I had no idea who I was dealing with." He leaned in, his voice dropping. "I knew of your parents' reputation, and I knew you were opening a cafe. That was the extent of my knowledge." His head tilted to the side, and a chunk of hair fell into his eyes. "So imagine my disappointment when things got out of hand with the review."

Aspen narrowed her eyes. "Imagine my disappointment when you attacked my family without actually knowing us."

Some of the arrogance on his face faded and he nodded. "You're right. That was wrong of me. The couch thing was an unfair tidbit to write about. My editor was looking for something to catch attention and that ended up being it." He held his hands out in a helpless gesture. "What was I supposed to do?"

"How about manning up and sticking to critiquing food?" she shot back.

One more step and they were practically nose to nose. Well...nose to chest. He was quite a bit taller than her. "I'm here now," he said, "to fix it."

Dang those butterflies. They were going to be the death of her.

"SO YOU JUST WANT TO make up for being a jerk?" she asked. The words would have hurt worse if they hadn't been so breathless. She definitely felt this attraction between them, and that only pushed Austin onward.

He slowly shook his head. "At first, I only came to your Goldilocks Game in order to obey my boss." He gave a little laugh. "Believe it or not, I was fully aware that you were trying to make a fool out of me."

Her lips twitched, but she held back the smile.

"But after we talked a bit, there was more."

Any semblance of the smile was gone, but there was a distinct lack of anger. Instead, she looked curious.

"Tell me you aren't interested," Austin pressed, making a very risky move. Her anger at his review was still fresh. He knew full well she could use that to push him away, but he hoped that wasn't the case. Yes, he'd been a little pushy about getting her to dinner, but he wasn't going to waste his time if there was no chance of her ever giving him a chance.

She was attracted to him, yes. But that wasn't a guarantee that she would ever let down her guard enough for him to get to know her or vice versa.

Her mouth opened and closed a few times, her eyes wide and caught off guard. She obviously hadn't expected him to come right out and ask such a question. "I..." Her lips closed and she swallowed hard. "I can't," she said in a low tone.

He kept his smile in check. "Then have dinner with me. Spend some time with me this week. And let's see if it's something worth working for."

Those dark eyes were so wide, Austin was sure he could get lost in them and he found himself holding his breath as he waited for her answer.

"Okay."

He forced his breathing to let out slowly, instead of completely deflating with relief like he wanted to. Turning, he held out his elbow. "Madam?"

Aspen rolled her eyes. "Let's not go overboard," she said saucily.

He chuckled. "Okay. But is it alright if I pull out your chair?"

Aspen smiled. For the first time, it was carefree and genuine. It was the smile he'd seen her give her friends and family, but had not once been directed at him...until now. "That would be fine."

He took the whole ten steps to their seats, then did exactly as he promised and pulled out her seat. "Is it too much to say you look lovely?"

Aspen snorted, watching him as he took his seat. "Flattery won't get you anywhere, Mr. Edwards. I know exactly what I look like."

"And what's that?" He settled into his seat, twisting his torso so he was watching her.

"Like a woman who's been on her feet all day," Aspen retorted.

"And do I look like a guy who's been sitting on his duff all day?" He laughed softly as she burst into amusement herself. The sound was loud and rang through the dining hall. How did such a loud noise come from such a tiny woman?

"Maybe," she finally replied, wiping at the edge of her eye.

"We ready for some grub in here?"

Austin nodded at Jayden. Aspen's cousin had been instrumental in helping Austin get tonight set up. Apparently, he worked at the inn as well as did photography. Since they'd met at the event this afternoon, it had made things run much smoother to have someone on Austin's side.

"Don't tell me..." Aspen said wryly. "You're in on this?"

Jayden grinned and gave his cousin a wink. "You'll never know, cuz."

Aspen sighed and leaned back in her seat. "Traitor."

Jayden walked through with two plates in his hands. "I like to think of myself as an opportunist," he said cheerfully. "Bon appetit!" The plates were set in front of Aspen and Austin and the smells emanating from them made Austin's stomach growl.

"Wow..." Aspen gave him a look. "You're still hungry after all that cake you ate?"

Austin rubbed the back of his neck, embarrassed. "What can I say? I like to eat."

"You must in order to do what you do." Aspen picked up her fork and dug into the roast beef. "Oh my goodness," she murmured. "Elvira totally outdid herself."

Austin followed suit, and soon he was moaning over the delectable dinner as well. "Who did you say cooked this?" he asked, helping himself to a large bite of potatoes and gravy. This was comfort food at its best and he wanted a second plate.

"Mrs. Torqson. She took over when my mom..." Aspen trailed off and looked away. "Um...she's fairly new, but she's been an absolute gem." Her smile was slightly sad as she waved at the plates. "You can see for yourself that she's really good at what she does. You should try her cedar planked salmon."

Ausitn leaned back in his seat. There was something she wasn't saying, or at least glossing over. Did she think he didn't know her mother used to work in the kitchens? That had all been in the profile he'd read on the family. Daddy Harrison mostly ran the bakery while Mommy Harrison kept the kitchens at the Gingerbread Inn serving wonderful fare, though she also helped out at the bakery when possible. At least that's how the media portrayed the couple.

However, Austin knew better than most that the media didn't always get it right.

"So, I'm guessing you're one of those kids that grew up peeling potatoes and chopping veggies before you could color between the lines," he teased, trying to bring back the contented mood they'd had only moments before.

Aspen laughed and tucked a piece of dark hair behind her ear. "You could say that. Only, I *wasn't* one of those kids complaining." She sighed. "I loved everything that has to do with the kitchen."

"So you cook as well as bake?"

Aspen made a face and tilted her head from side to side consideringly. "Sort of. I mean, I can cook. It's not where my heart lies, but I don't usually drive anyone away when I put together a meal."

Austin just grinned.

"And you?" Aspen raised her eyebrows in question. "For someone who obviously enjoys eating the food, did you also learn how to make it?"

Now, it was his turn to grow uncomfortable. "I can survive, but I'd rather not eat my own stuff if I don't have to." He tried turning it into a joke, but he prayed she wouldn't press the issue. It was uncomfortably close to the whole reason he brought Tye with him as a writer, not just a brother.

If word got out of his...problem...then he knew his career was gone for good.

CHAPTER 12

Aspen's head was having a hard time staying in the kitchen this morning. Last night, she had had dinner with Eat It Austin, who wasn't nearly as dog-faced as she'd been thinking of him in her mind. In fact, he was polite, witty, and far more handsome than any other dinner date Aspen had ever spent time with.

"Get it together," she scolded herself, mixing her cake batter a little too viciously. If she whipped it too much, it would ruin the density of her cake, and that just wouldn't do. *See what you made me do, Eat it Austin?*

Aspen grunted and got back to work, making sure she kept herself in check this time. It wasn't like this was going to become a regular thing. So they'd eaten dinner once. So what? People ate dinner all the time. Aspen worked for the inn, so in essence, it hadn't even been a date. It was just good business.

But then why can't you get his green eyes out of your head? Oh, let me guess. That's why we're using a green frosting on today's cake?

"Oh, my gosh, just stop!" Aspen put hands on the counter and shook her head hard. Why was this guy messing with her head so much? She had met handsome men before. She'd even dated a few. But none of them made her feel as upside down as Eat It Austin.

He frustrated her. He drove her crazy. He also sent her heart into overdrive and made her melt into a puddle. Was there a word for when a person's body couldn't seem to make up its mind?

"Yeah. Certifiably insane," she said to her empty kitchen.

"It *is* a little crazy to talk to yourself."

Aspen squealed and leapt into the air. Spinning, she glared at her sister. "That wasn't nice."

Maeve laughed and leaned her shoulder against the office door frame. "No one said I was nice."

"I thought the youngest were always supposed to be the nicest," Aspen argued.

"No. The oldest are. The youngest are the ones that get away with everything." Maeve pumped her eyebrows. "We're the mischievous ones."

"I'll believe that when I see it," Aspen grumbled, turning back to her cake. She could hear Maeve walking across the tiled floor until she reached Aspen's side.

"What's going on?"

Aspen shook her head. "Nothing I can't handle."

"Uh-huh..." It was clear Maeve didn't believe her.

"Seriously," Aspen pressed. "I'm just making cake. Nothing else."

"I can see that." Maeve looked at the mess on the counter. "Do we need to hire kitchen help? Maybe a teenager to wash dishes?"

Aspen laughed softly. "You must really hate doing it if you're willing to pull from the funds in order to hire another body. I thought we couldn't do that for six months." She gave her sister a look.

Maeve rolled her eyes. "I wash dishes. I just don't want to wash that many." She waved at the pile. "Not to mention, I have better things to do."

"How long does it take to crunch a few numbers?" Aspen teased. This was good. Arguing with her sister was going a long way to helping her get her mind off a certain set of strong muscles. Thank heavens Maeve hadn't heard the rest of the conversation. She would never let Aspen live it down.

"This is a full time job, thank you very much." Maeve glared over her glasses. "Sort of."

"Uh-huh." Aspen grinned.

"Okay, it'll be full time when I take on a few more clients," Maeve admitted.

"Then I guess you *do* have time for those dishes."

"Not happening!" Maeve called out, walking back toward the office.

"We're out of birthday cake!" Estelle hollered from the front room.

Maeve and Aspen both turned toward their oldest sister.

Estelle wiped the back of her hand across her forehead. "I can barely keep up. Maeve, why don't you come help me out? I could use a breather."

Aspen's eyebrows shot up. "Really?"

Estelle smiled. "Really. The place has been packed since opening."

Aspen had been so caught up in her own world, she hadn't bothered to look out front. She always arrived well before opening in order to start baking and decorating, and didn't always know how things were going out front.

After yesterday's spectacle, she felt a sputter of hope that the work they'd put into that was going to pay off.

"I was helping Aspen," Maeve said, walking toward the dishes.

Aspen rolled her eyes. Her introverted sister might hate dishes, but she hated crowds more.

"Nope. Those can wait," Estelle said firmly. "Out here now."

"Yes, Mother," Maeve grumbled, shoving her glasses into her hair.

"Who's the mother?"

Aspen's jaw about hit the floor when Eat it Austin came up behind Estelle.

Estelle gasped and stepped out of his way. "What are you doing?" she asked, recovering from the shock and putting her hands on her hips.

"I came to see how things were going," Austin said easily. He purposefully glanced over his shoulder. "I'd say the shenanigans yesterday were a hit."

"I suppose they were," Estelle said under her breath, a frown marring her beautiful face. She looked at Maeve. "Come on, Maeve. Let's get going before they riot." She turned her attention to Austin. "Mr. Edwards?" Estelle made a motion toward the front of the shop.

Austin looked unconcerned. His gaze landed on Aspen. "You look a little understaffed for this influx. How can I help?"

"Mr. Edwards," Estelle said, her motherly tone making yet another appearance. "We're doing just fine. You really shouldn't be back here."

Austin scurried past Estelle, fully standing in the kitchen now. "I'm an invited guest," he reminded her with a cheeky smile.

Estelle gave him an unimpressed look. "Be that as it may, you need to—"

"How good are you at doing dishes?" The words were out of Aspen's mouth before she could think better of it, but after they were free, she didn't feel too bad about them. So he wanted to be a part of the cake business? Maybe they should show him it wasn't all about eating delicacies and leaving harsh reviews. A dang lot of work went into what she did, and that included spending hours washing dishes at times.

A slow smile crept across his face. "I've been known to scrub a pot or two in my time."

Aspen tilted her head toward the pile. "You want to help? You start there."

Without losing eye contact, he unbuttoned, then began to roll up his shirt sleeves. The tight fitting button down shirt did a wonderful job of showing off his shoulders, but now, with his forearms on display, Aspen felt like they needed to turn on the air conditioning in the kitchen.

He walked toward her, walking so close, their shoulders brushed. "I'd be happy to," he whispered, his breath brushing against her ear as he passed.

Aspen tried to hold back her shiver, but when she heard his low chuckle, she knew she hadn't done a very good job. The man was too much. When she finally managed to look up, Estelle was staring at her with a resigned look. Aspen frowned. "What?"

Estelle shook her head. Her eyes darted to where Austin was starting the water, then back to Aspen. "Let me know when you've got another birthday cake." Without another word, Estelle disappeared with Maeve in tow.

Aspen slowly went back to work, doing her best to ignore the cheerful whistling coming from Austin's side of the room. *I'm going to regret this.*

AUSTIN COULDN'T HELP but look over his shoulder every few minutes. Aspen seemed completely intent on whatever cake she was making. All he could tell from his place in the kitchen was that it required a ton of dishes and it had a green frosting. The cake itself appeared to be white, but he wasn't sure as to the flavor.

"Is this a new flavor?" He might as well have screamed at her by the way she jumped at his voice. Austin couldn't help but laugh. "Sorry. A little jumpy today?" Truth was, he was a little on edge himself, though he was working hard to hide it.

Aspen had proved to be a wonderful dinner companion last night, at least after they'd gotten the awkward beginning out of the way. Once she'd settled in, they'd talked, teased, asked questions and enjoyed a chat long into the evening. It had been the best date Austin had ever had.

Though he was far from ready to admit that to Aspen.

From the tenseness in her shoulders, she wasn't quite sure what to make of their situation either. Austin had kind of pushed his way inside the shop without a real plan, but she'd offered him a lifeline and even if it left him with pruny fingers, he was going to take it.

The whole reason for staying in Seagull Cover for the week was so he could spend time with her. He didn't need the time in order to get his story ready to go. Tye had been there and seen and tasted it all. Austin's brother had opted to drive home this morning, but Tye would get the review written, then send it to Austin before it went to the boss.

No...this was purely personal, even if he wasn't willing to admit it out loud.

Aspen caught her breath. "Uh...yeah."

He raised his eyebrows, waiting for her to continue. When she didn't, he leaned forward. "And?"

"And what?"

"What flavor is it?" he asked very slowly, as if talking to someone hard of hearing.

Aspen rolled her eyes at him. "Who said you get to know?"

Oh, so we were playing coy, huh? He could do that. He left the sink, his arms dripping soapy water on the floor as he walked right up into her space. "Is it supposed to be a surprise revealing?" he asked, his tone slightly husky. That wasn't exactly planned, but what guy wouldn't have a reaction when this close to a gorgeous woman?

"N-no," she said with a shake of her head. Her dark eyes were so wide, they seemed to take over her face.

"Then why won't you tell me?"

She blinked, slowly, then more rapidly and seemed to finally get herself under control. Stepping back from him, Aspen glared. "Ever heard of personal space?"

He grinned unrepentantly. "Yes. Have you?"

"I wasn't the one bursting another person's bubble without permission."

"You invited me into your kitchen." Austin leaned in just slightly. He was beginning to understand that her eyebrows were always her first reaction. They were extremely expressive and their jump at his move let him know he'd surprised her again. With someone as sharp as Aspen, he'd have to keep her on her toes, or she'd lose any and all interest in him. "I believe that was all the invitation I needed."

She swallowed hard and he held back a victory smirk. "Green apple tart," she whispered.

He straightened. "Really?"

She let out a breath. "Yes."

"Can I try it?"

Aspen made a face. "It's not done yet."

"Well...hurry up!" He went back to the sink, ignoring her squeak of anger. "I'm only here for so long, you know." He could hear her grumbling under her breath and it made him smile. She must really be attracted to him if she wasn't bothering to kick him out, even with how much he was pushing the boundaries.

The problem was, even though a week seemed like a good sized vacation, it wasn't very long to get to know a person. He didn't have the time to take things slow and he had a feeling Aspen wasn't a slow mover either. For her to be willing to invite him down for the Goldilocks Game, she had to be a little impulsive, reckless even. The whole thing could have exploded in her face, but she'd been willing to take the risk. And from the looks of the shop this morning, it had paid off.

"When you're done with that one, are you going to get going on the birthday cake?"

"Uh...yeah. Probably."

He glanced back. "Probably? I thought Estelle said they were out."

Aspen shrugged. "They are, but I don't always keep the same cakes on hand."

"Ah..." He nodded slowly. "You keep them rotating, and that way, people come back more often. Either because they're looking for their favorite or because they want to see what's new." He smiled. "Brilliant."

Aspen glanced sideways at him. "Thanks...I think."

"It was a compliment."

She shrugged. "I know...but somehow you made me sound kind of, I don't know, devious, I guess."

He brought his attention back to the dishes. "I think the better word would be shrewd, and there's absolutely nothing wrong with that. Shrewd people tend to make good business partners."

"And what are you?"

Austin ticked his head back and forth as he thought. "Most would probably consider me shrewd as well." He glanced back. "And I don't say that to brag."

Aspen looked skyward and shook her head.

He laughed at her obvious disbelief. "What? You don't believe me?"

"Oh, I think you're shrewd alright," she shot back. "Otherwise, you wouldn't have seen through my rotating flavors ploy so easily." Her dark eyes shot his way, sending a frisson of electricity through his spine.

He wasn't sure he'd ever get tired of those soulful eyes.

"But you pretending to be humble? Yeah...not so much."

"You think I'm egotistical?" he challenged.

"I think you're good at your job and you're fully aware of it." Aspen carried a tray with several pans on it toward the large wall ovens and spent the next few moments putting them inside. Once done, she turned and put her hands on her hips. "So, there's no need to pretend otherwise."

Austin faced her, putting his back against the sink. "There's nothing wrong with being self aware."

"No. But I'm not a fan of people who think they're above everyone else." She moved as if to dismiss him, but Austin wasn't done.

"I don't."

Aspen turned. "Don't what?"

"I don't think I'm above everyone else," Austin said, tilting his head to the side. The humor was gone now. They'd just crossed a line he didn't like. "Being confident in my abilities is fine, but I've never once thought that made me more than someone else." As a kid who came from nothing, the thought simply wouldn't compute. Having a home and being able to hoard food was more than he could ever ask for. He had yet to feel so secure in his life that he felt like he was better than anyone else. Not to mention his dyslexia, which was the reason for his lack of reading and writing, was a stark reminder that he would *always* struggle where others thrived.

He turned around and went back to washing. Let her think what she would of that. He knew her defensive behavior stemmed somewhat from how their relationship started, but if she wasn't going to be willing to get to know him, then he wasn't going to waste his breath.

"I'm sorry."

The words were small and unsure, but it was an apology nonetheless. "Apology accepted," Austin said, not turning around. "On one condition."

She sighed, long and loud. "What?"

"You have dinner with me again."

"Again? Didn't you get sick of me last night?"

He looked over his shoulders, letting his intensity show. "Not even a little bit." They stared at each other for what seemed to be forever before he went back to the sink, breaking the spell. His face was overheated and the washing water almost felt cool in comparison. "We can go as soon as the shop closes."

There was a long pause, then... "Fine."

He didn't bother turning around. If he did, she would see his smile, which had been too much to contain. Okay...maybe they *were* giving this a shot.

CHAPTER 13

Aspen huffed and studied herself in the mirror. How in the world was she going out with Austin, yet again? Well, again might be strong. They didn't exactly go out last night. They'd eaten in. At her family's inn. The one where Aspen dropped off desserts every night.

Her almost black hair hung in waves down her back. She'd used a little dry shampoo to give it some volume. After being wadded up in a hair net all day, it was a wonder she could let it down at all. Her mother always described her hair as having beachy waves, but Aspen had always felt like they'd just been indecisive. They weren't curly, and they weren't straight. It was somewhere in the middle and that annoyed her.

Still, there wasn't much she could do about it.

She put on some nude lipstick, made sure her mascara hadn't smudged and declared herself done. "You shouldn't even have bothered getting dressed up," she grumbled.

She had felt so bad about telling Austin he was egotistical that Aspen had practically been ready to give him anything he wanted. She had assumed his caveat would have something to do with the cake. He did seem enamored with food.

She should have guessed that he would do something completely unexpected. He appeared to be a man who always got what he wanted. Maybe her little stunt with the chairs had knocked him off his game and he was trying to get back at her. Maybe she was dressing herself up just to be humiliated.

"You're thinking awfully hard," Maeve said from the hallway.

Aspen's head snapped in that direction. "Sorry." She closed her eyes and rubbed her forehead. "I, uh...I'm just a little freaked out, I guess."

"Why?"

Aspen took in a breath. "Why do you think Austin insisted on going to dinner with me again?"

Maeve shrugged. "Because you're beautiful and intelligent. Because you can keep up with him in a battle of the wits. Because you were the first person to knock him off his little social media high horse. Take your pick."

"You don't think he's just setting me up for revenge?" Aspen winced even as she said the words. They couldn't be true. She'd seen him with his fans. She'd seen him with a child. She'd watched him inhale enough food to feed three people and wash enough dishes for a dozen. What she hadn't seen was the jerk she knew online. The one who spoke without regard for others' feelings and used words as weapons.

Surely he wasn't going to try anything underhanded with her tonight. It just seemed out of character for the man she was starting to get to know.

Maeve yawned. "I'm not even going to dignify that with a response," she said. "Come on. He'll be here any second."

"And what are you doing this evening?" Aspen asked as they descended the steps of the house they'd grown up in. It made things so much easier that their parents had left them the home when they'd gone across seas. The reminder of why always hurt, but the lack of a mortgage was a huge boost while they were trying to get the business off the ground.

Maeve grunted and pushed her glasses up her nose. "Ethan came over. He's currently chumming up to Estelle, hoping she'll feed him dinner."

Aspen snickered. Apparently, she wasn't the only one having men issues tonight. She stopped and put on an innocent expression when Maeve glared over her shoulder.

Shaking her head, Maeve stomped the rest of the way down and headed to the kitchen. Aspen started to follow, but the doorbell rang before she could get there.

Her heart instantly started to pound against her rib cage and a light sweat broke out on her neck.

"Are you going to get that?" Maeve had poked her head back out of the kitchen door.

"Yeah." Aspen nodded, wiping her hands on the sides of her skinny jeans. The door seemed to loom in front of her and the fact that she was so nervous started to make her mad. Throwing back her shoulders, she grabbed the knob and jerked it open.

"Hey," Riley, Estelle's best friend, said with a wide smile. It was odd to see the woman without some kind of animal with her. She ran their local shelter and was constantly taking a pet home for the evening.

All the courage Aspen had built up fizzled.

Riley looked Aspen up and down. Her smile grew. "You look like you've got something interesting going on tonight." Her hazel eyes seemed to dance in the porch lights.

Aspen stepped to the side. "Sort of," she said. "Come on in. Estelle's in the kitchen, I think."

"It wouldn't have anything to do with that guy, would it?" Riley leaned to the side so Aspen could see another person walking up the front sidewalk.

Her breath caught in her throat. Austin looked...amazing. His peacoat was perfectly tailored to his fit body, and his long legs looked great in fitted jeans. A collar peeked above the coat and she was sure he would look just as delicious as he did this morning when arriving at the kitchen. If he was a cake, Aspen was sure she'd be a goner.

Riley laughed softly, then tried to cover it with a cough. "Sorry," she said quickly, looking down as if chagrined.

Aspen knew her sister's friend too well. She wasn't sorry at all.

"Hello," Austin said as he arrived at the door. His eyes swept over Aspen before turning to Riley. "Austin Edwards."

Riley nodded. "I've seen your picture before and I watched from a distance at the Goldilocks Game." She smirked. "You're better looking in person."

Austin chuckled. "So noted. And thank you."

Riley slipped past Aspen. "You two kids have fun!" Her calling them kids wouldn't have been so bad if Riley hadn't made kissy noises before ducking into the kitchen.

Aspen groaned and shook her head.

Austin looked to be fighting a smile as he studied Aspen. "Okay..." He cleared his throat and held out his elbow. "Ready?"

Aspen hesitated, then took his proffered arm. "I suppose so." She shut the door behind her and walked out into the cold to his waiting car.

"We're not going to a funeral," Austin teased.

Aspen forced herself to relax a little. "I know," she responded. "I just...haven't done this in a while. Especially not—" She cut herself off before admitting the rest of what she was going to say. It wasn't exactly a kind thought, and she had no reason to keep holding onto her preconceived notions where Austin was concerned.

"Especially not where enemies are concerned?" he asked, though his smile suggested he was teasing.

Aspen's shoulders fell. "I didn't say that."

"But you were thinking it."

Aspen tilted her head to study him. "I'm sorry," she said sincerely. "You've been nothing but kind since you arrived and I've been hold-ing onto a grudge." She held out her hand. "Can we start again?"

He smiled, his teeth a brilliant white even in the dark. "I think a dinner is the perfect place for that." He shook her hand. "I accept."

"Good." Aspen sat down in the passenger seat and looked up as he waited to close the door. "Because I was going to do it anyway."

"Of course you were," he said with a laugh. Shutting the door, he walked around.

Butterflies erupted in Aspen's stomach as she watched him. She could practically feel the brick wall she'd set up dissolving. She'd been so dead set on fighting her attraction that slowly accepting it gave her an odd sense of peace. She found herself eager instead of scared and intrigued instead of frustrated. Maybe she should have been willing to do this a long time ago.

BY THE TIME AUSTIN got in the car, something had changed. The very air between them seemed to vibrate a little differently than before. He glanced sideways as he drove, but he wasn't quite sure what it was. Maybe just the fact that she wasn't fighting him tooth and nail? Was she truly looking forward to their evening together or just biding her time until he left town? There was no way to be sure, other than to keep spending time together. Austin assumed he'd figure it out eventually.

"The Hot Pot?" Aspen raised her eyebrows. "You came to a coastal town in Oregon to take me to a Chinese restaurant?"

Austin grinned as he parked the vehicle. "What can I say? I'm a man of eclectic tastes." He grabbed the door handle. "I like to give everything a shot, no matter where I'm at."

"Fair enough."

He got out of the car and started around, but Aspen had beat him to it, climbing out of her door before he could get there. "How am I supposed to be a gentleman if you do it first?" he teased, though the question was a legitimate one. He hadn't been raised with the old fashioned standards he now tried to live by, but whenever his mom had managed to keep them in an apartment, Austin had spent all his extra time watching old shows. They finally had a place to sleep, but there definitely wasn't enough money for cable. But it hadn't mattered. He'd seen everything free television had to offer, and a lot of it involved food and good manners.

When they'd lost the apartment and gone back to living in their car, which had happened too many times to count during his growing up years, Austin had sworn to himself that someday, he would be like those men. He would eat good food and he would treat the women with respect.

It sometimes got him some odd looks, but very few complaints.

"Sorry." Aspen ducked her head a little. "I've gotten in the habit of doing for myself."

He nodded. "I know, but if you'll allow me, I'd like to offer you those courtesies."

She graced him with a small, shy smile. It was very different from the ones she normally wore, and the sweetness of it punctured Austin right in the middle of his chest. "I think that would be nice. Thank you."

He returned her smile, then stepped ahead to pull open the front door of the restaurant. Spices and chili permeated the air, greeting his hungry stomach with all it needed to know.

This was going to be good.

"Have you eaten here before?" he asked as they were seated at their table.

Aspen shook her head. "Nope. It's fairly new in town." She made a point of looking around. "As you can imagine, Seagull Cove is tiny and not much changes."

"Which means when something new comes along, I would expect the locals to descend in droves," Austin argued.

Aspen laughed softly. "Actually, it's just the opposite. The locals like it the way it is. This kind of thing appeals to the tourists, but that's about it."

They took a few minutes to order before Austin got back to the topic at hand. "So...you haven't come out of principle?"

Aspen rolled her eyes. "No. I haven't come because I've been trying to open my own shop without ending up in the poor house."

"Yes..." Austin played with the straw in his glass of soda. "I noticed the shop is a little short handed."

"Maeve is our brilliant accountant," Aspen explained. "She felt it would be a good idea to wait about six months before hiring help." She took a long drink of water. "That way, we started out less in the hole and could gain some ground financially as well as reputation wise before hiring out."

"And how's that going for you?" He hadn't meant to ask so many questions about the business, but right now that's just where the conversation was flowing. And since he wanted to know as much as he could about the beautiful woman across from him, that meant going along with the status quo, even if it wasn't his area of interest or expertise.

Aspen shrugged. "Most days, just fine." She smirked. "Until it's not."

He cleared his throat and shifted in his seat, slightly embarrassed. "Yeah...I'm guessing after your little stunt, you'll find business will be thriving, at least for the next little while." He laughed. "Maybe Maeve's six month plan will have to be shifted."

"I wouldn't mind," Aspen said. "It's hard being the only one in the kitchen."

He leaned his elbows onto the table. "Were you really that worried about the shop? I mean, it had been your father's, right? Surely, you know it would be fine."

Aspen nodded a little too quickly. "Yeah, we didn't figure it would be a quick failure or anything, but even coming from a well known family, we knew we'd have to earn our keep."

Austin frowned. The answer sounded...practiced. "Would you mind explaining that? I'm not quite sure I follow."

To his surprise, she shook her head. "Actually, I'd much rather change the topic to you." She threw her long, lush hair over her shoulder and smiled. "What made you want to be a food critic? How do you even get into that business?"

Crud. Why couldn't they have kept talking about Aspen's family? Her father was an interesting figure. World class chocolate sculptor living in small town America. Then he up and disappears from the scene. No one knew why he'd quit, but at the announcement that his daughters were taking over the bakery, the world went on.

There were definitely a few unanswered questions to that story. Ones that Aspen, apparently, didn't want to be a part of. Well, it just so happened that Austin wasn't keen on spilling his own past either. No one really knew how to take the fact that he'd lived in a car most of his life and his obsession with food came because he'd never had enough. Not to mention, the fact that he couldn't write because he could barely read was known by only a few people. It was a secret Austin planned to take with him to the grave.

"What can I say?" he said, trying to play off the situation with a little humor. "I love food. What better job than one involving eating the very thing I love?"

Aspen opened her mouth to ask more, but their server approached with all the supplies for their hot pot. After getting instructions on cooking and being careful not to burn themselves, the two dug in.

"I didn't realize this was going to be such an interactive meal," Aspen said as she used her chopsticks to stir the vegetables in the broth.

Austin shrugged. "Who says you can't play with your food?"

She snorted and it made Austin smile. A woman who was willing to make such an unflattering noise in public either had a massive amount of confidence in themselves, or didn't care what their current company thought of them. He hoped it was the former.

"Playing with my cakes would only lead to a massive mess. Trust me, I see brides and grooms fall down that rabbit hole all the time."

"Yeah...I've never understood that tradition," Austin mused. "Here a woman has spent hours trying to make herself as beautiful as possible for her wedding day, and then the groom goes off and ruins it all."

Aspen grinned and leaned in. "Want to know where it came from?"

His eyebrows rose high. "Yeah."

"The Romans. The grooms used to break a cake over the bride's head as a sign of good luck. Somehow over the years it's turned into smashing each other in the face."

He made a face.

"Not a fan?" she asked with a grin.

Austin shook his head. "No way. That's just a waste of good food." Her grin turned into a light-hearted laugh, which resonated through every part of Austin. It was clear that Aspen was starting to relax in his company. And he was finding himself more and more drawn to her. The sweet woman he'd seen interacting with family and friends was just as wonderful as she appeared from a distance. Though, he'd be the first to admit he didn't mind her feisty side either. The mix of both was slightly intoxicating.

"So you're a cake history expert as well as a baker," Austin mused. "I'm impressed."

"Oh? My peanut butter filling wasn't enough for you?"

The heat in the room rose a couple of degrees. Yeah...that sassy side was definitely enjoyable. Now he just needed to convince her of the same thing.

CHAPTER 14

"Want to take a walk with me?"

Aspen wiped her mouth on her napkin and leaned back in her seat. "I'm not sure I can. I might have to be rolled out of here." She fanned her face. "Not to mention, my mouth is on fire." She reached for her water glass while Austin chuckled.

"It did have a kick, didn't it?"

Aspen nodded. Little by little, as the night had gone on, all her inhibitions had slowly melted away. He was truly the gentleman he had asked her to let him be. He was sweet, funny, witty and loved many of the same things as she. It seemed the two of them had more in common than not. But still...she felt as if there was something he wasn't telling her.

Every time she asked about family, or his career, he clammed up. Just what was he hiding?

You've only known each other a few days, she reminded herself. *Give it time. If we continue to spend time together, some day he'll spill it.*

"That sounds like the perfect reason to walk," he said, pushing his chair back and holding out his hand to help her up. "I find when I'm overfull, walking helps settle it down."

"Have a lot of experience with that, do you?"

He shook slightly as he laughed quietly. "I suppose you could say that."

They left through the front doors, both ducking a little as a chilly wind beat at them.

"Brrr...you sure you want to take a walk?"

"Come on," Austin said, gripping her hand fully this time. "It'll be invigorating."

The pulse of electricity coming from where he touched her was enough to make Aspen want to pull away. It wasn't that it didn't feel good. It was that it did. In fact, it felt too good.

Had holding a man's hand ever felt so...right?

Heat seemed to travel up her arm and neck, warming her face right to the tip of her nose, which was Jack Frost's favorite place to nip when she walked in the cold weather.

Austin let their hands swing between them, as if they were a casual, romantic couple in the old times movies. Aspen couldn't help but smile a little. It was adorable.

She poked his side, laughing when he jumped a little. "You know, for someone who eats for a living, you sure don't seem to suffer from it."

He gave her a playful glare. "Are you saying I should be a lot heavier than I am?"

Aspen shrugged. "Not necessarily. But it's kind of disgusting that men like you can eat and eat and never gain a pound. Us women aren't so lucky."

"First off, I spend enough time in the gym to help overcome all the calories I eat." He squeezed her hand. "Second, it doesn't appear that your figure suffers either." His bright green eyes looked her up and down and even with a thick coat on, Aspen felt the heat of his gaze. "And you work with sugar all day long."

Aspen flipped her hair over her shoulder, hoping she appeared unaffected by his perusal, though inside she was a mess. "Flattery will get you nowhere," she said coolly.

"On the contrary," Austin said with a smile. "I'm pretty sure it gets people everywhere."

"Well, I'm not people."

"No..." His tone was low and intense. "You're not."

Aspen kept her eyes straight ahead. She couldn't look at him right now. The cold wind had ceased to have any affect on her at his flirting and insinuations. She was starting to understand just how in over her head she was with this man. She wasn't exactly shy and could usually hold her own in the world of dating and relationships, but right now she felt as if she were barely keeping her head above water.

The energy sizzling between them was either going to stop her heart or cause her to jump up and kiss him.

She wasn't sure which one she was hoping for.

"Hey, they got the corner with your chair decorated." *Yes. A change in topic. Perfect.*

"Really? That was fast."

Aspen glanced around, realizing they were only a couple blocks from the shop. "They did it while we were finishing the dishes tonight. Come on. I'll show you." She picked up her pace and began dragging him toward the cafe.

"I'm coming, I'm coming." His voice was tinged with laughter and it caused Aspen's pace to relax without conscious consent.

How did he do that? Aspen had always been driven and admittedly stubborn. Yet it took so little for this man she barely knew to calm her down and help her take an easier pace. She'd always rushed through life and this man made her want to take her time. To savor. To enjoy. What was happening to her?

"So who *did* the decorating of the shop?" Austin asked as they walked. His long legs kept up with her all too well and his hand kept her as warm as if she was in front of a fire.

Aspen snorted. "Now you're asking that? Do you really want to know?"

He glanced down. "Of course. I wouldn't have asked otherwise."

She shrugged. "Estelle is our decorator. She's got a marketing background, so she's really good at putting pretty things together." She gave him the side eye. "Despite what non-pink-lovers think."

His smile was completely unrepentant and completely charming. "Hey. I'm a guy. We don't like pink."

"I could find you plenty of pink ties and T-shirts that say otherwise."

Austin threw back his head with a groan. "Men only wear those because their women pick them out. But you're never going to let me live this down, are you?"

"Not if I can help it."

"You know...most women I meet try a little harder to get on my good side."

The words weren't nearly as egotistical as Aspen would have first assumed. In fact, she was pretty sure he was teasing her, though she could easily imagine what he said being true.

"Plied with lots of false flattery, huh?"

Austin shrugged. "Maybe. But I can't say I don't enjoy it."

"What man wouldn't?" Aspen couldn't wipe the smile from her face no matter how hard she tried. She was enjoying their banter far too much. "But I think we already established I'm not like most people, or women."

"Thank heavens for that."

Aspen laughed. "Tired of the status quo?" They'd reached the shop and she fished her keys out of her clutch.

"You could say that."

His presence at her back wasn't doing anything to help Aspen keep her wits about her, but somehow she managed to get the key into the lock and push the door open. She'd brought them through the front so he could see the little display Estelle had made with that horrid couch from the Goldilocks Game.

With little fanfare, Aspen flipped on the light and waved her arm toward the monstrosity. No one would ever say the couch was attractive, but...it did seem to be good for business.

But Handsome Faced Austin appears to be dangerous to my heart.

THE COUCH WAS SO UGLY that Austin wanted to close his eyes against the brightness. He did wince a little, though he hoped Aspen didn't notice. He'd chosen the small two-seater not because it was nice or even because it was comfortable, but because it had been the one Aspen had sat on when she'd fed him peanut butter cake.

He knew the likelihood of getting a repeat performance was slim to none, but a man could dream...and Austin was spending a lot of time dreaming about Aspen Harrison.

"Wow," he said, rocking back on his heels. "Estelle really went all out." The eldest of the Harrison women had turned the corner into a perfect spot for picture taking. Plants, curtains, it all turned the garish furniture into something social media followers would eat up like candy.

He hated it, but he had to admire the ingenuity that went into it.

Aspen burst out laughing, bending forward with the effort of her belly laugh. "You hate it," she said between her burst of noise.

"Well...I..."

She shook her head, silencing him, and pointed at his face. "You should see your face. It's so clear how you feel about it." Calming down, she wiped at the corners of her eyes. "Truth be told, it's not exactly our taste either." She glanced coyly at him. "But *someone* gave us very little to work with."

Austin put his hands in the air. "I was just playing your game," he argued. "You wanted me to pick a seat, so I did."

"Yeah, well, no one expected you to pick one that might be found in some eccentric billionaire's teenage daughter's room."

He chuckled, feeling better that she didn't seem to hold any hard feelings towards him. "I had very few weapons in my arsenal," he pointed out. "Revenge is best served in leopard print."

Aspen snorted again. "Well played, Mr. Edwards. Well played." Quickly spinning on her heel, she headed to the back. "Cake?"

Austin's eyes widened and he lunged after her. "Are you asking if I want a slice of cake? Because the answer will always be yes."

Aspen smiled, but didn't turn his way. "And here I thought you despised our small town establishment."

"Not liking the decor doesn't mean I hated the food offerings," he quickly explained. Reaching around her, he held the door open. The close proximity in which Aspen passed him had all his nerves on high alert. The more she teased and taunted him, the more he found himself wanting to take that mouth in a kiss that would knock the sarcastic socks right off of her.

Austin shook his head. He definitely wouldn't mind if the opportunity arose, but it was only their second date, after all. He wasn't sure exactly what the spitfire would allow.

"Too bad you didn't just say that in your first review."

Austin sped up to stand in front of her, blocking her way with his body. She skidded to a stop only inches from him. "I tried," he pointed out. "But other parts of the review became more popular."

Aspen's breathing had picked up and Austin took a chance by stepping closer.

"I'm under an obligation to my readers to share everything," he said softly. "I didn't bad mouth your baking, but the couch and I didn't get along. Can I help it if my fans picked out that part and ran with it?"

"I...hadn't thought about it that way," she said in a husky tone.

Was it hot in this kitchen? Surely, one of the ovens had to be on overdrive for him to be this warm. Only moments before, he'd been nearly shivering in the outside weather.

"But I can see your point." Her eyes looked like two pools of dark chocolate and Austin found himself leaning closer. They were here for dessert, after all...weren't they?

"Besides," Austin said softly, his eyes flicking between hers and her lips. "If I hadn't put up that article, I wouldn't have been treated to such a triumphant return." His mouth was within millimeters of hers now. The tension in the air was thick enough to choke him, but his heart only continued to speed up. "Plus, who would want only one slice of cake when they can have twelve?" Her lips quirked and Austin almost groaned as he waited to make sure she wasn't going to push him away.

"Who indeed." Without warning, she tilted her chin back and brought their lips together.

If a tsunami had crashed into the front of the building, Austin wouldn't have noticed. Right now only one thing was consuming every part of him and it was a five foot nothing brunette with a penchant for crazy cake flavors.

He brought his arms around to her back, tugging her into his chest. She followed suit and clung to the shoulders of his coat, letting him know without words that he'd better not stop now.

Time stood still and Austin found himself lost in the euphoria. No meal, no dessert, no heat or warmth had ever filled him with such utter contentment as this moment.

When she whimpered and raised herself onto her tiptoes as if to get closer, Austin found himself eager to respond, tightening his hold, but only for a few more seconds. It was easy to see that he would never be able to get enough. He would never be satiated and if he wasn't careful, he would stop being the gentleman he'd so proudly announced at the beginning of their date.

Pulling himself back, he forced himself to let go. His chest was heaving and he felt hot all over as he looked at the flush on her neck and cheeks. With how wide her eyes were, Austin was positive that she had felt all the same whirlwind of emotions that he had.

"Whoa..."

She smiled. "That's a good description."

Shaking his head, he pushed a hand through his hair. "So...cake?" His voice squeaked at the end, giving away the fact that he wasn't completely under control at the moment. He scowled when she laughed softly.

Stepping up to him, Aspen reached up and patted his cheek like a little kid. "Work up an appetite?"

He grabbed her hand. Gentleman, schmentleman. Sometimes the rules were made to be broken. Tugging on her quickly, he brought her back to his chest. "You have no idea," he said before claiming her mouth once more. Only this time, he was in charge. Aspen had started their first encounter and run with it. Now it was his turn. And he knew without a shadow of a doubt that he would walk out of this bakery a new man.

The week was going to be much, much shorter than he had hoped.

CHAPTER 15

A spen's lips were still tingling the next morning as she rushed down the stairs to get to work. She'd slept in longer than normal because she'd stayed out later than normal, thanks to Kissy Lips Austin.

And geez, the man could kiss. Aspen had never felt so overwhelmed and intoxicated by a man before. His hands had been gentle but strong, his lips caressing and enticing. The longer they had lingered, the more Aspen had wanted. She wasn't a complete shut in. She had dated and kissed men before, but none had gotten under her skin so fully that when they were gone, she itched to see them again.

If Austin were a cake, Aspen was positive she would have hoarded the entire thing for herself, refusing to share.

"Late night?"

Aspen froze, her hand on the front door knob. Slowly, she spun and gave Maeve a sheepish grin. "Maybe?"

Maeve pushed her glasses onto her hair. "By the color under your eyes, I'm going to say I was correct." She tapped the fake lenses. "I don't even need these to see it."

"You don't need those to see anything," Aspen argued.

Maeve only grinned.

"So..." Aspen tilted her head coolly. "How did things go with Mr. Next Door Neighbor last night?" It was a low blow. Maeve and Ethan hadn't gotten along in forever, though the disdain seemed mostly one sided. Aspen had no idea why Maeve had a bee in her bonnet about the surfer man, but whenever his name was brought up, Maeve flipped.

Maeve's expression tightened, but she didn't let the smile go. "As well as could be expected when someone's too lazy to fix their own dinner."

Guilt flooded her system. Aspen had been trying to turn the attention away from herself, but perhaps that hadn't been the right way to handle it. "Why are you so mad at him?" Aspen asked softly. "We've always gotten along in the past. Ethan played with us all our growing up years and was always a sweetheart."

Speaking of...why couldn't she have feelings for someone like Ethan? He was cute and friendly. His presence didn't make her heart skip a beat and give her mixed emotions about slapping him in the face with frosting or kissing him. He was easy. Why couldn't she like someone who was easy?

"Ethan is a mooch." Maeve sniffed. "He's an adult, but he's never bothered growing up and now, because his parents are gone, we've had to take over his care. It's ridiculous."

"His parents were killed in an accident," Aspen said, feeling defensive. Her sister was taking this too far. "Show a little compassion."

Maeve's face fell. "Right," she said softly. "Sorry." Spinning on her heel, she began to walk away. "I think I'll work from home today. See ya later."

Aspen rubbed her forehead. This did not bode well for the rest of the day. Last night had been the stuff of fairy tales and now she had awoken into a nightmare...of her own making. Shaking her head and trying to dispel the discontent, she headed out to her car. She had been the unlucky sister to get stuck in the driveway last night and now her car was freezing from the low temperatures. The worst part was it probably wouldn't even be warm enough to blast the heater before she got to work.

Tugging on her gloves, Aspen drove to town and parked at the back of the shop. They were set to open in a half hour and she needed to get a jump on things. Normally she'd have at least two cakes in the oven by now.

The light was already on when she headed into the kitchen via the back door, but Aspen hadn't noticed the other body in the room until she hung up her coat and spun around. "AH!"

Austin put his hands in the air in surrender. "Don't shoot!"

"Austin! What in the world are you doing?" she demanded.

A slow, delicious grin grew on his face. "I thought I was the resident dishwasher. Should I have slept in?" He looked around. "You haven't actually made a mess yet."

"Who let you in?" She chose to ignore his teasing.

"I did," Estelle said bluntly, coming through the door from the front of the shop. "You're going to need to do some extra baking today since we've got a media event."

Aspen stiffened. "Say what?"

"Our resident celebrity," Estelle waved at Austin, "has agreed to a photo shoot with the chair corner since he's still in town." Estelle smiled. "I think it'll look great on the website."

"You..." Aspen's mouth opened and shut several times as she tried to wrap her head around what was going on. "Why wasn't I informed of this?"

"Because I just thought of it early this morning." Estelle put her hands on her hips. "It'll be great publicity and Jayden said he's free, so he can do the pictures."

"Do you really think there'll be a crowd? This is pretty last minute," Aspen said, walking over to grab her apron. "And what's our inventory? I, uh..." She did her best not to glance at Austin, but failed miserably, "I haven't counted yet this morning."

Estelle's lips twitched. She wasn't fooled at all. "We have half a black forest, one-quarter peanut butter, one slice of cookies and cream and about three dozen cookies. Basically, we need just about everything."

"Wow." Aspen rubbed her forehead. She must have really been distracted yesterday. It wasn't like her to get so far behind in her baking. "Okay. I'm on it."

"I'll help."

Aspen jerked to a stop. She'd almost forgotten Austin was there. "Don't you have to get ready for the photo shoot?"

He looked down at his jeans and T-shirt, then back up. "You don't think I look good enough for pictures?"

Too good. Aspen bit her tongue to keep from saying those words out loud. Austin Edwards was simply a handsome man, no matter what he was wearing. "Your funeral," she replied, opting not to answer his question. It could only backfire. "I'm not going to fight your rabid fans if they say you look like you've been washing dishes all day."

Austin grinned. "I'll take that chance."

"Aprons are over there," Estelle said wryly. "I'm sure we can keep you looking just fine." She sucked in a long breath. "Meanwhile, I'm going to finish setting up shop and make sure that corner is ready to go."

Aspen gave her sister a salute and then walked with purpose toward the pantry. She began pulling ingredients into her arms until they were full and turned to walk out, almost losing everything when Austin was standing right behind her. "Geez." She gasped, panting slightly. "You almost gave me a heart attack." Shaking her head and glaring at Austin for chuckling, she straightened her shoulders. They might have had a fantastic date last night, but today was work, and she couldn't afford to be distracted. With a photo shoot, they might have larger than normal crowds. "Don't you have dishes to do?"

He raised a single eyebrow. "You haven't dirtied any yet."

Heat rose up her neck and into her cheeks. "Oh, yeah...right." Clearing her throat, she shoved a bunch of the ingredients at Austin. "Here. Make yourself useful."

He managed to arrange things in his arms without dropping them, then leaned down and left a quick peck on her lips before Aspen knew what he was doing. "How was that?"

Aspen blinked several times. The kiss had left her in a state of shock, but not an unpleasant one. The tingling sensation from earlier was back and her lips positively buzzed. "Uh...not so good. Now I'm distracted and can't remember what I was supposed to bake."

"Mission accomplished," he said smugly, turning to take the ingredients to the counter.

Ah, man...I'm in so much trouble.

AUSTIN KNEW HE'D PUSHED it with that kiss, but the shock on her face was priceless. He had every intention of spending the rest of his vacation at her side, no matter where she was. After last night, he could do no less.

The picture idea had been a surprise, but not unwelcome. He knew it would only boost the cafe's media presence and it would be a fun boon to his own following. They'd love to see him all cozied up on that disgusting couch.

He glanced at Aspen. *Can I convince her to join me on that monstrosity?* It was his whole reason for choosing that particular seat, after all. But how to get her in on the plan without spilling his stupid sentimentality?

"Hey, Austin?" Estelle poked her head in from the front room.

"Yep?" He set down the canister of flour, followed by everything else in his arms.

"I'm gonna need you to fill out a permissions form before the shoot. When Maeve gets in, can you remind her to get that out for you?"

Austin's heart stopped. "Uh..."

Estelle cocked her head. "I'm sure you've signed one before. I promise it's just standard. Just saying we have permission to use your likeness on our advertising avenues."

He swallowed hard. What could he say? This was why Tye was supposed to be with him, but Austin hadn't expected to be confronting a bunch of reading during his vacation to get to know Aspen. How was he going to get out of this without hurting people's feelings? His editor would kill him if he signed something without reading it first, and how could he read it without giving away the fact that he had dyslexia?

He coughed. "I'll be happy to take a look at it," he finally muttered. This was a disaster. They were going to figure out everything he'd worked so hard to hide. His eyes drifted to the pantry where Aspen was still gathering supplies. Surely the women wouldn't do anything underhanded, would they? He could trust that the document was legit?

"Great, thanks!" Estelle said easily, slipping back to the front.

"I think I got it all," Aspen said, her arms full of yet more supplies.

Austin ran over to help carry the load. "Let me get that," he said with a forced grin. He needed to act normal. If he stayed chill, he'd have a better chance of getting out of this unscathed.

Maybe he could take a few minutes to look at the contract and get Tye on a video chat? That should work. Right?

It wasn't much, but the idea had merit and it helped Austin calm down. He knew that if he ever had a serious relationship, he would have to share his secrets with that woman, but he barely knew Aspen, and Austin wasn't keen on becoming serious anytime soon.

She was fantastic. Their date had been fantastic. And Austin hoped for more time with her, but spilling every skeleton in his closet? Nope. Not even close yet.

"Okay. We're gonna be doing several cakes at once. Can you follow instructions?" she asked.

It was easy to see her mind was only on one thing. Work. Any fun, flirting or getting to know each other further was off the table. He grinned. *For now.* "I'm excellent at following directions."

"Great." Aspen's eyes didn't even look his way.

The challenge only made Austin laugh to himself. He enjoyed work as much as the next person and gave his all to his job, as shown by his willingness to come and be made fun of during the Goldilocks Game. But he also enjoyed playing. And his whole purpose for being here for the week was to play with Aspen. If she thought they couldn't play while working...she was going to have to learn.

"Grab the stack of metal bowls on that shelf," Aspen said, waving her hand in the general direction of the shelf.

Austin did as she asked, setting several bowls on the table in a row. He kissed her cheek. "Next?"

Aspen blinked as if coming out of a trance and turned to him with wide eyes. "What are you doing?" she asked.

He made sure he had on his innocent face and put a hand to his chest. "What? I followed your dema—I mean, direction."

She had the good sense to look uncomfortable. "Sorry. I kind of get in a zone when I'm working."

"Great. I'll work to help you stay in it."

Her smile relaxed. "You don't have to do this, you know. We barely know each other."

He tugged on her hair. "Maybe not, but I know enough to know I *want* to know more." He raised his eyebrows. "Am I overstepping?"

The fact that she shook her head so quickly gave him a burst of confidence. "No. I want to get to know you better as well."

"Then let's get these cakes going. You talk, I'll listen and while they're baking, we'll switch." *And I'll put off taking care of that form as long as possible.*

"Sounds good." Aspen rubbed her hands together and reached up to her head. "Oops. Forgot the best accessory."

Austin groaned. "Do we really have to use them?"

"Do you want a visit from an inspector?" she challenged. After popping a hairnet on her own head, she grinned and handed one to him. "Go on. I'm sure you'll look great."

Grumbling, Austin followed suit. Why couldn't someone come up with health protocols that didn't make people look like aliens in a compression chamber? Once finished, he turned back and held out his hands. "What do you think?"

Aspen tapped her bottom lip. "It's missing something." Her eyes widened. "Ah!" She pointed one finger in the air, then walked to the wall and grabbed a couple of aprons. One of them happened to be the same bright pink as the couch out front.

Austin took the offering as if it would poison him. "Why do I get the feeling this color isn't a coincidence?"

This time it was Aspen's turn to look innocent. "What? It's too big for me. It's probably the only one I have that will fit you."

The light laughter slipping from her tempting lips helped Austin feel marginally better about his new costume. He'd have to redo his hair before the photo shoot, but he was quickly coming to understand that he'd be willing to do anything this beautiful woman asked of him. No matter how humiliating.

Twenty minutes later, they had several bowls full of batter and Aspen was throwing her whole body into stirring one of them. Austin had already worked his way through a couple of bowls until they'd reached the consistency Aspen had advised, and now he glanced her way. He smiled at how her hips swung from side to side as she worked. His upper body strength had come in handy while stirring the extra large batches, but Aspen wasn't quite as big as him.

Deciding now was one of those times to add a little play to their work, he slipped up behind her. "Let me help with that," he whispered against her ear, putting his hand on the one she was holding the whisk with.

Aspen stilled and he could feel her breathing pick up now that she was trapped between him and the counter.

When she didn't say anything, Aspen began helping her stir the cake. Her back was against his chest and he savored the sensation and heat churning between them. After a few minutes, he helped her tap the whisk on the side. "I think that's just right, don't you?"

"Yep," she squeaked.

He smiled and slowly set the utensil down on the counter before spinning her around. Not bothering to wait, he brought his mouth to hers, stealing her breath the best way he knew how.

As much as he would have enjoyed staying there all day, Austin wasn't trying to get their business in trouble, so he pulled back too soon. "Time to get those cakes in the oven," he whispered against her cheek, then broke contact.

Aspen gasped for air and took a few seconds to collect herself. "Austin Edwards, I think you're trying to kill me." Her hands shot to her mouth as if she hadn't meant to say that out loud.

Laughing, Austin leaned in to leave a sweet kiss against her forehead. "Same, Aspen Harrison. Same."

CHAPTER 16

"Okay, lay your arm across the back and just relax," Jayden said from his place behind the camera.

Austin followed directions and managed to look cool and aloof while relaxed and at ease. It was a delicate balance and somehow the handsome reporter managed to pull it off.

Aspen wanted to roll her eyes, but she was too impressed. *He's so comfortable in the limelight. How does he do it? I hate being watched.*

"Work it, work it," Jayden said with a laugh.

Austin pursed his lips and began to shift his shoulders, throwing a few kisses at the camera. The audience was eating it up, laughing and catcalling, a few whistles ringing through the air.

Aspen felt her cheeks heat and she slapped her forehead. "Doofus," she muttered under her breath, though she couldn't seem to stop smiling. The guy could be a total dork, but he was certainly fun.

Jayden straightened. "Perfect!" He looked over the crowd and caught Aspen's eye. "Aspen! Come on."

All the blood drained from Aspen's head. "What?" she asked hoarsely.

Austin's smug grin grew. Had he known about this?

A nudge in her shoulder had Aspen looking over to see Estelle holding a plate of cake. Her deep brown eyes were snapping with humor. "For you," she whispered with a wink.

Aspen felt like she might faint. "What are you talking about?" she asked, looking around to a sea of faces and anticipation.

"Come on, Aspen," Jayden pressed.

"Go on," Estelle urged, handing her the plate. "Jayden had some ideas."

"They better be ideas on how he wants his funeral cake to look," Aspen snapped, feeling her anger build, overcoming the faintness from a moment before.

Estelle laughed, but luckily, no one else seemed to have heard Aspen's snarky remark.

She stomped toward the couch, doing her best to melt Jayden into the floor, but he only smiled brightly at her and waited patiently.

"Great," Jayden said as she finally stood next to the couch.

Aspen tried to hand the cake to Austin, but he didn't move.

"No," Jayden interfered. "You're going to feed it to him."

"Ooooh..." The crowd let out a dramatic call. This time the blood went straight to Aspen's cheeks, rather than draining. Every part of her was on fire at the moment and she wished for superhero powers to direct the flames at Jayden...or Austin...or maybe even Estelle.

"Just sit next to him, put your weight on your hip...that's right...and hold out a forkful of cake like you did at the Goldilocks Games." Jayden waited for Aspen to follow directions, then shot her a thumbs up and pulled up the camera.

Aspen kept her eyes on the camera, studiously ignoring the all-too-smug man at her side.

"It needs to be near his mouth," Jayden said wryly.

Aspen finally looked over and realized that her peanut butter cake was about to take out Austin's eye.

He apparently wasn't too worried since he was grinning. "I've always heard we eat with our eyes first, but I've never taken it so literally."

Laughter rang through the small cafe and the heat went up a notch. "Sorry," Aspen grumbled, bringing the fork down toward his mouth, but keeping her gaze away from his eyes. She knew if she looked too closely, she'd get caught up in the magnetic pull between them and get stuck like a deer in the headlights.

"Perfect. Now open up, Austin," Jayden instructed.

Jayden's command snapped Aspen out of her cool demeanor and she couldn't help but fall into his gaze. His green eyes held hers and the room seemed to hold its breath. It was as if everyone there could feel the tension building between the two people on the obnoxiously bright couch and wanted to be witness.

Slowly, Austin opened his mouth, holding it just right as if he were actually going to eat the bite of cake.

"Great..." Jayden murmured as he leapt around the space, taking pictures from all sorts of angles.

It should have been obnoxious, but Aspen barely noticed. All her attention was on the man to the side of her. She couldn't seem to look away. Yes, she'd kissed him. She'd spent time with him and even gone on an official date, but right now they weren't back in the kitchen, away from prying eyes. She hadn't planned to announce to the world that she was changing her opinion of the normally taciturn food reviewer. Her private life was just that...private. And now, with a few presses of Jayden's finger, Aspen knew that there would be no going back.

There wasn't a single person in that cafe that couldn't see what was happening. The room was overly warm and the air felt thick as molasses. Only an idiot wouldn't recognize that there was much more going on than just Jayden's photo taking. The amount of clicks going through the room and murmured words let her know the entire social media world was privy to this moment.

She felt the thought press her panic button and Austin must have seen the reaction in her eyes because he quickly reached out and snatched her hand, holding it in place when Aspen wanted to retreat.

He subtly shook his head, his open mouth turning into a crooked grin. Slowly, ever so slowly, he pulled himself closer to her hand.

Aspen felt her breathing pick up and the people in the room melted away. Her eyes widened and her heart nearly beat out of her chest.

Just before the fork reached his face, Austin opened his mouth again and pulled the bite inside. He closed his lips around it and slid the fork out, not letting go of her hand.

Was it possible to die from attraction? Aspen was sure she was about to expire. She couldn't catch her breath, and yet, she now had no desire to go away. All she could think about were the lips right in front of her that she had touched before, and she wanted to taste them again.

Letting their hands fall, Austin was once again on the move. But this time, his face came closer to hers, rather than the plate.

Aspen's hold on the plate began to shake and Austin quickly shifted his weight, using his free hand to steady hers. Her eyes fluttered closed as his lips pressed to hers, but it was the gasps, giggles and snapping of cameras that kept her from fully giving in to the moment.

"Kiss me," Austin breathed against her mouth before pressing in again.

"They're watching," Aspen whispered back, letting him move his head to change the angle.

"Who cares." He obviously didn't since his next kiss was far less sweet than the first couple.

The fork clattered to the ground as Aspen brought her hands up to cup his head and his shot straight to the back of her neck, pulling her to him. The cake landed in her lap and for the first time ever, Aspen cared nothing for the waste.

THE ROOM WAS ERUPTING with catcalls and whistles, and Austin knew he needed to pull back, but how? How did any man let go when he had a willing woman in his arms who had just about sent him through the roof by feeding him cake?

He might have started the moment, but Aspen had him by the nose and she didn't even know it. When he'd grabbed her hand and pulled the cake into his mouth, his only thought had been to tease, maybe make her blush, and have a flirty photo op.

The moment had completely backfired and he was struggling to regain control.

"Austin," she whispered, pulling back a little.

He kept their foreheads together. Yes, she was right. They needed to pull back, but he wasn't ready to lose contact just yet. "Sorry," he whispered just as softly. "That kind of got out of hand."

"I have the feeling that the entire world knows we...like each other," she said.

Austin pulled back and laughed, helping fix her hair where it had gotten mussed during their amorous exchange. "That's an understatement."

He was afraid to look at the crowd. Their noise said they were happy to see them as a couple, but there were always a few individuals on the opposite side of the majority. "Dare we look?"

Aspen's nose scrunched. "If we can't see them, does that mean they can't see us?"

Austin grabbed her hand and squeezed it before turning to the crowd. Most of the faces were bright with news of gossip and eager for more, but a few of Aspen's family members looked slightly uncomfortable. He couldn't exactly blame them. Clearing his throat, Austin stood, taking Aspen with him.

The plate of cake landed on the floor, completely forgotten during their moment in the spotlight. Austin looked down, looked at Aspen, then looked at the crowd. "I guess I should just be grateful she didn't smash it in my face, huh?"

The crowd erupted in more laughter and even Estelle and Jayden relaxed a little, smiling at his quip.

Austin held their hands in the air. "And the cake is officially out of the bag. Thanks for joining us today."

Ignoring the cake and the clawing hands of the people who wanted to speak to them, Austin led Aspen into the kitchen, where he promptly shut the door and leaned against it. His head fell back and he closed his eyes. That was wonderful and terrible all at the same time. Yes, he wanted to date Aspen, but he hadn't exactly planned to tell the world about it. He had no idea how the fans of Eat It Austin would respond to the news.

He got ribbed all the time for being single, but it was always easy to push the teasing away. But being the face of the review blog meant people wanted to know his business and Austin had just shared far more than he normally would.

His fans saw the face he showed. They actually knew very little about him as a person. They had no idea that he'd grown up in his mom's car. They had no idea that his starving childhood had led to his love of food. They also had no idea that he was dyslexic and that he didn't write any of the reviews. His face had simply been considered the better of the two to put in front of the public.

He snorted. *How's that for egotistical?*

The clanging of pans caught his attention and Austin opened his eyes to see Aspen with her head down, starting to mix a batter. He swallowed. She didn't look happy.

Pushing off the door, he walked to her side, but she wouldn't look at him. "I'm sorry," he finally said softly, breaking the quiet.

"Hmm?" She still didn't look his way.

Austin sighed and grabbed her shoulders to turn her toward him. She resisted, but only a little. The look she gave him, however, once they were finally facing each other wasn't nearly as friendly as she had been only moments before. "I'm sorry," he said again. "I hadn't planned all that." His arm waved toward the door.

"All that." The words were flat and without emotion.

Any man worth his salt knew to be wary when a woman had that kind of tone. It was the one where they said "I'm fine," though they were anything but. "Yes. All that." He tilted his head. "I don't usually put the woman I'm dating in the spotlight and throw her to the wolves."

She raised an eyebrow and folded her arms over her chest. "So you've done this before."

He scowled. "What? No. I just said I *don't* normally do that."

"But that means you *sometimes* do."

Austin closed his eyes and rubbed between his eyebrows. "Okay, let's break this down a little." He looked at her, dropping his hand to the side. "What's really bothering you?"

"What do you mean?"

"I mean..." He opened his eyes wide. "You're ticked off, but I'm not exactly sure why. Call it being a man, call it being dumb, I don't care, but I do care about figuring out why I just walked in here after having the best moment of my life and you're banging pots like you want to take my head off." Guilt began to trickle down his spine when he saw her eyes getting misty. Why did a woman's tears always hurt so bad? He hung his head and sighed.

Aspen sniffed and wiped at her eyes. "I'm sorry," she said quickly, as if trying to hide the evidence of her emotions.

"What are you sorry for?" he questioned, reaching out to wipe the dampness from her cheeks. "Not only did I just out us, I made you cry. I think that makes me more than sorry."

She shook her head. "No...I just..." She held up a finger and walked away toward the office space.

Disappearing inside, Austin heard her blow her nose before coming back out.

"I guess I was worried that it meant nothing to you," she admitted, staying near the door.

He scrunched his eyebrows together. "Meant nothing? Do you mean that kiss?" His tone became incredulous. How in the world did she get *nothing* from *amazing*?

She nodded, sniffling against and using a tissue to wipe at her nose. "I got so caught up in the moment, I didn't think until afterwards that maybe it was all just a publicity stunt. That you were using me for ratings or to further your career." Her head was down and she looked up at him through damp lashes.

He pushed a hand through his hair and blew out a breath. "I don't know whether to be offended or relieved." He barked out a sarcastic laugh.

"But then you said it was the best moment of your life and I realized how ridiculous and insecure I was being." Aspen threw her arms out to the side. "I'm sorry. I wasn't sure how to react after something so...public." She dropped his eyes again. "Despite the thing with the Goldilocks Game, I don't usually put myself in the spotlight." She snorted. "There's a reason I bake in the back where no one can see me."

Austin groaned and walked over, wrapping her in a tight hug. "This is new territory for me too," he admitted. "I've dated a few women, but always kept it in the background. And I hadn't planned any kind of announcement about us either, it just kind of happened." He shrugged, still rubbing her back. He was grateful when she melted into his chest, letting him know she wasn't mad anymore. "Maybe we can work on navigating it together?"

She nodded against his chest. "Okay."

"Is that a real okay, or just...okay, I'm trying to get him to shut up?"

Aspen laughed and pulled her head back to look up at him. The fire wasn't quite as bright in her eyes, but it was definitely better and it took the rest of the stress off Austin's shoulders. "A real okay." She patted his chest. "I don't like to do things halfway."

He nodded. "Me either. So...we're all in? We're going to really give this a go?"

A slow, soft smile spread across her lips and she nodded. "Yeah. I guess we are."

"Great." He kissed the tip of her nose. "Because I need a slice of cake. One bite wasn't enough and it would have been awkward to ask for it if you'd broken up with me."

Aspen rolled her eyes, but pulled away and walked to the door leading to the front. "Men...it's always about their stomachs."

CHAPTER 17

"A ll I'm asking is how much you really know about him,"
Maeve said with a shrug. She took another bite of toast and
Aspen fought the urge to walk away.

Why did her logical sister always have to rain on her parade? "I
thought you were excited for me to get out more," Aspen challenged.

Maeve's eyes went from her phone to Aspen. "Is that what you
called that kiss? Getting out more?"

Aspen pinched her lips together. "That wasn't planned."

"It sure didn't look like it was your first kiss," Maeve said.

"Enough, ladies," Estelle said coolly, breezing into the kitchen.
She went straight to the cupboard to grab a mug, then poured hot
water and dipped in a tea bag. "Aspen is an adult," Estelle said. She
turned and leaned her back against the counter, cradling the hot mug
in her hands, fixing her gaze on Maeve. "If we can trust her to bake
all the goods for the cafe, why can't we trust her with her own love
life?"

"Thank you!" Aspen practically shouted, waving a hand at Estelle. "At least someone isn't treating me like a kid."

Estelle stepped toward the stool where Aspen was sitting. "However, I have to say that like Maeve, I'm worried about how fast things
are progressing with the two of you." She paused and Aspen felt her
confidence deflate. "I didn't mind pushing you two together at first.
I mean, the whole world could see the chemistry, it nearly burned
down the cafe, but..."

"But what?" Aspen demanded. She could feel the heat on her
cheeks and she found herself struggling not to be defensive. How
dare they both encourage, then try to dump cold water on her. It

wasn't how sisters were supposed to be. Whatever happened to good old fashioned support?

"But…" Estelle was looking inside her mug, then looked up from under her lashes. "But I worry that his life on social media might be influencing your dating more than you."

"Agreed," Maeve said. "I'm not saying, don't date him. I'm saying, find out more about him." She took another bite. "Not all men are what they seem on the outside." Her words were soft, but they hit their mark as intended.

"Isn't that what dating is all about?" Aspen demanded, trying and failing to stay strong in her conviction. She hadn't expected to be defending herself this morning. "We spend time together, we get to know each other and we see if we want to continue. How am I supposed to do that if we're not dating?"

"And him eating you alive?" Estelle asked dryly.

"He didn't eat me alive," Aspen argued.

"Did you watch the video?" Maeve threw in. She fanned her face. "If you weren't my sister, I would have watched it over and over again. It was better than any romance movie I've ever seen."

"That's because it was real," Aspen said tightly. She'd already been through this with Austin. He wasn't just using her for social media. He had enjoyed and even wanted their kiss. This…tension…chemistry…energy…whatever a person wanted to call it, was thick between them. More so than it had ever been with any other man. Aspen would be a fool to not see where it led.

Besides, the more time she spent with him, the more she wanted to spend time with him. That, in and of itself, should be a clear sign of her growing feelings. In fact, if Aspen was being completely honest with herself…and she wasn't going to be to her sisters yet…she was falling, hard and fast.

His kisses were wonderful, but there was more to it. She enjoyed seeing him with his fans. She enjoyed his banter. She enjoyed being kept on her toes. She enjoyed his appreciation for her baking and his eagerness to be a part of the process. And she also enjoyed his appreciation of her. He made her feel beautiful and that her passionate nature was a good thing, rather than something that drove men away. Instead of backing off, he pushed harder, and it was everything she needed.

"I can see we've lost you," Estelle said in a teasing tone. She grinned over her teacup, blowing into the hot liquid.

"Sorry," Aspen said, rubbing her forehead. "Look. Thank you for your concern, but as you pointed out, Estelle, I'm an adult. I'm not sure where this will lead with him, but I have hope and I want to give it a try." She slumped in her seat. "Is it too much to ask for support rather than condemnation?"

"Of course not," Estelle said quickly, coming to her sister's side. Just as she sat down, Estelle's phone rang and she pulled it out, her eyes wide. "It's Mom." Before anyone responded, Estelle had turned on the speaker phone. "Mom! How are you?"

Aspen held her breath. Her parents called every couple of days, but each time, her heart began to pound with worry that it would contain more bad news.

"Hello, my lovely daughter." Antony Harrison's voice was still just as deep as it had been before, and Aspen knew full well how much her mother loved it.

"Dad," Estelle said reverently, leaning into the phone. "You're, uh, on speaker phone. We're all here."

"So I'm speaking to three beautiful women instead of just one?"

Aspen laughed, trying to hold back tears. Her father was such a charmer. No wonder her mother always said she didn't stand a chance.

"How are things going?" Dad asked.

"Just fine," Estelle assured him. She glanced up at her sisters, holding out the phone.

"We're good, Dad. It's nice to hear from you." Maeve called out.

"Wonderful. And you, Aspen? How's my best kitchen helper?"

Aspen swallowed the lump in her throat. "Good, Dad. I'm taking care of your baby." Had that been a wobble in his voice? Was his disease progressing? Did they have access to doctors in Italy that would know how to treat him?

Aspen wanted to ask all the questions swirling in her head, but she knew it wouldn't help. Her parents were her parents. They would share with them when they felt the time was right and there would be no convincing them otherwise. A lifetime of arguing had taught Aspen that, at least.

"My babies are all grown up," Dad said with a laugh. It broke off and he coughed harshly.

Aspen jerked upright, along with Maeve, and even Estelle looked worried. "Dad? Are you sick?" She almost slapped her forehead. What a stupid question. Of course, he was sick! That's the whole reason they were visiting family!

"Good morning!" Mom said as she took the phone. "Sorry about that. Your dad has a cold and needed a drink of water."

"Is he going to be okay?" Maeve asked, sounding much younger than her age.

"He's fine," Mom said quickly. "Just a chest cold. He's got lots of family around to smother him in love and help him get better, so don't you worry your beautiful heads about it."

There was a pause on the line.

"We miss you," Estelle said softly.

A long sigh followed the admission. "I miss you too," Mom said. "You don't know how much." She cleared her throat. "But we're doing great. Your grandmother, great aunts and uncle and extended cousins are taking great care of us. Your dad is all smiles and always telling everyone about you girls taking over the bakery. He's positive Aspen's cakes are going to become world famous."

Maeve grinned. "I don't know about her cakes, but—oof!" She cut off when Aspen threw a piece of bread at her sister. Maeve snickered and the whole mood lightened.

"Okay...do I need to fly all the way back to the U.S. in order to break up a fight?" Mom demanded. "Can't you three get along for five minutes?"

"We're fine, Mom," Aspen said loudly, giving her younger sister a stern look. "Maeve was just being silly. And we're not fighting. It was just a sister squabble."

"Last time I looked, squabble and fight were synonymous," Mom said.

"Don't worry," Estelle said primly, giving her best impression of their mother. "I've got it handled, mom."

"Of course, you do, sweetie. You always could run the household better than I could." Another sigh, this one a little more upbeat. "Now...I need to go check on your dad and make sure your aunt isn't stuffing cannoli down him. We'll chat again soon, okay?"

"Okay, thanks for calling," Estelle responded.

"Love you!" Mom made kissy sounds and then the line went dead.

Estelle set the phone down as if it were a bomb that could explode any second and the room stayed somber and quiet, each sister staring at the device like it was a foreign object. There was nothing to say. They all heard it, they all felt it and soon Aspen felt herself get restless. She needed to be up and doing something and since she couldn't cure her dad, taking care of his business was the next best thing.

Time to bake.

AUSTIN SPIT THE TOOTHPASTE into the sink, then rinsed out the residue. Just as he was putting things away, there was a pounding on his door. He frowned. Who in the world would be coming by? He glanced at his watch. Aspen should be heading to the cafe right now, not attacking his door.

The pounding picked up again and Austin sighed. Grabbing a towel, he walked across the room and opened it. "Tye?" Austin jerked back as his brother shoved his way through the door. "What are you doing here?"

Tye threw himself on the edge of the bed. "We're in trouble, man."

Austin's heart stuttered. "What do you mean? How are we in trouble? I've been watching the numbers and the fans have been eating up all the publicity from down here."

Tye shook his head. "That's not it. Our numbers are fine and the Stan the Man is happy with that."

"Then?" Austin raised his eyebrows, leaving the question open-ended for Tye to finish.

"Mom showed up at the office."

Austin froze. "Excuse me?" he choked out.

"You heard me," Tye said in a low tone.

"Why didn't you call me?" Austin said through gritted teeth. His mother only came out of the woodwork when she wanted something...and it was usually money. Her addictions were the reason they'd spent so many years living in a car and his stomach had come to appreciate a good meal. When he was young, it didn't matter what meal it was. He'd eaten at the school cafeterias as if they were five star restaurants since it was often the only meal he got.

Yet, whenever someone noticed his...healthy appetite, his mother had always been very good at covering her tracks. She always seemed to be able to get her act together for just long enough to convince the school system that Austin and Tye were safe and well and being looked after in a happy household.

She somehow managed to make Austin appear as the trouble-maker, which was easily believed since he struggled so much in school. His dyslexia made him a terrible student and his hunger made him restless. It was surprisingly easier than it should have been for his drug addict mother to convince the system that he was simply a troubled child and needed to stay with her.

The truth was, Austin was her meal ticket. She never worked, but she received government help and without a child in the house, it would have been much less. She needed her boys and was willing to fight to keep him.

Now, however, things were different. Austin was grown, he'd made a good life for himself, using his strengths and his weaknesses to his advantage and he did everything he could to cut off ties with the woman who had used him his whole life. Including taking care of his anxious brother.

Being a face in the public eye though made it nearly impossible to get away from her. Like a dirty penny, she somehow always managed to pop up at the most inopportune time. Her favorite story was to threaten to tell the world about his dyslexia unless he funded her current needs.

A check usually saw her disappearing for another six months to a year, but he had given her money just a few weeks ago. Why was she showing up now? And why hadn't anyone called him?

Tye shook his head. "I didn't think a phone call would have been enough."

"How many people saw her at the office?" Austin asked in a low tone. Stan was the only one who knew about Tye and Austin's arrangement. If word got out that Tye was the voice and Austin only a face, they would be ripped to shreds. Not to mention, having dyslexia made him even more of a freak. Aspen would kick him to the curb if she realized how broken he was.

Tye scrubbed his face. "I don't know. She wasn't subtle by any means, and she was high, so she was shouting all sorts of things. Most of them were incoherent, but some were clear."

Austin groaned and sank into a seat. "What did she want?" he asked, feeling like the whole world was being swept out from under him. He was on the verge of the best thing that had ever happened to him and now this. Fate couldn't be that cruel...could she?

"What does she always want?" Tye pressed. "Money." He swallowed audibly. "But this time she wants more. A lot more."

Austin jerked his head upright. "How much?" His voice was flat...dead. He had a feeling he wasn't going to like what his partner had to say.

Tye stared for a moment before naming a number that made Austin sick to his stomach.

"You can't be serious." Austin pushed his hand through his hair. "Where the heck does she think I'm gonna get that kind of money?"

Tye shrugged and shook his head. "I don't know. Like I said, she was high." He pushed out a long breath. "There's more."

"Of course there is." Austin fell back against the seat and waved a hand in invitation.

"Stan said to get rid of her, or we're done."

Austin closed his eyes. "We're the reason his magazine is doing so well. Why would he threaten something like that?"

Tye seemed to grow smaller with each bit of news he shared. "He said she's bad for business and we won't be worth it if she doesn't disappear."

"What does he want me to do? She's our mother," Austin all but shouted.

Tye held up his hands. "I know that, but Stan doesn't care. She's not related to him and you know he has no tolerance for outside attachments." Tye made a face. "He's already ticked about you being down here. If you hadn't had that publicity thing with the chair and the kiss, I think he might have fired us both." The face turned into a grin. "That was pretty hot, by the way. I had no idea things had progressed so far."

Austin glared, but there was little heat in it.

Tye's smile fell. "This isn't..." He paused, then shook his head. "Nevermind."

"No...you've already delivered bad news, might as well get it all out."

"You're not dating her just to get ratings, are you?" Tye hurried on as if he was afraid he wouldn't be able to get it all out. "I mean...you, of all people, know what it's like to be used by others. I don't think it's right to do it to someone else."

Austin wasn't sure whether to be offended or impressed. His shy brother didn't usually stand up to people, but the fact that he thought Austin capable of that made their relationship seem a little less genuine. "I'm falling for her," Austin said simply. He chose to ignore the other insinuation. Really...considering how public their relationship was, it was probably a legitimate question. Far too many people in the public arena started out as good people and the fame turned them into someone else entirely.

Tye's eyebrows shot up. "No kidding?"

Austin shook his head.

"Wow." Tye huffed slightly. "I didn't see that coming."

Austin's foot began to bounce. "Yeah, well, neither did I, but here we are." He glanced at the wall clock. "In fact, I need to get going. I've been helping out at the cafe."

"What are you going to do about Mom?" Tye asked, not moving from his spot on the bed.

"I don't know," Austin answered honestly. "Maybe she was just on a bender. We'll give it a couple days and hope she calms down."

"And if not?"

Austin sighed. "I'll figure it out."

CHAPTER 18

Aspen's mind had been churning all morning. She had expected Austin to come by now. They only had a few days left before he headed back to Portland and she had assumed they would spend it together.

"You've grown too used to him," she scolded herself. The fact of the matter was, the situation scared her. She was falling for the snarky reviewer...fast. But the phone call with her mother and father today was a good reminder that loving someone wasn't all sprinkles and frosting.

Sometimes it was hard. Sometimes it hurt. Sometimes it broke a person's heart.

Aspen wasn't sure she wanted that kind of stress in her life, and yet she found she couldn't quite walk away either.

"Good morning, Beautiful."

Austin's deep voice hit a spot in her chest that, until that moment, had been empty. As if it had been waiting for his presence to feel content and full for the morning. She closed her eyes as he came over and kissed her cheek. "You call this morning?" she teased, trying to cover up her internal emotional reaction to his presence. "I've been working for hours."

Austin chuckled and walked to the wall to grab an apron and a hairnet. "Not all of us rise with the sun," he teased. "Some of us need a little more beauty sleep."

Aspen looked over and smiled. "You left yourself wide open for that one, but I'll refrain."

"And I appreciate it," he said with another cheek kiss. "Now...what are we working on today?"

Aspen laughed softly. Always so eager. There was something so wonderful about him being interested in her life. As if he truly wanted to experience all the same things she did. It made the kitchen warmer than normal. "I'm working on creating new recipes today." She gave him a coy sideways glance. "In fact, I have one I'd like your help with."

His eyes widened like a little boy staring at the tree on Christmas morning. "Really?" He rubbed his hands in glee. "Where do we start?"

"By creating the cake, of course." Aspen waved her hand at the counter full of ingredients.

"What flavors were you thinking?"

Aspen swallowed back the desire to share with him that she had been the inspiration for this flavor profile. She often found ideas in daily life and right now, that revolved completely around Austin. Her chat with her parents had led her to her most common stress reliever...baking. But Austin's sweet kisses and childlike enthusiasm had led to her idea for flavors.

"I thought we'd start with a peanut butter cake base."

"Yessss." Austin nodded. "Peanut butter is my favorite."

Aspen had gathered that from his response to her other peanut butter cake. "Perfect. Let's do that first, and then we'll talk fillings and frosting." She reached across the space. "We need to sift the dry ingredients first."

She set Austin to sifting flour and baking soda and when he was set, she began mixing together the wet ingredients. Once the butter and sugars were whipping, she began to stir the eggs.

"Why do you mix the butter and sugar first?" Austin asked, his hand hitting the side of his sifter. "You do that every time."

"It's called creaming," Aspen answered. "We cream them together at a high speed because it creates pockets of air. That translates into a fluffy, light batter."

"Making a fluffy, light cake," Austin said with a sage nod. "Got it."

Aspen smiled. "Stick with me, kid, and we'll make a baker of you yet."

Austin chuckled. "Did you spend a lot of time with your dad in the kitchen?"

Aspen's smile fell.

"Sorry... Was that too much?" Austin immediately tried to backtrack. "I wasn't trying to get too deep too soon."

Aspen shook her head. There was nothing wrong with his question. She was just a little sensitive from the reminder of her big, amazing father becoming crippled this morning. "No, it's fine." She plastered her smile back on. "Yes. I spent a lot of time in the kitchen. In fact, he tried to teach me chocolate sculpting." She laughed softly. "He would have loved it if I had followed the same kitchen path as him, but..." She shrugged.

"But?" Austin pressed. He bumped hips with her. "I'm guessing there's a story or two that I haven't heard."

Aspen shook her head, her smile becoming more genuine. "Maybe. But you're a reporter. How do I know it won't end up on some blog somewhere?"

Austin put a hand in the air. "Scout's honor. This is completely off the record."

Aspen gave him a playful glare before smiling again. "Okay, well, there *might* have been a disaster or two in the kitchen before we figured out I wasn't a sculptor."

"I feel like I need a bowl of popcorn or something," Austin said with a laugh. "This is gonna be good."

Aspen rolled her eyes. "Gah. You meanie. Always thinking of your stomach."

"Hey! Food makes everything better."

"Dessert makes everything better," Aspen corrected.

"I don't know..." Austin finished his sifting and set down the metal colander. "I enjoy a nice savory meal as well. It doesn't have to be sweet."

"Blasphemous!" Aspen cried. "I think maybe you need to leave."

Austin stepped up behind Aspen and wrapped his arms around her waist, leaning his head down by her ear.

Her heart immediately reacted to his nearness by jumping into overdrive. Her skin flushed and she found a shiver of anticipation working its way down her spine. The involuntary reaction was all the evidence she needed to know that her earlier worries were completely valid. She wasn't just falling for Eat It Austin...she had fallen. Her body was no longer her own and her heart was taking the same path.

The sound of his voice, the feel of his warm breath, his touch against her skin...that's all it took for her to be putty in his hands. She'd never reacted that much to any other man in her life, neither had she wanted to. Austin was different. He was interesting, intelligent, caring, funny...he pushed her and drove her crazy, but also made her want to be better.

Yeah...her fears were valid, but at the same time...why would someone want to miss the opportunity to experience something so beautiful?

Their relationship wasn't ready to say those three little words out loud, but Aspen knew that when the time came, no matter how frightened she was...she would do the same thing she'd done her entire life.

Jump in with both feet.

Eat It Austin was definitely worth it.

HER HAIR SMELLED LIKE mint with some kind of citrus on the backend and it nearly made Austin's eyes roll back in his head. He hadn't planned to get quite so close right now. They were supposed to be working, but Aspen had left herself wide open after demanding he leave. What else was a man supposed to do?

"Are you sure you want me to go?" he whispered against her ear. He grinned, making sure she couldn't see him, when he watched goosebumps run down the side of her neck. She couldn't hide her reaction to him and it gave his ego a boost.

He ran his nose along the shell of her ear. As he got closer to her skin, the smell of sugar and baked goods began to overrun the mint. It was purely Aspen and it was a scent he would never associate with anyone or anything else.

"Aspen?" he cooed.

"Hmm?" Her eyes were closed as a shiver ran through her, bumping her into his chest.

"Do you really want me to go?" He tried not to let her hear the smile in his voice. Convincing her to let him stay was serious business, after all.

She tilted her head to the side. "Mmm...maybe?"

He pressed a kiss just below her ear, lingering just a touch. "Are you sure?"

A slow smile spread across her face and she spun, bringing them nose to nose. "Well...since I can't afford to pay another helper and you work for free," she sighed dramatically, "I suppose you'll have to stay."

"I don't work for free," he said in a husky whisper.

Her dark eyes widened. "You don't?"

Austin slowly shook his head. "Nope."

She frowned. "Then what are you getting paid?"

There was only one way to answer her. Grabbing the back of her head, he stole a fierce kiss. As always happened when their lips met, Austin found himself rocked to his core. This woman. The more time he spent with her, the more he was positive there would never be another like her.

His mother had left a gaping hole inside of him, and while some of that would never be filled, the woman in his arms had helped heal those lonely pockets more than anyone else.

Slowly, he pulled back, letting their lips linger as long as possible. "Throw in a piece of this cake and we'll be even," he whispered against her mouth.

Aspen laughed under her breath. "Done deal."

Austin forced himself to pull back. "Then let's get baking." He moved back to the table. "Next step?"

Austin listened, asked questions and followed directions for the next half hour until the cakes were in the oven.

"Now...the filling," Aspen said, heading toward the pantry.

Austin followed in her footsteps. "Chocolate?" he asked.

Aspen shook her head. "No...let's do something different. Chocolate is too easy."

He frowned. "What else goes with peanut butter?"

Aspen held up a jar of corn syrup. "What about marshmallow?"

His eyes widened. "Don't tell me you're going to use bananas next?"

Aspen continued grinning. "No. If we were using bananas, it should have been in the cake. Banana filling is too soft."

"Then...what?"

Aspen handed him the corn syrup and tapped her lips, her eyes roaming the large pantry.

Austin watched her with interest. She didn't like to think within the box, that was for sure. No wonder her cakes were so impressive. No one else thought of the same combinations that she did.

"Got it!" Aspen grabbed a couple of jars and a cookie package, then waved him back out into the front room.

"Wait, I didn't see what we were doing," he said.

"Marshmallow buttercream," Aspen explained, setting her armload on the counter. "Apple pie filling, and a Biscoff crumble."

Austin whistled low. "Holy cow. Where did you get all of that?"

She glanced at him sideways, as if slightly embarrassed, before answering. "Well, the peanut butter was for fun. The marshmallow was because the flavors compliment. The apple gives us a tart break against the sweet, but still blends with both flavors and the Biscoff is because I didn't want to do graham crackers."

Aspen shook his head. "Your mind is a beautiful thing."

Aspen elbowed him lightly. "Flatterer."

"Nope. Just an admirer," he said, leaving a quick kiss on her temple. Man, he was a goner. He couldn't seem to get enough of touching or kissing her. Even with the weight of his mom bearing down on him at the moment, the most important thing on his mind was spending his time with Aspen well.

In just a couple of days, he had to go back to the real world. The world where he dealt with drug addict mothers, a hidden learning disorder, demanding bosses and a public who thirsted for more reviews and set downs. But right now...he was enjoying every moment of his bubble and he planned to squeeze every last bite out of it.

An hour later, the cake was done and ready to be taken to the front. During the baking and subsequent breaks for cooling, he and Aspen had also spent time popping cookies and brownies in the oven in order to fill the display case.

"Ta da!" Aspen said, stepping back from her work of art.

And it was art. It might not be paint on a canvas or plaster formed into an object, but it was Austin's favorite type of creativity. The edible kind.

"When do we get a piece?" he asked, bouncing on his toes.

Aspen laughed softly. "We don't."

"What?" Austin put a hand to his chest. "You can't be serious!"

Aspen shook her head, her smile still in place. "At the end of the day if there's any left over, you can try it."

"How do you know it'll taste good though?" Austin challenged. "This is the first time you've made this one."

Aspen pointed to the counter mess. "I put the piece together with a bite of scraps." She leaned in. "It's great."

"And yet I didn't get any." Austin put his hands on his hips. "I'm feeling unpaid."

Aspen laughed and grabbed a small plate from the cupboard. She proceeded to put scraps of cake, a bit of the apple, a sprinkle of the cookies and finally a dollop of the buttercream on top. She held it out. "Messy, but it'll let you know what's up."

Austin still glared while he took the offering. However, after stuffing the whole thing in his mouth, there was no way to continue pretending to be mad. "Oh my gosh." He moaned, closing his eyes in bliss. "I think this is my favorite one yet."

Aspen picked up the cake stand and began walking toward the door to the front. "You realize you say that about everything, right?"

He shrugged and began gathering more scraps. "Then maybe it's just the woman who's my favorite." He gave her a scorching look and Austin absolutely knew that if she had lighter skin, it would be flaming red right now.

The look she sent back his way, however, let him know that his compliment hadn't been amiss. She was just as attracted to him as he was to her. Now though, Austin was beginning to hope that her feelings went well beyond outer looks. His definitely were, but was she feeling the same?

There would come a time to ask that exact question, but right now things were still too new. Yes...he was falling hard and fast, but he wouldn't force her to do the same. They'd begun at odds with each other, only an insane chemistry pulling them together, but now? Now he wanted more. He'd work to build the foundation while here, and then he could only hope that would be enough to continue when distance and real life tried to pull them apart.

CHAPTER 19

Aspen flicked the switch which turned on the fireplace in her family room. She was exhausted. She and Austin had baked until they couldn't bake anymore today and they'd ended up making three more of her new peanut butter, marshmallow cake. It had been a massive hit and she was now considering keeping it on the full time menu.

Her eyes drifted to Austin. He had gone straight for the couch once they'd gone home for the evening and was currently laying with his head back and his eyes closed. She had grown so used to having him around in the kitchen that she wasn't sure what she was going to do when he left in a couple of days.

Her heart clenched at the thought. She wasn't ready for him to go. He not only helped ease her load at the cafe, but he made her feel better as a person as well.

None of the snarky, snappy personality that she saw on his review blog seemed to seep through in his real life. And Aspen had been watching. At first she didn't believe his behavior. She thought he had to be putting on an act, but there was no way anyone was that good. Even when he thought she wasn't looking, he was as sweet and genuine as she could ever hope for.

So how did a guy like that become famous for being a jerk?

Aspen shook her head, her eyes going back to the fire crackling in the hearth. Something about it all didn't make sense, but she wasn't sure what to do about it. Did she dig? Ask him outright? Just continue to watch?

The problem was, she was already a goner for him. Only a few days with a handsome man who made her feel things she had never felt before and Aspen had no control over her heart anymore. So what did she do about the obvious discrepancy in who she knew him to be and who the public knew him as?

"I'm starving." Austin moaned.

Aspen couldn't help but grin. "You ate like four slices of cake today. How in the world is there room for anything else?"

Austin's left eye cracked open. "I'm full of sugar. But my savory tank needs filling."

"What? We're not cows. Humans don't have separate stomachs."

Austin crooked a finger in her direction.

Aspen glared.

A small smile tugged at his mouth, but he continued urging her to come.

Rolling her eyes, Aspen walked over and plopped on the couch next to him. He smelled like the bakery and she wanted to put her nose in his neck and take a deep sniff, not coming back up for air. "Yes?" she said with a bit of a bite.

Austin wrapped his arms around her and pulled her into him, causing Aspen to squeak. Her hands landed on his chest as she worked to hold herself up so she could see his face. "Perhaps my sweet tooth hasn't been satiated after all," he said, both of his eyes open now.

Aspen felt her face heat up. "You're incorrigible," she said breathlessly.

He shrugged. "I don't deny it."

Aspen laughed under her breath, then got louder when his stomach growled. She pushed off of him. "Come on. Let's grab dinner and then we can curl up by the fire."

"That sounds amazing," he gushed. He followed her into the kitchen. "What are we fixing?"

"You still have the energy to cook?" Aspen gaped. "I've been baking all day. I have no desire to do more."

"You? The great baker is all baked out?" Austin put his hands on his hips and tsked his tongue. "Something is wrong with this scene."

Aspen punched his upper arm. "Estelle usually makes dinner and leaves it for me in the fridge." She pulled open the door. "All we have to do is warm it up." She paused. Was it weird to feed the guy she was dating leftovers? It felt...familiar. Like something a couple would do when they were so comfortable with each other that there was no need to impress anymore.

He's seen me in a messy apron, with flour in my hair and hairnet head. Surely it doesn't get any more familiar than that.

She glanced over her shoulder, trying to gauge the situation, but Austin didn't seem the least bit put off by her announcement. Taking a deep breath, she pushed the worries out of her head and grabbed the container out of the fridge. She opened it and smiled. "Looks like pasta tonight."

Austin stepped up behind her. "Carbs! My favorite."

Aspen chuckled. "Everything is your favorite."

He shrugged and began grabbing plates out of the cupboard. Apparently, he was perfectly comfortable with their situation. "That's probably more true than I'd like it to be," he admitted. "But some of us were made to fix the food and some of us were made to eat it." He grinned over his shoulder. "What fun would your gift be if there was no one there to appreciate it?"

Aspen's smile never left her face as she dished up the separate plates and they put them in the microwave. The idea of Austin being there just to enjoy her gift of baking cakes seemed wonderful. Exactly what she would ask for in a partner in life.

Her hands froze.

A partner in life? Slow down there, Sparky.

Her mind-wandering was getting completely out of hand. Yes, she was falling in love, but they weren't ready to say that yet. And they still had to deal with the fact that he was going to be leaving in two days. Who knew what would happen to their relationship when they weren't in each other's company all day every day? Plus, Aspen still wanted to solve the mystery of the nice versus rude Austin. There had to be a story there.

So maybe tonight is the night to start asking those questions?

Her stomach tightened at the thought. She had been so happy being with him. Did she really want to risk ruining it all by asking questions she wasn't sure she was ready for the answers to?

The microwave beeped and Aspen pulled the two plates out. "Ready?" she asked, walking to the small breakfast table. Her large family usually ate in the dining room, but right now it was just her and Austin. They could sit in the breakfast nook just fine. Her sisters had come home long before she had, and Aspen was grateful they were being nice enough to allow her and Austin some time alone.

"Always," Austin said cheerily, bringing two glasses of milk to the table.

"Thanks," Aspen murmured as they each handed the other their offerings. She sat and folded her hands in her lap. After a short grace, they dug in. But despite the amazing pasta, Aspen's mind wouldn't move away from her questions and concerns. She might not work up the courage to ask them tonight, but they would have to come up. And truthfully, any time was going to be too soon for comfort. Especially since she worried that the answers she was looking for might ruin the best thing she'd ever experienced in her life.

SOMETHING WAS OFF. Austin could feel it, though he wasn't sure what it was. Aspen was smiling at the right time, she was looking at him just as she was before, but there was something slightly...hesitant about her behavior tonight.

His phone buzzed in his back pocket for the billionth time that night and Austin found his worries shifting from from Aspen to his other problem.

Tye.

And his mother.

Those thoughts sent any warm feelings he had from a stomach full of pasta skittering out into the cold evening.

"Is that your phone?" Aspen asked, looking pointedly at his waistline.

Austin shrugged. "Yeah. But I'll get it later."

Aspen paused slightly, then nodded. "Okay." She wiped her mouth, her plate empty. "What did you want to do tonight?" She stood with her dishes in hand and headed to the sink.

Austin jumped up to join her. "I thought you promised me cuddling in front of the fire?" he teased in her ear.

Aspen shivered slightly and it made him smile. "I think I said we could curl up by the fire." Her eyes were full of mischief when she looked over her shoulder. "That doesn't necessarily mean we're doing it together."

He wrapped his arms around her waist and began tugging her toward the family room. "I'm afraid separate isn't an option," he said.

Aspen squealed slightly, trying halfheartedly to dig in her heels, but he just kept pulling her back. Finally, with a huff, she gave up and let him pull her along.

Austin pulled them to a cushy chair and pulled Aspen into his lap, nestling his face in her hair. It smelled of cinnamon and sugar and all the wonderful baked goods they had made that afternoon. He was completely exhausted from the day. He had no idea how much work went on behind the scenes of a bakery.

Somehow the cakes, cookies and pastries had always just magically appeared in the case and he'd been privileged to eat them to his heart's content. But now he was seeing a different side of things. He saw the thought, work and love that went into creating something to truly make people happy, and it was as fascinating as it was tiring.

He loved his job as a food reviewer, but in the back of his mind, Austin was slowly coming to realize that he wouldn't mind going to work with Aspen for a lot longer than this week would allow him. Making that new cake today had been exciting, and watching her had been more so. She thought outside the box in a way that was new to him and he liked it. He liked her.

I more than like her... He shook his head. *Too soon.*

Especially with his mom and his job breathing down his neck. When he went home in a couple of days, there were going to be a lot of things to fix before he could move his relationship with Aspen forward the way he would like to.

"So you just want to sit like this for the rest of the evening?" she asked, leaning into his chest. "Seems sort of boring."

"Obviously, you've never held a beautiful woman in your arms," he said with a grin. "It's anything but boring."

Aspen laughed and shook her head. "Did you want to put on a movie or watch a show or something?"

Austin glanced at the wall clock. "Actually, as much as I hate to admit it, I probably better head back to the inn." He leaned forward to leave a quick kiss on her cheek. "My temporary boss is running me ragged and the morning comes all too soon."

Aspen sighed dramatically and stood up. "Man...this boss sounds like a tyrant. Keeping you up until all hours of the night and bringing you in early in the morning..." She tsked her tongue. "What will she think of next?"

"Who said it was a she?" Austin asked. He chuckled as Aspen rolled her eyes. Taking her hand, he walked toward the door. "Walk me out?"

She smiled. "Of course."

He wrapped her up in a hug, ignoring another buzz in his back pocket. "Thank you for a wonderful day," he whispered against her ear. It would be all too easy to get caught up in kissing her until he didn't know up from down, but tonight...Austin had other things to worry about.

Unfortunately.

HIs time with Aspen was limited, so he wasn't about to leave without a proper goodbye, but it wasn't nearly as long lasting as he wanted it to be.

Pulling back, his heart racing and his body screaming for more, he left a gentle kiss on her forehead. "See you tomorrow," he said, his voice husky.

"Okay," she whispered breathlessly. Her eyes were wide pools of chocolate and Austin wanted to jump in and never emerge.

If she only knew how much power she held over him. This early in their relationship, it would probably frighten her, so rather than spill all his secrets, Austin tore himself away and walked outside.

The cold, bitter wind bit into his skin, waking him up from his Aspen-haze and snapping him back into focus. His car sat in the driveway and it only took a few moments to be seated and turning on the engine.

Before hitting the road, he punched a number on his phone and put it on Bluetooth.

"Are you ever coming back here?" Tye asked angrily. "I think we have things to discuss."

"I told you I was spending the day with Aspen," Austin said, aiming for calm, but there was still an edge to his voice. "You didn't have to stick around."

"We're about to lose our shirts and you don't think I need to stick around?" Tye scoffed. "Might I remind you that our *mother* is causing these problems? If it weren't for her, no one would ever figure out how we run things and our secrets would be safe."

Secrets would be safe...

The words felt like sticky tar in Austin's mind. He hated holding onto them. He hated hiding that he'd grown up on the streets. He hated dealing with his drug addict parent. He hated hiding his dyslexia, and he especially hated that he lied to the public and Aspen each and every day in order to keep a job.

The thoughts of just how many skeletons were in his closet made him feel dirty, and after basking in Aspen's presence, it made him want to slink away with his tail between his legs and lick his wounds in private.

He didn't deserve her.

She needed someone who could love her freely without worry of public consequences. What would she think if she ever found out he could barely read? Or that his award winning blog had nothing to do with him? Or that his obsession with food came from being traumatized as a child? What would happen if Aspen ever visited him and his mother showed up?

Dread landed in his stomach like an unleavened loaf of bread.

How was he going to do this? Yes, their relationship was still new. He had no idea if it would get beyond these early stages, but the way his heart beat when he was around her told him that he definitely wanted it to get past these first stages.

He had thought that he could fix his problems before trying to move to the next step, but the more he thought about it, the more Austin realized that these were problems that would never go away.

"Are you even listening to me?" Tye growled.

Austin forced a breath through his frozen lungs. "Yeah..." he finally stammered. "I'm almost back. Give me a minute and then we can talk."

The phone line went dead and Austin punched the button to turn it off. He took a deep breath. He needed to make a plan, figure out how to move forward, what to do with Aspen.

But for the first time in his life...he was at a complete loss.

CHAPTER 20

Today was the day.

Aspen took in several deep breaths to try and calm her racing heart. The day at the shop was over, she and Austin were about to head out to dinner and Aspen was going to let him know how she felt.

She wanted him to know that her feelings were much more than just a little crush. Although she enjoyed his company in the kitchen, she enjoyed getting to know him as a person even more. And she had decided the best way to do that was to open up her own past and hope it spurred him into sharing his own.

No one outside of her family knew about her father's illness. Not even the media. For all intents and purposes, he had simply decided to retire and leave the bakery to his daughters.

Only the family knew the truth. Aspen, her siblings, the family around Seagull Cove and now the family left in Italy that he had gone to visit.

But at dinner, Aspen had decided to take a leap of faith. Especially with Austin's job within the media, she knew that trusting him with this secret was going to be a big deal. At least...it was to her. She hoped he understood the significance of it as well.

A warm presence came up against her back. "Ready to go get dinner? I'm starving."

Aspen smiled, hiding the anxiety growing inside of her. She turned and wrapped her arms around his chest. "I think that's a constant state of being for you."

He grinned, kissed the tip of her nose and let his hands rest at her hips. "Then I suppose we'll just have to do something about it."

He made a face and Aspen froze. "Do you mind if we hit a restaurant about thirty minutes down the road?"

"A restaurant? I thought we were going back to the house?"

He nodded and pushed a hand through his flattened hair. "I know, but I got a call from my boss. I've been contracted to do a review on a seafood restaurant just south of here." He shrugged. "I figured I could take care of that with you, rather than having to leave early tomorrow."

"Sounds like a plan to me," Aspen said, forcing some extra cheer into her voice. She had hoped to have a more private setting to talk to him, but...this would do...she hoped.

"You aren't allergic or anything?" he asked, backing up to take her hand. He started walking to the door.

Aspen shook her head. "Nope. That would certainly be tragic. Living right on the ocean and being allergic to seafood."

Austin nodded. "Yeah...that would stink."

She looked down at her clothes. "I'm not really dressed to go out." She rubbed at a smear of flour on her jeans.

Austin used their combined fingers to tug her in so he could leave a kiss on her head. "You look beautiful. Don't worry about it."

With a sigh, Aspen nodded. She loved how much he worked to make her feel special, but she would love it even more if she'd had some advance warning that she was going to be seen in public. *Oh, well...nothing to do about it now.*

The drive south was comfortable and quiet. Their hands stayed connected over the center of the car and Aspen allowed herself to relax against the seat. The scenery was too dark to enjoy, but the lights of town and houses sped past, seeming almost like low hanging stars, surrounding them as they made their journey.

The trip had been so pleasant that Aspen found herself loath to ruin that as they were ushered to a seat. The restaurant had low lighting, with small candles on each table and soft overhead bulbs. If it had been during the summer and the sun had been setting outside, she could only imagine how beautiful the view would be.

The restaurant was right on the edge of a short cliff that led to the water and Aspen was sure that if things had been quiet, she would have been able to hear the waves crashing into the rocks below.

All in all, it was a much nicer restaurant than she usually frequented. This was a special occasion restaurant and suddenly it seemed perfect for their last night together.

"This is beautiful," Aspen murmured, settling herself in her seat. "Much fancier than my restaurant."

"You have a cafe," Austin said with a wry grin. "There's nothing fancy about that and there's not supposed to be."

"Good to know it won't be held against me," she teased, but her smile fell quickly. Now that they were seated, she was starting to feel those stirrings of anxiety again. It was hard...telling him all her dark secrets...but she wanted there to be no barriers between them. Long distance relationships were hard enough as it was and Aspen refused to let her own insecurities make it harder.

If they were going to have a chance at this, she needed to be fully open. And that meant sharing her past and her plans.

She waited until their orders had been taken before scooting in a little closer to his chair.

Austin smiled and reached out to take her hand. He pulled it up and kissed her palm, then rubbed her fingers between his in a contented manner. "This is nice, huh?"

Aspen cleared her throat. "It is," she agreed. "But...I have something to tell you."

His humor faded. "Oh?" His words were hesitant, as if he were bracing for a blow.

"Nothing bad," Aspen hurried to say. At least, she hoped he wouldn't see it as bad. This was supposed to be a step forward, not a punishment. She leaned into the table and brought her free hand to cover his. "I just...wanted to share something with you."

He relaxed, but only slightly.

Aspen couldn't blame him for his reticence. No one liked to hear the dreaded words *we need to talk*. Clearing her throat again, Aspen forced herself into motion. "I'd like to tell you the real reason my sisters and I took over the bakery."

His eyes flared and he leaned in. "Are you saying your dad didn't retire?"

Aspen shook her head. She hesitated, that one final doubt creeping in that he would spread the news worldwide before she shoved it away. "We kept the real reason from...well, from everyone."

Austin squeezed her fingers, his warm ones helping bring heat back to her cold skin. "Tell me," he urged.

There was no hint of excitement or eagerness which Aspen would associate with someone about to get a juicy story. In fact, she couldn't see anything but sympathy in his gaze and it proved to be exactly what she needed in order to loosen the binding around her chest and open her mouth.

"It all started last year when he ruined one of his sculptures..."

AUSTIN'S MIND SPUN. The great chocolate sculptor, Antony Harrison, had Parkinson's disease? How? It seemed so incredible. What a tragedy to lose such an artist to something so early in life.

But the more Aspen shared, the more Austin understood. He understood why Aspen had been so determined to make him retract the harsh words against the cafe. He understood why she was so dead set on creating the perfect cake. He understood why they'd redecorated and why the sisters were determined to keep the bakery in the family.

So many revelations in such a short amount of time. When she finally finished, he had no words. What in the world was he supposed to say to a story like that?

Luckily, their food arrived before he could say anything, giving him just a few more moments to try and figure out what Aspen needed from him.

She'd offered everything. She'd told him her darkest secrets, shared her heart, her worries, her triumphs, her hopes for the future...and he couldn't do the same.

His secrets were different. His weren't simply a matter of protecting his family's privacy. No...his secrets would break everyone around him. His secret would show him to be a liar, a freak, a broken man who had unresolved trauma from his childhood.

Aspen's dark eyes stared at him expectantly. She had a right to expect a response. Austin just didn't know which one to give her.

Taking a deep breath, he let his fork sit untouched at the side of his plate, instead pulling both of Aspen's hands up and kissing her knuckles. "Thank you for sharing that with me," he said in a low voice. "I know we haven't known each other long, but...my feelings for you are stronger than anything I've ever felt before, and knowing you trust me enough to share all that..." He shook his head, his heart heavy and elated all at the same time. "I promise to keep it to myself, but I'm also eager to help you any way I can." He winked. "Although, I'm not sure how a food reviewer can do anything to help your dad, but...you never know."

Aspen laughed softly and squeezed his hands before letting go. "Thank you," she said. "I appreciate that."

They were quiet for a few moments while both began to eat their dinners.

"Do you want a bite of mine?" Aspen asked. "You know...for research purposes?"

He chuckled. "I doubt it'll change my mind, but sure."

Aspen frowned as he took a bite of her salmon. "What do you mean?"

Austin poked at his plate, letting the flavors of the fish coat his tongue. "I mean, it's not that great and tasting yours doesn't change that."

Her frown deepened. "I think it's pretty good."

"And that's the point," Austin pointed out. "It's *okay*. Not great, not delicious, not amazing." He shrugged. "It's just okay, and that's not what I'm looking for in a restaurant."

"So you're going to leave them a bad review?" Aspen's voice was small.

Austin was sure that she was remembering Tye's scathing post about her own place. In that case, it wasn't the food that had driven him off, but still...it had to have stung, especially considering the story she had just told him. "I can't leave them a recommendation if I don't love the food," he explained. Surely she understood that. People relied on his opinion. He wouldn't send people to a restaurant unless it was worth their time and money. This wasn't bad, but it wasn't worth a trip out of their way.

"But you also don't have to rip them apart."

Austin paused, then looked up from his plate. "You're upset."

Aspen blew out a breath. "I don't know," she said, setting her fork down. "I just...do you have to be one or the other? Can't you just leave a review that says it's good but not great? You always seem to either gush or gut. There's no in between."

He wiped his mouth on his napkin. Austin was starting to feel as if this conversation had been inevitable. Their little bubble this week was coming to an end. She'd shared parts of herself as a show of good faith, but he wasn't able to share back, and now some of the obstacles between them were rearing their heads. First up was his job.

This was exactly why he couldn't tell her the truth. She didn't understand that the words weren't his. She didn't understand that without Tye's snarky personality, no one had paid any attention to him. She didn't understand that food was the only thing that made him happy.

Until her.

The words floated through his mind with a ring of truth, but Austin shoved them aside. Yes, Aspen made him happy. She teased, she pressured, she challenged, but it was still too soon. He couldn't allow himself to have such soft thoughts or he would end up sharing the skeletons in his closet the same way she had. And if he shared, he'd lose everything.

Aspen, his job, his reputation...all of it would disappear.

"I'm sorry you don't like what I do for a living," he said carefully, "but this is who I am. You can either take me or leave me."

The words sent a sharp pain through his chest. He didn't mean them, but he'd gotten awfully good at lying over the years. He wanted Aspen. But he needed security.

Aspen huffed and picked her fork back up. "I guess we'll just have to agree to disagree."

Taking her at her word, Austin went back to eating. The meal was over quickly, neither one of them wanting to linger, even though the atmosphere of the restaurant was made for lovers.

Taking a chance, he took her hand and let out a quiet sigh of relief when she didn't resist. The argument, however, was a sign that maybe this wouldn't work out the way Austin had begun to hope. Maybe the obstacles were going to be too great. It made him grateful he hadn't risked sharing anything with her. The first hiccup in the road and they were already unsure.

"Did you want to stop somewhere for dessert?" he asked as he opened the passenger side door.

Aspen huffed a laugh, the tight lines of her face easing as she buckled up. "I think we deal in dessert all day. You sure you want more tonight?"

He gave her a significant look. "Are you really asking me that?"

Aspen threw back her head with a groan. "I've created a monster."

"Not true," he pointed out, a teasing tone in his voice. "I was this way long before we met. Your cake has just made it worse."

"I'm not sure whether to be offended by that or delighted."

"When in doubt, always take it as a compliment," he said before shutting the door. The walk around to his side felt much longer than it should have. Three seconds wasn't much time, but it felt like forever as his mind immediately turned to the issues at hand.

Tomorrow he would go home. He wouldn't be at Aspen's side anymore. He'd have to deal with real life, with his mother and his job. He'd have to find a way to better hide his past and make sure his and Tye's secret was secure.

For the last time in a while, he would enjoy Aspen's attention and baked goods, but come tomorrow...he'd have to face his demons.

CHAPTER 21

"What kind of cake would you like?" Aspen hollered over her shoulder as she entered the kitchen. She headed straight for the counter where the cakes were tucked up for the night. Grabbing a couple of plates along the way, she stopped at a drawer for a large knife. "Or did you want a cookie or something?" Austin didn't answer right away and Aspen spun around.

Austin was staring at his phone. His cheeks were red and his muscles tense. Whatever he was reading was not something that made him happy.

"Austin?"

He jerked as if he'd forgotten she was there. "Yeah. Sorry." Stuffing his phone in his pocket, Austin scrubbed his face with his hands and a smile spread across his face.

Even from across the room, Aspen could see it wasn't genuine. Things felt slightly awkward between them at the moment. She still wasn't sure what to think of their conversation at dinner. While she understood his argument about having to be honest in his assessment of restaurants, Aspen didn't understand why he couldn't grasp the fact that these places were people's livelihoods.

Not everyone had the courage to fight him publicly like she had. Most of the restaurants would simply take whatever he dished out, or maybe grumble on their social media, but otherwise, what Eat It Austin said was considered law.

He was such a nice guy. He was good with people and he made her feel wonderful, despite the fact that she was a bit of a workaholic. He hadn't made fun of her dreams for the shop or suggested they share her father's story with the world. In fact, he'd been a little stoic about her story. She'd expected a little more interest on his part, but after all was said and done, Austin had left the story on the sidelines, not particularly engaged.

So why would such a nice guy purposefully build up a reputation where the public saw him as a jerk? A famous and funny jerk, but still a jerk. It still made no sense.

"Work problems?" she asked as he drew closer.

His brows pulled together. "I suppose you could say that."

When he didn't say more, Aspen plastered her own fake smile in place. "Well, I guess there's a bright side to you going home tomorrow, huh? You can put out all the fires that cropped up while you were gone."

He nodded, his eyes on the cake. His usual excitement over the sweet treat was absent.

"I'm...going to miss you," she whispered. It was still too early to tell him about her real feelings, and after their chat at dinner, Aspen needed time to come to grips with her thoughts.

She loved him. But could she dedicate her life to a man who put others down? If only everyone could see the man she saw. If only he had chosen to be his true self on social media.

Or maybe that is his true self and this week has been the facade...

No. Aspen shoved the thought aside. There just was no way he was that good of an actor. No one could be.

Austin's face relaxed. "I'm going to miss you too," he responded. Stepping up close, he tenderly kissed her cheek. "But maybe a little time apart will be good for us both."

Aspen felt as if she'd been slapped. "What?" The doubts came rushing back with a vengeance. "This week was all your idea," she reminded him.

Austin brushed a hand over his head and nodded. "I know, and I don't regret it, but...we've spent a lot of time together. Spending time apart will help us know our real feelings. That's all I meant."

Aspen stared. Her mouth had gone dry and she had no words. Things had been slightly awkward at dinner, but now it had gone even further. It wasn't awkward, it was downright hostile. "You're breaking up with me," she said bluntly.

"No!" He shook his head and blew out a breath. "That's not what I meant at all." When he reached for her, Aspen stepped away.

She could read between the lines. Apparently, she'd been wrong. He was that good of an actor. Why else would he be trying to ease their separation now that it was here? He stuck like glue during his vacation, but now he was going back to his life and didn't want a barnacle sucking the life out of him.

"Aspen." He groaned. "Don't take it that way. That's not what I meant."

She folded her arms over her chest as if that could stop the pain that was radiating a spot suspiciously near her sternum. "Oh? Then what did you mean? Because when a man says the distance is a good thing, it certainly doesn't make a woman feel like he wants to be around her anymore."

He threw his head back. "Why does it all have to be so complicated?" he muttered to the ceiling.

"No one is making this complicated," Aspen snapped. "No one except you, that is. If you only stuck around to learn my secrets and eat my cake, then fine. Just admit it and we can call it quits. It was only a week, after all. I'm sure I'll recover." Every word tasted like burnt chocolate on her tongue. Lies, lies and more lies. But what was a girl to do? With words like that, she had to protect herself. It was self preservation at its finest.

Austin's shock was immediate and he backed up a couple of steps. "Is that really what you think of me?" he asked hoarsely.

Aspen threw her arms to the side. "No," she argued. "It wasn't. At least until you started telling me that a break would be good for us. You waited until the very last minute to tell me that, after I shared everything with you at dinner. I..." She blew out a breath. "What am I supposed to think?"

Austin deflated. "You're right," he said softly. "My timing was all wrong. I just...I was just trying to save us some heartache, I suppose."

The sharp pain in her chest intensified. "You *are* breaking up with me."

"Would you stop saying that?" Austin snapped. He closed his eyes and shook his head. "Sorry. I'm feeling a little wound up at the moment and this conversation isn't helping."

"Austin," she said carefully. "What's going on? Something's wrong, I know it. Is it because of your job? Because I don't agree with how you handle your reviews?"

He shook his head. "No, though that's something that'll be hard to overcome, won't it?" His laugh held no humor.

Aspen opened her mouth to ask another question, but a loud pounding on the door stopped her. "Who in the world would be coming by at this time of night?" she asked, walking toward the door to the front.

Austin followed her to the door, but when Aspen continued into the front room, he stalled. "Aspen," he said, the hoarse tone back. "Don't worry about it."

A tall, lanky man was pounding on the glass, his face peering inside. "Open up, Austin," the man shouted. "I know you're in there."

Fear skittered down Aspen's spine. "Do you know that man?" she asked.

Austin nodded, his eyes glued to the door. "He's my...brother."

"Oh. Tye. I remember him." Aspen blinked as the man pounded again. She hadn't recognized him in the dark. "I'll just let him in then."

"No...wait..." Austin said half heartedly.

"We can't let him wait in the cold," Aspen argued. She gave the man a small wave, but his anger didn't abate. Aspen began to wonder if she should truly open the door, but he was Austin's family. She couldn't leave him outside, could she? She unlocked the door and started to push it open. "Hey, Tye," she said warily. "Is there something I can help—oh!" She nearly fell when he jerked the door from her hands.

"We solve this now!" Tye shouted, storming inside.

"ASPEN!" AUSTIN RUSHED around Tye to make sure she was alright. When he'd checked her over, he ushered her back inside and put himself between the woman he loved and his angry brother. "What is *wrong* with you?" Austin shouted. "You can't just come barging in here like this."

"How else am I supposed to talk to you?" Tye argued. He put his hands on his head and blew out a breath. Leaning around Austin, he dropped his voice. "I'm sorry, Ms. Harrison. I don't normally go around screaming at people or pounding on doors late at night."

Aspen didn't respond and Austin didn't blame her. Tye looked wild at the moment and it worried Austin. "What do you need?" he demanded.

"To talk to you," Tye said, his voice tight. "Stan called again with more threats. Years of work is about to go down the toilet and you can't be pulled away from your sugar mama long enough to fix it!"

Aspen gasped and Austin felt her step away from him.

"Let's not do this here," Austin tried to say, but Tye wasn't having it.

"Stan said Mom came to the office almost every hour today. Every time she came in, she was out of her head and shouting all our secrets to the entire office."

"Why didn't he call the police?" Austin asked, his heart pounding against his rib cage. If it pulsed any harder, it was going to break through. Would the office take it as the shouts of a mad woman? Did anyone actually know it was his mother? Or would they believe the stories she was telling? There was no way for him to know.

"He did," Tye cried. "But she always managed to slip out before they arrived. When the police left, she would come back." Tye paced away, his hands nearly tearing his hair out by the roots. "She's gonna ruin it all! By the time we get back to the office, they'll have packed up our desks and we'll be out. OUT!"

Austin put his hands in the air. "Bring it down, Tye. We'll figure this out."

"How?" Tye demanded. "How? Every few months, this happens. Always demanding money to keep quiet. She's killing us! When will it end? She's gonna expose everything."

Tye finally collapsed on the leopard print loveseat, his head in his hands.

Normally, Austin would have walked over and wrapped his arm around his anxious brother, bringing him down from an episode, but this time there was another person to consider. Slowly, Austin turned to Aspen.

Her eyes were wide and fear, mixed with curiosity, sat on her beautiful face.

"What's going on?" she asked. Her voice was quiet but filled with steel. There would be no squiggling out of this one.

Austin nodded reluctantly. Despite their earlier argument, he hadn't planned for this to be the end of their relationship. He'd known an end might come, but he had hoped it would be far in the future. He'd fallen for Aspen in a way he knew he would never fall for another woman. A week simply wasn't long enough.

But with Tye showing up literally on her doorstep, there was no way to hide the truth from her any longer. And truth was, he was tired of it anyway. Tired of shouldering the burden. Having his mother out his secrets was almost a relief, even if it did mean his job was more than likely forfeit.

He felt his own panic try to rise as he wondered what he would eat, but Austin pushed it down. He still had a house and a bank account. He'd be able to feed himself and his brother just fine until he got a new job. It just more than likely wouldn't allow him to eat at the fancy restaurants he frequented now. But he knew how to make a dollar stretch. It had been a necessity of life. He'd done it before, he could do it again.

"It's apparent you've been holding back," she said tightly. "What I want to know is why?"

Austin felt his chest deflate. "Because I didn't want you to know."

"But *why?*" she pressed. "I don't understand. Why are you so worried about me hearing what Tye is saying?"

"Because he didn't want you to put two and two together," Tye said, jumping to his feet. "Spending any time with me would ruin it all." He glared at his brother before going back to Aspen. "If you read our blog, then talking to me for any length of time would let you know exactly who does all the writing."

Austin tried to swallow the lump in his throat as Aspen's mind worked. He could practically see the wheels turning as she put it all together.

Her eyes grew impossibly bigger as she finally looked at him. "You don't do the reviews."

Here it was. The moment he'd been dreading his whole life. The moment his weakness turned him into something worthless. "No."

"But you went to that restaurant with me." Aspen shook her head, still missing a couple of the pieces.

"Austin is the face and the taste buds," Tye said, his voice growing quieter with each word. His bravery was quickly fading. Adrenaline and fear had been the only reasons he had a voice at all.

"And you're the writer," she finished.

Tye nodded, then folded into himself. He might have been taller than Austin by an inch or two, but when he slipped into his scared place, no one could tell.

Aspen's head jerked back and forth between the two men. "So Tye, you wrote the review on the cafe." It was a statement, not a question, but Tye nodded anyway, refusing to meet Aspen's eyes.

"I still don't get why any of this matters." Aspen clutched her head. "Why does it matter if people know that one brother does the writing?"

The words didn't want to come. They would change everything. Right now he was still somebody. He had a job, a reputation and confidence. In a moment, it would all be over.

"Because I'm dyslexic."

A pin could have dropped and no one would have missed it. Aspen stood stockstill, as if she hadn't heard him.

Her lack of movement sent an inappropriate surge of protective anger through Austin. "You want to know why our jobs and food are so important?" he asked, gritting his teeth. Logically, he knew it wasn't Aspen's fault, but right now he felt like an animal cornered. The only way to freedom was to break out, and there was no way to do that without shedding blood. In this case...it would be his own.

"Our mother is a drug addict," Austin said softly. "We grew up living in a car. Food was hard to come by."

Her wide eyes began to shine, slowly filling with tears. "Austin," she breathed.

He didn't want her pity, or her eventual goodbye. He'd do it himself. "I was the oldest, but Mom always made sure I knew I was worthless. I couldn't read, I couldn't write and I was always getting in trouble at school because of it." His smile was far from happy. "Stubborn. Troublemaker." He scoffed. "All because a hungry little boy wasn't ever taken to the right doctor." Austin straightened his shoulders. "But we grew. We survived and we grew up. I had an unhealthy obsession with food, but couldn't write. Tye had words but crippling anxiety."

Aspen opened her mouth, but Austin didn't give her the chance to say anything.

"So we put both of our talents together and created Eat It Austin. But it didn't take off until Tye got a little snarky with one of our reviews. The post went viral and..." He held his hands out to the side. There was nothing else to explain.

The public liked snark. They liked poking fun. And it had put food on the table and clothes on their back in a way they had never experienced before, and the two boys had never looked back.

"So now when our mother comes around, we pay her off to keep her quiet, and we go about our business." Austin took a deep breath. "And we never let anyone close enough to know our secret." His heart was shriveling with every word. The fear of what she was going to say was so heavy, he couldn't breathe.

It was time to leave.

"Come on, Tye," he said soothingly, helping his struggling brother to his feet. "Let's go home."

CHAPTER 22

Numb. That was the best way to explain how Aspen had been moving about life and generally feeling for the past two days. Ever since Austin walked out of the cafe as if she was nothing more than crumbs on his plate.

But why?

It was a question that Aspen still didn't have the answer to. The only thing she could think of was that he was scared. Scared of how she would react. Scared of the fact that he had lied to her and the rest of the world for years.

She closed her eyes, breathing deeply through her nose. She could still see his face when he told her about his dyslexia and she felt more confident in her thoughts. He was scared of how she would react to his learning disability.

She shook her head, forcing her limp hand to move back to the cake and keep decorating. She had been hired for a custom anniversary cake and the cute couple celebrating their twenty-fifth year together didn't deserve something subpar just because Aspen's heart had skedaddled back to Portland.

She carefully cupped the frosting, swirling it along the straight edge of the cake. Normally such a movement would be soothing and seeing her progress would lighten her heart. She would imagine the crowd cutting into the delicacy and enjoying each and every bite. The goal was always for it to taste as good as it looked...but today her heart wasn't in it. Her heart wasn't even in the building with her.

Her vision blurred as she ran Austin's story through her head for the millionth time. Homeless...drug addict...protective older brother...hoarded food...struggles with learning...

Eat It Austin Edwards might have run out of her cafe with his tail between his legs, but he was one of the bravest men Aspen had ever had the pleasure of knowing.

She sniffled and set down the frosting tube, heading to the office to blow her nose. This was starting to get ridiculous. She needed to speak to him. She should have told him early how she felt about it. She should have assured him that her feelings were strong and true.

But she'd held back. Aspen had been her own sort of coward that night and had worried that what she felt was happening too soon, and when the inevitable bump in their relationship hit, they weren't prepared for it. Austin had run because he didn't know that she cared for more than just his fame. He didn't know she wasn't worried about his dyslexia or even how they set up their blog. None of that mattered to her as much as just being with him.

The kitchen felt empty without his large presence and no new cake ideas had come to her since his departure. Almost as if he'd been her muse. She shook her head and pushed open the office door. There she was, getting all stupid again.

If only he'd answer his phone or one of the million texts she'd sent. His voicemail was full of her pleas for him to call her back. She'd shed all pretense of self respect in an effort to get him to respond to her, and it had all been in vain. Austin was gone and it appeared as if he'd never come back.

It took a moment for Aspen to realize that Maeve was crying when she entered the office. Aspen's feet stuttered to a stop. "What's going on?"

Maeve wiped her eyes with her fingers, coming away with smeared mascara. "Dad had to go to the hospital last night," she whimpered.

What little was left of Aspen's heart nearly stopped. "What?" she breathed. Her knees began to shake and it felt as if she would hit the floor. Gripping the threshold of the door was the only thing keeping her upright at this point.

"He was walking down the stairs and Mom said his foot...stuttered...and he fell."

"His foot stuttered?" Aspen was trying to grasp everything coming out of her sister's mouth, but this morning she was having a hard time keeping up.

"One of the symptoms of Parkinson's is that their muscles are slow to react," Maeve explained as if she was talking to a small child.

Aspen grit her teeth, but forced herself to not snap. When she was upset, she went quiet. When Maeve was upset, she went into lecture mode. It was best to let this play out.

"He was walking by himself and his leg didn't move as quickly as it should have," Maeve explained. "And he fell."

"Is he alright?" Aspen's voice was hoarse, but her throat felt as dry as the Sahara.

Maeve shrugged. "He broke his wrist and has several bruises, but otherwise he's okay."

Estelle came up behind Aspen. "I'm flying over tomorrow."

"What!" Aspen screeched. She jumped and spun, glaring at her sister for the scare as well as the news. "You knew about this?"

Estelle nodded curtly.

"And no one thought to tell me?" The tears were back, and the pain. Apparently, she wasn't as numb as she thought.

Estelle's voice was soft but firm. "We thought you had enough on your plate," she explained.

"There is *nothing* that would ever land on my plate that would keep me from wanting to know what was happening with Dad," Aspen snapped. She paused and closed her eyes. "I'm sorry. None of this is your fault." Shaking her head, Aspen stomped to the tissues, grabbed a couple and stomped back out. "Maeve, I guess that puts you on front counter duty."

Aspen didn't stick around to hear her younger sister's response, instead throwing herself back into her work. The cake turned out beautifully, for which Aspen was grateful, since her heart was a pulpy pile of mush. It was amazing it even functioned at this point in time.

She glanced at her phone for the time and sighed. Early that morning, the idea of possibly taking a day off to drive up to Portland had been percolating at the edges of her brain. But now? There was no way.

Aspen sighed and stuffed the phone back in her pocket. Family came first. They had to. She had fought hard for this cafe, even going so far as to demand an apology from a social media star, and now she would have to fight again. But this wasn't a fight that was happening in the public eye. No one would be tweeting about it and no one would be capturing it with a camera.

No...Aspen knew that in order to help her family, the best thing she could do is let go of her connection with Austin and focus on keeping the business alive while her sister went to Italy. Estelle would help set things right and take care of Dad so Mom didn't have to carry the whole burden. And Aspen would stay here. She would bake, she would clean and she would sell when necessary. She was the next oldest and the responsibility of the home fell to her shoulders.

No more dates, no more dreaming of a future that could never be. From now on, she would have to eat, live and breathe the business, because the only thing that could hurt their father more than what he was already going through would be to lose the shop.

And Aspen refused to be the one to take that away from him.

DISASTER. THIS WHOLE thing was a disaster.

Austin buried his face in his hands, listening to Stan's yelling. Apparently, Austin's boss didn't need to breathe because he hadn't stopped his ranting in anything less than thirty minutes.

"If you can't keep her out of here, you're through! Do you hear me, Edwards?" Stan put his hands on his desk and leaned over it. "Through. Washed up. If I ever see her face again, I'm calling the cops to have her hauled away."

Tired...so tired.

Austin could barely nod at Stan's demands. His boss had every right to demand his mother stay off the property, but most of Austin was just so darn tired of fighting it all. Somehow, miracle of miracles, no one in the office really understood what she'd been spouting for days and all thought it was the delusions of an addict. In some ways...it was. But what they didn't understand was her cries of stupid, freak, troublemaker were all pointing to one thing.

Austin's lies and disability.

He blew out a breath. The dark bags under his eyes were a testament to how much sleep he'd gotten since arriving home from Seagull Cove. He'd walked out of the Three Sisters Cafe without a backward glance, taken his brother straight home and been trying to patch a thinning web of deceit ever since.

There weren't enough hours in the day to keep pulling the pieces of the puzzle back together. It was like trying to put a sandcastle back together. The more he tried, the more of it slipped through his fingers.

And he was so tired...

"Edwards!"

Austin's head snapped up. "Yeah?"

"Get out and get it fixed," Stan growled.

Austin climbed to his feet, but had to hold still for a moment when a dizzy spell hit. He really needed to get some sleep. His feet shuffled, barely lifting off the carpet. If he was being honest with himself, he was afraid to go to sleep. He knew that when he did, hiding behind those eyelids would be Aspen's face. The hurt look in her eye when he snapped at her. The pity, the tears, all of it.

He rubbed his forehead as he left the office. It felt as if the weight of the world was on his shoulders and Austin had no idea how to fix it.

"What did he say?" Tye asked, his voice quavering ever so slightly.

Austin sighed. This headache was quickly becoming a full blown migraine. "I'm sure the whole office knows what he said by now, T."

Tye nodded sadly. "I know. But I just..." He blew out a breath and pushed his hair back. "I don't know what I thought."

The clipping of heels had Austin snapping his mouth shut before he could respond. Izzy was just as put together as always as she sidled up to the brothers. "Trouble, handsome?" she asked, tapping her fingernails on Austin's chest.

He backed away from her. After experiencing Aspen's tenderness, Izzy's touch almost made him sick to his stomach. This whole environment was making him sick. He wanted out. He wanted...

Shaking his head, Austin stepped back further. It didn't matter what he wanted. He and Tye needed this work just like they needed to eat.

"Everything's fine," he said stoically. Aspen, with her melted chocolate eyes and silky hair, would just end up being another casualty in this war to stay afloat.

Along with my heart.

"Come on, Tye. We have work to do," Austin said, pulling his drooling brother away from the temptress. Izzy wasn't good for either of them, but Tye wasn't always very good at recognizing that. He'd learn sooner or later.

"Where are we going?" Tye asked.

Austin's jaw clenched. "To find our mother."

Tye jerked back. "What? Why?" He stopped. "I don't want to see her."

Austin also stopped and formed his words very carefully. "I understand that, but we need to end this." He looked around, making sure they were alone. "We either need to pay her off, or let the police deal with her," he said under his breath. "We can't keep going like this."

Tye wrung his hands together, his face pale. "I don't know if I can."

Austin closed his eyes. Why was he always so alone in this? He'd been taking care of Tye since they were boys and somewhere along the line, his younger brother was supposed to grow up. Why had it never happened? Why was he always pulling Tye off the ledge? When would he be an adult?

A flare of anger sparked to life in Austin's chest, but he pushed it away. That wouldn't get him anywhere. Anger had never been a good friend and it certainly wouldn't help now.

"Come on, Tye. This is our life. Let's take care of it."

Tye took a deep breath, then nodded. "You're right. Let's go find her."

Once in the car, Austin began heading toward his mother's favorite haunt. She had a small apartment that Austin paid for, but she rarely stayed there. Her activities took her from home and once high, Austin knew she struggled to get back to the apartment.

Not knowing where else to start, he drove to the building and headed to her door. Five minutes of knocking led to no answer, so he came back to the car.

"Where to next?" Tye asked, his fingers tapping a frantic rhythm against his knee.

Austin sighed. He was so broken. He shook his head. "I don't know," he admitted. "But we'll drive around and see what we can find."

By the end of the day, Austin was no closer to solving his mother issues than he was getting back together with Aspen. Right now, both of them seemed equally impossible.

"You going to sleep tonight?" Tye asked as he headed down the hall of their house.

Austin nodded, the movement making his vision shake. Man...he really needed a break. "Sure." There was no way he'd sleep any more tonight than he had since he got back from Seagull Cove. His body was crashing, but his mind couldn't stop. There were still too many things to fix.

He cradled his cell phone in his hands. There were a dozen messages from Aspen that he refused to listen to and about a hundred text messages showing unseen, but it hadn't slipped his notice that none had come through today. Three days and she had already given up on him?

Can you blame her? You walked away, haven't answered her messages and you expect her to keep reaching out?

Just once he wanted someone to bridge the gap from their side. For her to push the way he always had to push. He was always the one trying to help his mother. He was always the one trying to help Tye. He was the one saving the blog, or smiling at the cameras, or...

"How do I do this?" he whispered to the dark house. It was all too much. Too many problems, too many heartaches, too many pieces to keep juggling. He had a dreadful feeling that at any moment, all of them were going to come crashing down on his head. His hurt feelings toward Aspen were unfounded, but he couldn't get them to stop.

But with the way things were going, it was only a matter of time before it didn't matter anymore.

CHAPTER 23

"How bad is it?" Aspen asked, pinching the bridge of her nose. Somehow, they'd managed to go three days before news of her and Austin's breakup hit the internet. She had thought that they might actually get away with keeping it under wraps, but the internet had eyes everywhere.

And ears, apparently, Aspen thought wryly. She hadn't talked to anyone about the breakup except her sisters and she was positive they hadn't shared the news with anyone. So either Austin was using it for social media fame, or somehow another person had gotten wind of the situation and shared the juicy tidbit. Aspen hoped it was the latter. She didn't want to believe that Austin would spill it all online, especially after the way they broke up. His confession about his childhood and learning disability were the very things he was hoping to keep from the public. Surely, he wouldn't want to spread it all over.

Maeve made a face. "Kinda bad," she said.

"Just say it," Aspen snapped. She took a deep breath. "Sorry. I'm not mad at you, Maeve. Just frustrated with the situation. This is actually all my fault." Aspen rubbed her throbbing forehead.

Maeve sputtered, leaning forward in her office chair. "What? How in the world is this your fault?"

Aspen dropped into the metal chair across the desk. Her legs felt shaky and she was slightly nauseous. "I *knew* I shouldn't have dated him," she whispered, her eyes on the carpet. She couldn't bring herself to look her sister in the eye. "It was a conflict of interest. I shouldn't have let my guard down, I—"

Maeve huffed. "Enough with the drama," she said. Leaning forward, her elbows on the desk, Maeve pinned her sister with a glare.

"The fact of the matter is, you finally found someone who meant more to you than cake." A small smile tugged at her lips. "I don't know if you've ever paid attention to yourself, but that's quite the feat. We've all been sure you would never fall for anyone simply because they didn't come wrapped in fondant."

Aspen jerked back automatically. "I hate fondant."

Maeve rolled her eyes. "Not the point, Aspen."

Aspen slumped and nodded. "I know. I suppose I've always been a bit of a workaholic."

"That's putting it mildly." Maeve smiled and held up a hand to stop the argument. "My point was...that we were all excited for you. Yes, we thought it was moving fast, but that's who you've always been." She shrugged. "You don't do anything by halves. You always jump in with two feet and it totally makes sense that any relationships you have would be the same way."

"But now look where that got us," Aspen pointed out. "Now our name is being smeared all over the internet...again...and it's because I didn't look before leaping."

"You looked," Maeve said with a snort. "We all did."

Aspen's eyes widened. "What the heck is that?"

Maeve shrugged again. "Are you telling me you didn't notice your boyfriend was totally delectable? I think the whole of the internet has."

Aspen tugged on her ponytail. "I suppose I did."

"Suppose?" Maeve gave her sister a look. "You're a terrible liar."

"Okay...he was hot. Is that what you want to hear?"

Maeve threw up her hands. "Well, at least you finally admit something."

"I admitted this was my fault."

"Which was just another lie," Maeve argued.

Aspen closed her eyes and took a deep breath. "What do you want from me, Maeve? I've admitted I was wrong. I'm willing to help keep our business going, even with Estelle in Italy. I don't know what else I can do."

Maeve shook her head. "I'm really not asking you to do anything," she said softly, drawing Aspen's gaze. "The internet is in an uproar right now. It won't last. Some celebrity will get booked for drunk driving and we'll be old news." She sighed and pushed her glasses up onto her head. "All I want is for you to either admit you still love him and figure out how to get him back, or to let go and use this as inspiration to make more cakes."

Aspen couldn't breathe for a couple of heartbeats. "What?" she croaked.

Maeve's look was decidedly pitying. "You still love him, don't you? Even after he confessed to lying about his job and admitting he has dyslexia?"

"Of course," Aspen gushed. "What kind of person would I be if I let the fact that he struggles to read keep me from loving him? And as for the job..." Aspen opened and closed her mouth a few times before the words finally came. "I don't know...I don't really care. I always thought there was something off with the fact that he was so sweet but his words were so harsh. This just lets me know why. I still wish he didn't act like he was that snarky person in public, but I'm willing to work around it." The pain she'd been struggling with ever since he left hit her chest again, robbing her air. "That is, if he'd been willing to do the same."

Maeve nodded. "And therein lies the problem. *He* thinks it's enough to have you running." She huffed and leaned back, folding her arms over her chest. "I actually think I'd be offended if someone thought that about me."

"Can you really blame him?" Aspen said with a tired sigh. "You heard about his mother. It doesn't really sound like the women in his life have been very supportive. Why would he think I was any different?"

"Because you are."

Aspen felt the prick of tears, but she shoved it away. She'd cried enough. "But we didn't date long enough to know that."

"Maybe," Maeve conceded. "So...what are you going to do now?"

Aspen shook her head. "I don't know. Keep the bakery alive? Try to survive until Estelle gets back or someone gives us news on Dad?"

Maeve nodded. "Good ideas. But what about Austin?"

Aspen held her hands out to the side. "What do you suggest?" she asked, a slight edge to her tone. "I've called and texted until he has enough evidence to get a restraining order. Obviously, he doesn't want to give me a chance." She swallowed hard. "Or maybe he just doesn't want me." She dropped her gaze again. The doubts that Austin had simply used her were coming back stronger than ever, but Aspen was doing her best to fight them. She didn't want to believe that of him, and considering how the breakup happened, Aspen was *almost* positive that his feelings had been real.

Maeve grinned and it was far from the sweet one the academic woman usually wore. "Then maybe we need to get his attention another way."

Aspen froze. "What do you mean?"

Maeve rubbed her hands together. "I think we should have the gang out for dinner tonight. We have some brainstorming to do." She grabbed her phone and began to text madly.

"Even Ethan?" Aspen's eyebrows shot up while Maeve's shot down.

Maeve grumbled and glanced up with a short glare. "Yes, probably even the next door joker."

"Huh." Aspen could barely move. If Maeve was willingly bringing Ethan into this, then they were desperate for sure. *You are desperate for sure,* her inner voice snapped. Aspen let out a long breath. She had to admit, her sister was right. Aspen still loved Austin and she didn't want to give up on them, especially since his reasons were ludicrous.

But just how would they get his attention if direct calling and texting didn't work? Aspen stood and walked back to the kitchen. Their friends wouldn't be coming over until dinner and she would need to ply them all with sugar if she was going to get their help. Her fingers twitched and for the first time in a few days, Aspen was ready to bake.

"HAVE YOU HEARD ANYTHING?" Tye hissed as he walked past Austin's desk.

Austin looked around to make sure no one had heard the question before shaking his head. "No. No one's seen her."

Tye sighed and plopped into his seat, pushing a hand through his hair. "I can't live like this," he said softly. "The not knowing is killing me." His hand dropped to his lap.

"Edwards!"

Austin winced. He had a bad feeling he knew exactly what his boss was going to want to talk about. It had only been five days since he'd gotten back from Seagull Cove, but they had been some of the worst days of Austin's life, and that included his hellish childhood. "Coming."

Austin stood and gave his brother a significant look. "Try to relax. We'll know before she does anything, *if* she does anything."

Tye nodded. "You're right. You're always right. Sorry."

Austin squeezed his brother's shoulder before heading to Stan's office. "Heya, Stan," Austin said, hoping his voice sounded easy, though his life was anything but.

"Sit down," Stan demanded, his chair squeaking as he settled himself.

Austin sat, trying to relax his muscles, but it was hard. He hadn't relaxed since getting home. He still ached for Aspen in a way that wasn't normal. His fun week had turned into something so much more and now, he knew he'd never be the same. His heart was back in Seagull Cove and since her texts and calls had finally tapered off, Austin was positive he'd never get any of it back.

"Have you looked at the numbers recently?"

Austin nodded. "Yes. They're pretty high at the moment."

Stan snickered, the sound grating rather than enjoyable. "You could say that. That breakup of yours is hot news."

Pain lanced through Austin's sternum. His fist clenched and he found himself struggling not to explode at Stan. The fact that Austin's boss took joy in his heartache just showed the type of man that Austin worked for.

For years, Austin had been putting up with the demands, the rudeness and the fear of losing his job. Never had Austin been so close to simply calling it all quits. Losing Aspen had done something to him. But he knew he still had to take care of Tye. He knew he couldn't afford to let his secrets out to the world. He just couldn't afford to put his own wants ahead of everything else.

He wasn't supposed to walk away from everything so he could bake at Aspen's side for the rest of his life. He wasn't supposed to stop caring about his food storage or his brother's anxiety or whether or not his mother outed the fact that he was dyslexic and couldn't write worth a darn.

But he had fallen in love. And he wanted to spend the rest of his life baking next to Aspen. He was caring less and less about taking care of his brother's problems and his mother's refusal to sober up.

Austin gave himself a mental shake. His whole life had revolved around keeping secrets and taking care of his family the best way he could. He couldn't stop now...no matter how tired he was or how much he wanted life to be different.

Austin leaned back in his seat, choosing not to respond to his boss's snarky remark.

"So..." Stan folded his hands on top of the desk. "What do you have planned next?"

Austin blinked. "Excuse me?"

"The ratings are fine *now*," Stan said slowly, as if talking to a small child. "But they never stay that way. We need something big. Something fresh. New." He slapped the top of his desk. "Where's that review from when you were down in that podunk town?"

Austin swallowed hard. This was the problem with social media. The constant need for content. Striving to be the next big hit, plus the need to be bigger and better every single time. "I...don't have it," he admitted.

The truth was, he *did* have it. But Austin was having a hard time turning it in. Tye hadn't been in a good mood when he was doing the writing and it had come out in the review. No, the restaurant wasn't amazing, but after talking with Aspen, Austin couldn't quite bring himself to post the mean words.

"What?" Stan snarled. "What do you mean, you don't have it? It should have been out days ago." His bushy brows pushed together. "The only reason I let it slide was because your breakup was a better boost."

Austin held back the wince. Every time Stan brought it up, it was like he was re-stabbing Austin all over and again. "I'm not quite ready," he said. "I need some time. From the breakup." That was the first time the breakup sort of worked in his favor.

Stan laughed harshly. "Don't tell me you're upset about that? You were only there a week." He chuckled. "I thought it was all a fling...for the blog."

Austin didn't laugh. "No. It wasn't," he said flatly.

Stan chuckled a little more. "Huh. I had no idea."

Austin kept his eyes pinned on his boss, but Stan didn't look the least bit repentant about his comments.

"Well, the past is done with," Stan said, waving his hand through the air in a dismissive way. "We need to move on. I want that review on my desk in the morning. Got it? Get your brother off his duff and get it done."

Austin ground his teeth together.

A nasty smirk hit Stan's face. "You're not going to make me threaten your job, are you? If you won't keep working to keep rankings up, I'm sure I can find someone who will."

"No," Austin said tightly. "I got it." He wasn't sure what he was going to do. He wasn't sure he could bring himself to post that review. Maybe he could get Tye to rewrite it? Or maybe Austin would rewrite it himself?

No...that would never work. His writing was terrible. He couldn't spell to save his life and the amount of editing it would need wouldn't be worth it, not to mention Austin didn't have the way with words his brother did. There was a reason the reviews hadn't taken off until Tye became the writer.

Stan pointedly looked at the door, then down at his desk, effectively dismissing Austin.

Without a word, Austin stood and left the office, not bothering to close the door like he normally would. He had to figure this out. He either needed to get back to being the calloused reviewer he was before, or he needed to figure out a different way to run their job.

But with Stan breathing down his neck, his mother still on the loose, and Tye growing more and more anxious, Austin felt less and less hopeful that life would ever get back to normal.

CHAPTER 24

Aspen's eyes were wide as Maeve brought the meeting to order. She hadn't expected nearly as many people to show up. *What did Maeve do?*

"Alright, everyone," Maeve called over the chatter, her hands high in the air. "Let's get this brainstorming session started."

"Care to share why we're all here?" Harper whispered in Aspen's ear.

Aspen jumped. She hadn't heard her friend sneak up. Her mind had been too shocked to hear the fork hitting the plate as Harper ate a slice of cake.

"Oh, good heavens." Harper moaned. "This new marshmallow cake is divine."

Aspen swallowed hard. "Thanks. It's new." She closed her eyes when Harper smirked.

"Mind on something else?" Harper teased.

Aspen gave her friend a look, but before they could talk more, Maeve continued.

"I'm sure you're all wondering what's going on, so for that, I'm going to turn the stage over to Aspen."

"What?" Aspen screeched. This whole thing had been Maeve's idea and now the brat was throwing Aspen to the wolves? She glared at her sister, who looked a little too pleased with herself.

"Come on, Aspen!" Jayden called, giving her a slow clap. "Let's hear it!"

Aspen's cheeks were flaming by the time she got to the front of the room. She had almost ten friends over and they were all giving her trouble. She turned her glare on the crowd. "Why do I feel like I'm walking the plank?"

Jayden whistled. "I'd pay money to photograph that."

"You hush," she called to her cousin, pointing a finger at him. "You were in on this from the beginning."

Jayden put his hands up. "Hey, no one said playing matchmaker was easy." His easy smile got him out of a lot of predicaments, but Aspen had grown up with him and knew better. Jayden was a Class A troublemaker. Too bad he also had a heart of gold. It made it hard to stay mad at him.

She sighed and rubbed her forehead. "Look. Thank you for coming out tonight. I really appreciate the support."

"As long as there's cake, I'll always come running," a deep voice called from the back.

Aspen smiled at Mason. His voice matched his lumberjack looks. He had been a great friend to have around in middle school. Her eyes traveled around to the rest of the crowd. Ethan stood against the far wall, his face relaxed, while Maeve stood six feet away, a look of complete indifference on her face. *What is up with those two?*

Aspen shook her head and waved the thought away. She had work to do. "Again, thank you for coming." She took a deep breath. "As many of you know, I started dating Austin Edwards while he was here."

"I think the whole world knew," Michael muttered. Another of Aspen's cousins, he came from her Aunt Hope and Uncle Enoch's side. His quiet demeanor made him a wonderful listener, but not much of a socializer.

A murmur of agreement ran through the room.

Aspen clasped her shaking hands together. "Yes, we didn't really plan for that to be something that went viral, but..." She shrugged, refusing to apologize for it. It had been real and it had been great publicity. She refused to cower. "What you probably also saw on social media is that we broke up."

"Hang on." Jayden had his hand in the air and Aspen gave him an expectant look. "You're not asking us to help you get him back, are you?" He made a face. "Matchmaking only goes so far."

Here it comes. Aspen swallowed past the thick lump in her throat. "Actually...I am."

"What?"

"Aspen...be realistic."

"Sweetie..."

She heard each and every response and most of them were the kind Aspen would have expected. A smart woman would know she'd been dumped and leave it be, but Aspen's heart was in too deep to let it go. Especially since she believed that Austin had only left because he was ashamed of his situation.

"HEY!" Maeve shouted, grabbing the room's attention. She pushed her glasses up her nose and scowled at the room. "Let her talk." Relaxing against the wall yet again, Maeve nodded at Aspen.

"Thanks," Aspen said softly. Her courage was quickly failing her. She wasn't the scared type, but dealing with matters of the heart was a different story. "What you don't know is that Austin is the one who broke up with me," she offered. "But only after his brother spilled some secrets that I wasn't supposed to know."

The room was dead silent.

"And no...in case you're wondering, I'm not sharing them with you either." She held back a grin at a few grumbles of discontent. "Suffice it to say that during that week, I fell in love."

Harper gasped, her beautiful blue eyes wide. "Oh, Aspen."

Aspen blinked back tears. She wasn't going to break down...yet. "And I think Austin feels the same."

"If that was the case, don't you think he'd still be here?" Michael's voice was soft and tentative, as if he knew the words would hurt, but they needed to be said anyway.

Aspen nodded. "I know that must be what you're all thinking, but I truly believe Austin feels for me the same way I feel for him, but that he's too..." She shrugged. "Embarrassed? Ashamed? I'm not sure what else to describe it as. Once his brother shared those things with me, Austin shut down and left."

Jayden's hand was up again.

"Yes, Jay?"

"You do realize this is Eat It Austin, right? If we're going to help you get him back, I have to be sure that you want a guy who can sometimes be a jerk at your side."

Aspen had been prepared to scold her cousin for yet another interruption, but after that, she couldn't. She bit her tongue to keep from spilling the secrets she held, then splayed her hands to the side. "He's everything I've ever wanted." There. That would have to be enough. If they ever found out the truth, so be it, but it wouldn't come from her.

Jayden studied her, then finally nodded. "Okay. What do you want us to do?"

She bit her lips between her teeth. "I'm actually not quite sure. Austin won't take my texts or calls and I can't leave the shop with Estelle out of the country."

"So we need another draw to force him to talk to you?" Harper clarified.

Aspen nodded. "That's what we were hoping for." She put up a finger. "But *not* one that will end up with another hideous couch inside my shop," she said firmly.

Chuckles came from around the room.

"Social media is the only way to draw him out then?" Ethan asked.

"I think so," Aspen responded.

Ethan's bright blue eyes wrinkled at the edges as he grinned. "Then I think I've got an idea for you."

"THERE SHE IS," AUSTIN muttered. He closed his eyes and shook his head, just to make sure his eyes weren't playing tricks on him before stepping out of his car. It had been a solid week since he'd walked away from Aspen and he had barely slept for more than a couple of hours.

His job was hanging on by a thread and his sanity along with it. Tye was in an uproar about rewriting a nicer review, Stan was threatening to sue, Aspen refused to leave Austin's brain alone, along with his heart, but finally, *finally*, he had caught a break.

Every day at lunch he drove around the city looking for his mother. Her threats to out his skeletons were something he could take care of, if only he could find her, but she had been slipperier than an eel since his time back.

"Mom!" Austin shouted, rushing down the alley.

Wide, bloodshot eyes jerked his way, then continued on as if they hadn't recognized him.

Austin slowed as he reached her side. "Mom," he said more softly this time.

The woman before him looked nothing like the woman who had raised him. Her skin was stretched so tightly over her bones, it looked like she hadn't eaten in weeks. Dark circles under her eyes were even more prominent than the ones under Austin's, and that was saying something. Her fingers twitched and her mouth opened and closed several times without words coming out.

Austin rubbed a hand over his face, not sure what exactly to do. She needed help. Not just another check, but honest to goodness medical help. But how could he convince her to go in? He had no control over her.

And Tye wonders why I couldn't let Aspen any further into our lives.

He groaned at the reminder of the woman he loved. It was partly her fault he was standing where he was. He had built a wall of immunity to this. Years and years of being disappointed by his single parent had taught him to not care what she did to destroy herself, as long as she didn't try to destroy him along the way.

But as he stood above her shivering frame, buried inside an old, holey coat, he found an emotion that had been lacking in his life for a very long time.

Compassion.

It almost felt foreign, and yet...not. He had never been one to hurt people on purpose, but he'd allowed his public persona to do so, rationalizing that it didn't matter since he wasn't really the one saying it. It had seemed fine at the time because it had put food on his table and given him a security he'd never known before.

But Aspen had shown him behind the scenes. She'd stood up for her own respect and then demanded he give it to others. Which meant simply making sure his mom had enough money for a hot meal wasn't going to cut it anymore.

Austin squatted to the ground. "Mom?" he asked softly. "Do you know who I am?"

Her eyes twitched to his again, then away, unable to hold his gaze. A single tear slid down her cheek and a bout of shaking nearly brought her to the ground.

Sighing, Austin reached out and gripped her too-thin elbows. "Let's get you taken care of, huh?"

It was a testament to how bad she was that she didn't put up a fight. Normally, Ina Edwards wouldn't let anyone tell her what to do. She ran her own life and refused to be under anyone's mercy.

But as Austin walked his mom to his car and got her settled in front of the heater, he realized something. This wasn't really his mother. His mother had died a long time ago, a victim of poverty and drug usage, and he had spent most of his life mourning her, letting his bitterness keep him from seeing the truth around him.

Ina Edwards was dead, and in her place was a shell of a human being that wasn't cognizant enough to help herself.

But I am.

Austin started the car, blasting the heat as high as it would go. "Don't worry, Mom," he said softly as he drove to the nearest hospital. "We'll get you taken care of."

Somewhere in his head, he was sure this was all a waste of time. That bitter little voice saying that she would only get sober long enough to be released and go back to the usage, but Austin found he didn't care.

He *needed* to do this, and not because she was always threatening to ruin his career. But because he wanted to be the person Aspen thought he was. The person she had pushed him to be.

He couldn't have Aspen, but maybe, he could still hold a piece of her close, one that would be proud of the man he was working to become.

He pulled up to the emergency room doors and came around to help his mom inside.

"What's going on?" the nurse behind the desk asked, rushing around to help him. "Daryl, bring that wheelchair over here."

"This is my mom," Austin said in a low tone. "She needs help."

Ina moaned, her head falling to the side, suddenly too heavy for her to hold upright.

The nurse narrowed her eyes at him. "I know you..."

Austin shook his head. "No. I'm nobody. I'm just here for my mom."

The nurse took in a deep breath and nodded. "Right." She looked over her shoulder. "Daryl!"

A security guard rushed over with the requested chair and they got Ina settled. Austin watched them rush her to the back, his feet rooted to the floor. Should he follow them? Was she going to make it? He'd never seen her quite so out of it before, but then again...how often did he hunt her down?

"I'll need you to fill out some paperwork," the nurse said, coming back to the front and plopping herself at her desk. She began rifling through different piles. "Does she have insurance?"

Austin shook his head. "No. I'll take care of the bills."

The nurse looked at him in surprise, then nodded. "Alright. We'll put you as guarantor. Any idea what she's been taking?"

He shrugged. "No. I'm sorry. I haven't been....very involved in her life."

The nurse kept nodding. "I can understand that. Addict parents are difficult to handle." She paused. "Why don't you have a seat, hon. This might take a while."

Austin sank into the hard chair next to the desk. *This is for you, Aspen,* he thought as he fought his desire to bolt and hide his face.

A warm feeling began to swirl in his chest and he realized something. *And maybe, this is also for me.*

CHAPTER 25

"**I** don't like this," Aspen muttered, folding her arms over her chest. "Don't you think we should have someone else issue the challenge?" She dropped her arms, then waved them through the air. "This just makes me look desperate, like I'm trying to get him back."

"You are," Jayden said wryly.

"I know that," Aspen cried. "But that doesn't mean I want the whole world to know it."

Jayden rolled his eyes and turned to Harper, who was watching the two of them with interest. "Sweetie, Jay's right," Harper said in her most soothing tone. "This has to come from you. You're the one who bakes the cakes, you have to be the one to issue the challenge."

Aspen threw her head back and groaned. It was one thing to man up and share her desperation with her friends. It was another to announce it to the entire internet. She blew out a breath. "This is going to be harder than I thought," she admitted softly.

Harper stepped up and gave Aspen a tight squeeze. "If anyone can do this, it's you," she said softly. "You're amazing, and if Austin really feels for you the way you think he does...then we're about to witness a fairy tale come true."

Aspen rubbed her throbbing forehead. Her stress levels had been exceptionally high lately and she didn't see that changing any time soon. "Let's just hope my gut doesn't let me down."

"It won't," Jayden said, readjusting his camera. "Aspen, I'm your cousin. I'm supposed to drive you crazy and push you to do stupid stuff."

"Hey!" Aspen cried, giving him a look. "Not helping."

He grinned. "See? I'm excellent at this job."

Harper held up a hand to stop the approaching fight. "Enough," she said in her soft voice. "Aspen. You know why this needs to be you. You're trying to catch his attention. Use the strength of the media to pull him back and then don't listen to the naysayers who only want drama. We're already giving them drama. They can take what we have or they can look somewhere else, but the point is we're trying to catch his attention and if he loves you, then he won't be able to not watch and his followers won't let him not come." She clapped her hands. "It's a match made in foodie heaven."

Aspen laughed softly. "I didn't realize you were such a cheerleader."

Harper shivered dramatically. "Ugh. Don't call me one of those. I won't wear a short skirt for anyone, but I also won't let my best friend let go of the man she loves just because he's convinced he's not good enough." She shook her head. "'That's just dumb and I kinda wanna give him a talking to for not giving you a chance to respond."

Aspen pursed her lips and nodded. "Me too."

"And on that note, let's get this thing recorded," Jayden interrupted. He held up the camera. "Ready?"

Aspen closed her eyes and took in a deep breath. She filled her chest, threw back her shoulders and opened her eyes. "Ready."

"On three..two...one... Go!"

Aspen smiled. "Hello, Eat It Austin. Long time no see." She paused, knowing watchers would find the joke funny. "For those who don't remember me, I'm Aspen Harrison, daughter of renowned chocolate sculptor Antony Harrison. My sisters and I just renovated and reopened his bakery, with my own personal creations." She leaned in, hoping she looked conspiratorial. "Creations that I come up with on my own, inspired by the lives of my friends and family...and love interests."

Here we go.

"Austin...I have a bone to pick with you." Aspen straightened. "While you were in town, most everyone knows that we spent some time together, dating, eating..." She grinned. "And I don't think anyone missed that kiss where your cake fell on the floor." She gave another pause, waiting until Harper had stopped snickering. "You were in town because I issued the Goldilocks challenge. You found our furniture offensive and wrote a rude review about it." Aspen put her hands on her hips. "Now that you and I are no longer dating, I wanted to share something I found offensive about you."

Jayden's grin was so wide, Aspen was afraid it would split his face, but even as her cousin enjoyed this, Aspen was sweating bullets. She wasn't one to back down from a challenge, but for the second time in a couple of months, she wasn't just standing up to a challenge, she was issuing them and it terrified her. Almost as much as not living up to her father's expectations did.

But this time, it wasn't her business on the line, it was her heart and that brought with it a whole new set of rules and risks.

"I discovered while you were here that you...Mr. I Eat Everything...cannot cook." Aspen put her palms in the air. "You go around critiquing others' cooking but can't do it yourself." Aspen slowly shook her head and tsked her tongue. "So...in the interest of keeping things fair, I've got another challenge for you."

Dramatic pause...wait for it...wait for it...

"I dare you to bake a cake. You obviously found me and mine lacking, so I want to see you cook your own." She grinned coyly. "Even after the Goldilocks Game, your choice in furniture is questionable, so let's see what people think about your ability to put flavors together." She clasped her hands. "You put a cake together and I'll put one together. A panel of independent judges will eat them anonymously and determine a winner." She pushed her grin to become a full fledged smile. "May the best connoisseur win."

Jayden held up a countdown with his fingers, then punched a button. "And that's a wrap." He laughed. "I don't even think we need a second take, Aspen. You're a natural."

Aspen wiped at her sweaty forehead. "Please don't ever ask me to do that again."

Harper gave her another hug and Aspen melted into the warm embrace. Her friend was small, but fierce. "There's no way he can ignore that," Harper said, holding Aspen at arm's length. "Not to mention you were a total temptress!"

"Oh my gosh, stop," Aspen said, though she smiled through the scolding. She certainly hoped Austin felt the same way. She wanted him to see what he'd left behind, but didn't want to come across as a stalker.

"I think it was great," Jayden agreed. "Coy, tempting, but challenging all the same. His followers will totally eat it up and I didn't think you sounded like this was all a ploy to get him to talk to you."

Aspen's shoulders deflated. "Good. Because that would be the worst."

Harper patted her shoulder. "None of us think you're desperate."

"Thanks, but it's the public I'm worried about."

"And it's a worthy thing to worry about," Jayden said under his breath as he worked with the camera. "But I think we can make this work." He looked up. "There'll be a few who say rude things, but for the most part everyone will just be circling for blood, and a challenge from an ex will bring that. So, no worries."

Aspen rubbed her forehead again. "I just don't want to see it."

"Maeve and I will keep an eye on things," Harper assured her. "And the rest of the gang is keeping an eye out as well. Plus, they'll help set it all up when he accepts the challenge."

Aspen smiled despite her headache. "You guys are the best."

"I know," Jayden said easily. He winked and blew a kiss to his cousin. "I'm gonna go see Maeve and get this taken care of. Good luck!"

Aspen swallowed. She was definitely going to need it.

"EDWARDS!"

Austin jerked upright. He wiped at his mouth, making sure there was no drool moving down his chin. He'd fallen asleep...again. He rubbed his face, trying to remember what had woken him up. If only he could get Aspen's sad eyes out of his mind, he might be able to sleep through the night.

"EDWARDS! NOW!"

Austin jumped to his feet. "Coming." What in the world could his boss be upset about now? Tye had rewritten the review, they'd turned it in and though Stan had huffed about it being too nice, it had gone over okay with their followers. Austin's mother was currently in rehab and on twenty-four-seven watch since she was considered a flight risk, but that meant no more unannounced trips to the office.

In the last forty-eight hours, life had calmed down considerably, though Austin himself still hadn't recovered. Stan should have been ecstatic though. As far as he knew, everything was back to normal.

Austin walked into his boss's office and shut the door behind him.

"Have a seat," Stan huffed, throwing a hand toward the chair.

Austin slumped into it. He really needed to get a good night's sleep. His body was trying to shut down on him at all hours of the day. It gave him a new appreciation for mothers of newborns. They probably felt exactly like him, minus the broken heart part.

Stan chortled happily and Austin's eyes darted up to meet his. "Have you been on the site today?"

Austin shook his head, then froze and waited until the spinning stopped. He rubbed his temples. "No. I was looking up restaurants this morning." Sometimes if their schedule was slow, he would send invitations for reviews to new places. Right now he had a ten day gap. It was the perfect excuse for him to throw himself into the work.

Stan leaned back in his seat, looking a little too pleased with himself. "Well, it looks like you're headed back to Seagull Cove, or whatever the heck that tiny place is called."

Austin stiffened. "Excuse me?"

Leaning forward, Stan spun his monitor around. "Take a look for yourself."

A still of Aspen was on the screen and Austin felt as if all the air had been sucked from his lungs. Even in the grainy shot, she was stunning. He could still feel her soft fingers in his, running through his hair and giving him all sorts of feelings that he had no business feeling. The sweet taste of sugar hit his tongue as if he were in a Pavlov experiment. Aspen Harrison would always mean dessert to him, in more ways than one.

Stan clicked a button and her voice came bursting out of the speakers. The longer she spoke, the more Austin's eyes widened and his heart threatened to burst from his chest.

"I have a challenge for you..."

Finally, *finally*, the video ended. Austin couldn't take his eyes away. What in the world was this? Why was she pushing him so hard? It had taken every bit of strength he had to cut off ties from her. She was supposed to be mad at him. She was supposed to hate him for lying and despise him for his weakness. And yet here she was, using every tool in her disposal to pull him back.

Could she possibly still have feelings for me?

The thought hurt and soothed at the same time. Taking action on it could lead to the best reward ever...or the worst heartache ever.

"Are you listening to me?"

Stan's snapping words caught Austin off guard and pulled him from his daydreaming. "Excuse me," Austin said, clearing his throat. "I didn't hear you."

Stan rolled his eyes. "I said, I want you to go down there and do the baking thing." One side of his lip curled. "The whole of social media following this, it went viral within two hours. There's no way we're missing this publicity."

"You actually want me to cook?" Austin shouted.

Stan pierced him with his nearly black gaze. "Are you refusing to go?"

Austin swallowed. Things might have calmed down, but that didn't mean he wanted to lose his job. "Not necessarily, but can't we respond a different way? Why are we letting her dictate all the terms?" His leg began to bounce. The idea of facing Aspen again was tearing him apart. He could barely breathe. Did she, or did she not, hate him? Was she calling him back to humiliate him? Or did she want to reconcile? Maybe she just wanted the last word? Maybe he should have listened to her messages. It would have given him a clue as to her thoughts.

Aargh! Why was it all so complicated? And why did she have to get Stan involved? Nobody needed him sniffing around when Austin's entire future was on the line.

"Need I remind you that in the case of your career, I hold all the cards?" Stan sneered.

The usual flash of anger began to burn inside of Austin. He was so *tired* of being treated this way. Why couldn't he just say *to heck with it* and walk away? Why did he have to be so afraid of losing his job? His stability?

What about losing Aspen?

He closed his eyes. If she hadn't been turned off by his secrets, she probably hated him now. He had put his job and his precious food supply ahead of her. No woman deserved that. He didn't deserve her and he couldn't let himself hope that she wanted anything other than to bring him to his knees. He knew how feisty she was. She had already called him out once, and now she was doing it again. The first time she had sparked a flame that had nearly consumed them both. This time, Austin was worried the flame was so cold that it would freeze him in place.

"Get out a response this afternoon," Stan continued, completely oblivious to Austin's inner turmoil. "Plan on leaving tomorrow. And take Tye along. We need every bit of this recorded."

Austin stood without saying a word. He was just a pawn here anyway. His thoughts wouldn't matter. Stan had no idea that he was sending Austin to his ultimate demise.

No matter how many cameras they had on the dog and pony show coming up, Austin knew it was the invisible show that would be the most lasting. Aspen's little stunt would give her another boost in sales and they'd be the talk of the town for another few weeks. But his heart? His life? Whatever damage this trip inflicted would be permanent.

And he hated that he deserved it all.

CHAPTER 26

Aspen was sure she was going to pass out. Austin's page had posted a reply to her video within hours and today was the day they were going to film the competition. She couldn't believe she had let Ethan and the rest of her friends talk her into this. It was far worse than when they'd held the Goldilocks Game.

"Okay," Harper said, stepping back and sweeping a critical eye around the kitchen. "It looks perfect." She checked her cell phone. "Oh my goodness, he should be here within a half hour." She blew out a breath. "We barely made it."

Aspen's eyes widened at her announcement and she squatted down, trying to catch her breath. "I...think...I'm...hyperventilating." She gasped, her hand fluttering to her throat.

"Aspen," Harper said firmly, kneeling in front of her friend. "Sweetie." She pulled Aspen's face up, Harper's blue eyes flashing with determination. "You're better than this. You've got to pull yourself together and show the world who you are. If Austin loves you, this will open the door to your happy ever after. If he doesn't, then this will be a harsh lesson, but good for business." She smiled, though it didn't quite reach her eyes. "Either way, you come out a winner."

Aspen forced her lungs to move, sucking in air and pushing it back out. At first, the movement was painful, but she kept at it and each breath became a little easier and a little more relaxing. "You're right," she finally managed. "At least this way, I'll know the truth, instead of being left hanging."

Harper smiled for real this time. "That's my girl." She took Aspen's elbows and together they rose from the floor. "Besides," Harper said with a wink, "you're going to run circles around him in here."

Aspen laughed softly. "You do realize we're setting him up for humiliation? The chairs were supposed to do that, but instead he turned it around and it became a viral sensation. This time, we targeted something he can't get out of by being charming."

"All the more reason for him to beg your forgiveness," Harper called out over her shoulder. "If he's good, he might be able to get out of making a cake by getting back together with you."

"I don't want him to confess his feelings just to get out of baking a cake," Aspen grumbled.

"Grow up," Maeve hollered from the office. "And stop complaining. It's getting on my nerves."

Aspen blew out a breath and sent a prayer heavenward that she wouldn't say anything rude to her sister. "Sorry. I'm just nervous and I'm letting it out through my mouth."

Jayden had just stepped through the door and chuckled at her comments. "Best to get it out now," he said with a grin. "Because lover boy has arrived."

Aspen's lungs ceased again, but when Maeve cleared her throat, Aspen forced the fear down. She'd never played such difficult odds before. Her hope that Austin felt the same about her was just that...hope. The way their last conversation had ended had been so difficult and sad and incomplete, there just had to be more than she knew.

It was his silence after that that was giving her doubt though. Why wouldn't he talk to her? Why not be willing to hear what she had to say? Why not let her form her own opinions instead of deciding how she should react?

It was those questions that left her unsure of how today was going to go. It could end up being wonderful or a complete disaster.

But at least it'll be good publicity.

The words were ridiculous, but they helped lift Aspen's spirits just a touch. Harper always had been good at finding silver linings.

"Come on back, Mr. Edwards," Jayden said with a flourish.

Aspen stiffened her muscles just in time to keep her knees from buckling and sending her to the floor. Austin's face was like a punch to the gut. He looked, in a word, exhausted. Dark circles were under his eyes and his skin was paler than before. They had only been separated for two weeks, but it had obviously taken a toll on the food reviewer.

"Aspen," he breathed, coming to a halt in the kitchen. His green eyes softened and looked her up and down like a loving caress.

"Austin," she said carefully, keeping her tone neutral. It was too soon to hope she was detecting warmth in his tone. "Thank you so much for coming."

Austin glanced over his shoulder as someone spoke from behind and he nodded, stepping farther into the kitchen. Tye stumbled in behind him. "You remember my brother...Tye?"

Aspen nodded and smiled tightly. "Hello, Tye. Welcome back to Seagull Cove."

Tye waved and stuffed his free hand in his pocket. His other hand was holding onto a case she assumed held a camera.

Austin walked a little farther inside, his eyes surveying the space. He whistled low. "You guys went all out. It looks great in here."

Aspen nodded to her friend waiting in the corner. "Harper is an artist. She set everything up so it was easy to record and easy to look at as well." Aspen shrugged and gave a sheepish grin. "It's less efficient, but more viewer friendly."

Austin shook his head. "I doubt that'll change the outcome of this little shindig." He chuckled low. "We both know I have no chance of beating you."

She shrugged again. "You never know. The judges might prefer simpler. Not everyone enjoys unique combos."

His face grew serious and he took a step closer. "I did," he said softly.

Her bravado fled and hope fluttered like a newborn bird in her chest. "Then why did you leave?"

"You know what?" Harper called out, clapping her hands. "I think Jayden and Tye should have a little chat about what all they want to record." Her smile was wide as she began pushing everyone but Austin and Aspen out of the kitchen. "We'll just go have a meeting in here and you two figure out when you're going to be ready to start, okay? Okay."

It took less than ten seconds for them to be alone in the kitchen and Aspen felt slightly shell shocked. She wasn't sure whether she should strangle Harper or hug her. But still...the woman knew how to get things done.

Austin laughed again. "I take it we're supposed to address the...elephant...or should I say cake...in the room?"

Aspen put her fists on her hips. "We don't *have* to address anything," she said boldly. "But I think we'd both feel better if we did."

Austin stared at her, his eyes wounded as if he was afraid of the outcome of this meeting.

Me too, buddy. Me too.

"You're right," he agreed. "It's time."

"Then let's start with the question already sitting between us," Aspen pressed. "Why did you leave?"

He took two breaths before responding. "Because I couldn't stand to see your reaction."

She frowned. "My reaction to what? The fact that Tye is a writer and you have dyslexia?" Aspen stepped back. "You really think that would matter to me?"

"Doesn't it?" Austin challenged. "Can you really say that you're not put off by the fact that I lie to the public every day? That I can't read a recipe to save my life? That I've allowed my need for security to overrun my need to live an honest life?"

Slowly, Aspen nodded. "You're right. It does bother me."

He blew out a breath and stepped back as if he'd been hit.

Aspen held up a hand. "But not in the way you think."

AUSTIN WAS HAVING A hard time breathing. Despite his best efforts, he had truly hoped that the competition hadn't really been about another publicity boost. That it had been Aspen's way of getting his attention and trying to work things out between them.

But the answer she had just given him blew out those hopes like a birthday candle. Still, he felt he owed it to her to hear her out. It wasn't like he could simply walk away again. If he went back to Portland before getting this video, Stan really would fire him.

Aspen's mouth opened and closed a few times before she seemed to gain the courage to speak. "I don't like being lied to," she said softly. "But I understand that you were keeping secrets that you felt were dangerous for people to know about." Her shoulders slumped. "No one can fault you for wanting to protect your family. Heaven knows I've done enough of that myself." She splayed her hands to the side. "After all, outside of myself and my cousins, you're the only person who knows about my dad."

Austin swallowed hard, then nodded. His hope was starting to try to reignite, but he held it back. She wasn't done yet.

"We haven't exactly *lied*, but we've certainly omitted certain truths in order to maintain privacy and keep my dad's reputation intact." She sighed. "So I understand what it's like to not want to share."

"But you did share," Austin said softly. His hands clenched and unclenched by his side. His dream woman was right in front of him and if they weren't having such a serious conversation, he would pull her into his chest and never let her go. He didn't have that right, though he wanted it. But first, they had to get past all the hard truths in front of them. "You eventually trusted me enough to share."

"And you did too."

Austin shook his head. "No, Tye just had a panic attack and shared it all."

"Are you telling me that you would have continued to have a relationship with me and hope I just ever noticed that you couldn't read or write?" She tilted her head in a beguiling manner and pinned him with a glare.

In for a penny... "Truth is, our relationship wasn't supposed to last."

Aspen blinked and she paled slightly. "What do you mean?"

"I've...never allowed myself to get close to a woman," Austin said quietly. This was going to hurt, but if there was even the slightest amount of hope for anything between them, she needed to know it all. "You were...intriguing to say the least." He laughed darkly and dropped his gaze to the floor. "I'm not exactly a playboy, but I certainly have had my share of first dates." He looked back up at her reaction, which was unreadable at the moment. "You were beautiful, sassy and didn't back down when challenged." He shrugged. "I wanted to get to know you. I thought I'd have fun for a week and then go back to my life with a couple of enjoyable memories."

"So I was supposed to be a passing fancy," she said in a barely audible tone.

He hesitated, but finally nodded. "Yes." The word was like slivers in his throat. It physically pained him to say it. He was such a selfish jerk. He had always thought he was doing women a favor by not getting too close. After all, who would want to be saddled with someone like him? A boy from the streets with a compulsion to buy food, who couldn't read or write any better than an elementary student?

But now he realized that it wasn't a courtesy, it was selfish. It was cowardice. It was nothing but a way to protect himself. And it shamed him to think of it.

He watched the emotions play over her face, her eyes moving around as if watching a movie. Pain, anger, betrayal, longing and finally...something unexpected. Determination.

Clearing her throat, Aspen stuck her chin in the air. "If I ask you a question, will you be completely honest with me?"

He nodded immediately. "I'm doing that now. That's why I shared that with you."

Aspen nodded regally. "Then, I want to know how you felt by the last day we were together." She took a step toward him. "Before our little tiff at dinner. Before Tye came and spilled the beans. Before you left."

By now, she was only inches from him, looking up with her chocolate gaze so fierce he couldn't pull away even if he wanted to.

"How did you feel?" she whispered.

His muscles twitched, his body coiled. Austin wasn't sure how she was going to react when he told her everything, but she had asked and he had promised.

"Scared."

Her brows pulled together and disappointment flashed through her dark eyes. "You were scared? Why?"

"Because for the first time ever, I didn't want to walk away." He couldn't stop himself anymore. His hands moved without his permission, slowly reaching until he felt her fingertips and he rejoiced at the softness of her skin. "For the first time ever, I considered trying to make it work."

He slid his touch up her hand and arm, feeling but not seeing the goosebumps on her skin. Her eyes grew softer and softer the farther his hands went.

"For the first time ever, I wanted to tell someone my past, my burdens...my truth."

He'd reached her neck and he could feel the rapid pace of her pulse. It was just as fast as his and he was sure that if he took the time, he'd find that their hearts were beating in sync.

"For the first time ever," he whispered as his hands framed her face, "I fell in love."

Her eyes flared and her hands shot to his shirt, gripping it tightly. "You love me?" she asked hoarsely. "Then why did you leave?"

Austin nodded slowly. "These last couple of weeks have been a living purgatory," he responded. "But I couldn't stay and see your disgust when you discovered who and what I was. So, I left. I convinced myself it was better that way. That it saved you from me. That you deserved better. That I was the only one hurting. That you would never forgive me for lying to you."

Aspen's head was shaking. "You...are an idiot," she said with a small, teary smile.

He chuckled. "I was hoping that this invitation to bake was actually your way of asking me to be *your* idiot."

Her smile grew. "It was. After you left, I felt as if my heart had been torn in two. But you wouldn't answer my calls."

He dropped his forehead to hers. "I know. Again...I was running on fear." He sighed. "I'm so far from perfect, Aspen, it's actually quite funny, but I've learned a lot about myself these last couple of weeks, and not all of it is pretty." His thumbs began to trace her cheekbones. "But I've also realized how much I want things to change. How *I* want to change." He took in a fortifying breath, enjoying the sweet, familiar scent of her kitchen. "If you would be willing to forgive me, I can't promise to never do something stupid, but I can promise that I'll never simply walk away again, and that I'll never hide anything from you..." He smiled. "Unless it's a surprise for your birthday or Christmas."

A girlish giggle escaped and the sound went a long way into lightening the situation. "If you can promise that, then I can easily forgive," she responded, her voice thick with emotion. "But what I won't forgive is if you don't kiss me right now. Because if you don't take advantage of this moment, you really are an id—"

There was no need to have her finish that sentence. He might actually be an idiot, but he was an idiot willing to learn. And he was determined to be a star pupil.

CHAPTER 27

"**K**nock, knock!" Jayden's voice interrupted their moment much earlier than Aspen was ready to be interrupted.

She reluctantly pulled back and smiled at the sour look on Austin's face. Apparently, he felt the same way. "Yeah?" Aspen called over her shoulder. "We're here."

Jayden's head came in from the front. "But are you decent?"

"Jay!" Aspen scolded. She turned and put her hands on her hips. "What did you think was going on in here?"

Jayden pumped his eyebrows. "I don't think I should say."

Aspen glared even as Austin chuckled.

"I hate to be the bearer of bad news, but if you two are done making up, we need to get set up. Recording needs to start in about ten minutes."

Aspen hung her head. She didn't want to do this. She didn't enjoy making these videos and now that her goal had been accomplished and she and Austin were back together, she wanted to leave the social media aspect behind. "Do we have to?" she asked, scrunching up her nose. She squeaked and jumped when Austin wrapped his arms around her from behind.

"I'm the one being made fun of in this challenge," he whispered in her ear. "You have nothing to worry about. "You just be your normal creative self."

She sighed. "Fine." Aspen stepped out of his arms. She wouldn't be able to concentrate at all if he kept touching her. She threw her shoulders back. "Let's get this over with."

"You make it sound like a prison sentence," Austin said with a grin as the room filled with their crews. "The fact of the matter is, you invited me. Why do it if you didn't want to create the video?"

Aspen gave him a look. "Do you really have to ask?"

He leaned in and kissed her forehead. "I love you," he whispered for her ears only.

"And I love you," she whispered back, closing her eyes and enjoying the sensation of his lips against her skin.

His smile was playful as he looked down. "Then let's bake."

Aspen couldn't help but smile back. "Okay."

"We're on in five, people," Jayden hollered. "Positions."

"What ingredients do you need?" Harper asked in a rush, looking slightly frantic.

"I have all my things," Aspen responded. "Austin?"

He was unloading a bag that Tye handed him. "I didn't bring butter or milk. Can I borrow some of yours?"

"Of course." Harper scurried across the room. "Aspen, you need to fix your hair!" she called over her shoulder.

"Yeah...sorry about that," Austin said with a wink. "That might be my fault."

Aspen put up her hands. "I can't see it!"

"On it." Maeve came over and did a little adjusting. "Perfect. Okay...I'm out." She hurried behind Jayden and put her thumbs up.

"Where's Estelle?" Austin asked as he finished his set up.

"She's in Italy," Aspen said off handedly, then paused. *He doesn't know.* She turned to him. "I'll have to tell you about it later."

Austin studied her serious expression and nodded. "I look forward to hearing it."

Aspen released her breath. He had been fairly dismissive before, as if afraid to get involved in her life, but with their current confessions, she had every hope that things would be different between them.

"Thirty seconds!"

Panic hit Aspen's lungs and she struggled to breathe. She really hated being on camera. *If you're going to date Austin, then you better get used to it.*

"Remember, this is only the introduction," Jayden said quickly, Tye right beside him with his own camera. "We're going to get started live, then cut out until the end with the judges." He shrugged. "I doubt everyone will want to watch cakes rising in the oven."

"You'd be surprised," Austin muttered under his breath.

Aspen snorted.

"And three, two, one!" Jayden pointed a finger at Aspen.

"Hello!" Aspen said in what she hoped was a cheery tone. "This is Aspen Harrison, part owner and baker at Three Sisters Cafe. I'm here with Eat It Austin." She turned to acknowledge her cohort.

Austin waved. "Thanks so much for joining us today." He grinned. "I know how many of you are eager to see me make a fool of myself, so..."

Aspen laughed lightly. "I have to admit I was surprised you accepted the challenge. How much experience do you have in the kitchen?"

Austin scrunched his nose. "I learned how to make Top Ramen as a kid. Does that count?"

Laughter rang through the room. "It's not quite baking, but we'll put it on your resume," Aspen responded. She turned back to the camera, feeling a little more at ease. Austin was so relaxed and easy to banter with. It was helping soften her nerves with each moment. "Should we get started?" Aspen asked him.

Austin nodded. "And don't worry," he said to the camera. "We know watching us live the whole time would be boring, but we'll be sure to check in over the next couple of hours to give updates. We have a two hour time limit and the judging will be immediately following. If you just want to see the results, that's the video you want to keep an eye out for."

Aspen nodded. "Right. So for now, we'll say 'see ya later' and we'll check in in thirty minutes." She waved. "See you then!"

Jayden held up his hand, then clenched his fist. "Awesome." He fiddled with his camera. "That was a great start."

Tye nodded, his eyes on his camera as well. "There was a good chunk of viewers during that first clip. I'll get the replay uploaded and we'll take it from there." He glanced up, then immediately dropped his eyes again.

Aspen walked toward him, knowing she needed to clear the air with him as much as she had with Austin. "Tye?" she asked softly, trying not to spook him.

He kept his face down and looked up from under his lashes.

"I'm sorry things got so out of hand that night," she said careful-ly. "Can you forgive me?"

Tye's face fell. "I think that's my line," he whispered.

Aspen smiled. It grew when Austin's hand landed on her low back. "I'm ready to let it go if you are."

Tye gave her a shy smile, then stuck out his hand. "Deal."

Aspen shook it, then turned around. "Come on, Eat Everything Man. We have work to do."

WELL...IT WASN'T PRETTY, but it was finished. Austin stood back to look at his cake. It was slightly uneven, the frosting could have been done by a five year old in art class and the color was not quite as vibrant as he'd wished, but...he'd done it.

He leaned in, smelling the cake. "It smells okay," he declared to the room.

"Good thing," Tye muttered, eyeing the finished product. "At least you'll have one thing going for you."

Austin jerked forward, pretending to go after his brother, but they both broke into laughter. "You make one and then we'll see whose is better."

Tye put his hand in the air. "As long as you didn't mix up the salt and the sugar, I'm calling it a win."

Austin nodded. "Yeah...I'm hoping that too."

The door from the front opened. "You two ready?" Jayden asked. He looked at the cake. "Looks finished to me."

Austin had to give Aspen's cousin credit for being nice about it. He nodded. "Yep. Should we do a reveal, then cut the slices?"

Jayden nodded and came in the rest of the way. "That's the plan." He moved aside as Aspen, Maeve and Harper all filed in as well.

Aspen's face lit up. "You did it! And you thought you couldn't follow a recipe."

He was grateful she used the word *follow* instead of *read*. Being honest with her didn't mean he was ready to announce his flaws to the whole world. "Let's just hope I don't poison any judges by the end of the day," Austin joked.

Aspen smiled and shook her head. "I doubt it." She stood beside him, bringing her own stunning creation next to his. "Ready for another video?"

"If you are." He made a face. "Do we have to have them next to each other though? Yours makes mine look bad."

"It has nothing to do with hers," Maeve teased.

"Maeve!" Aspen scolded.

"No, no...she's right." Austin gave a dramatic sigh. "I knew this was coming. Humiliation at the hands of the woman I love. Every man experiences it before too long."

"Too bad I didn't get that on camera," Jayden responded. "It would have definitely gone viral and the ladies would have eaten it up."

"You two are ridiculous," Aspen grumbled.

Austin laughed and kissed her temple. "Let's get the cameras rolling. We're almost done here, and then I can spend the evening doing everything I missed while I was away."

She gave him a coy smile. "Sounds like a plan to me."

"In three...two...one!" Jayden gave them the signal and Austin found he didn't have to pretend to be happy for the camera. "Welcome back, everyone! We've reached the end of our little baking bonanza and are ready to show you the finished product." He splayed his hands in front of the cake. "Behold, the Big Blue."

Jayden and Tye both carefully moved around, getting the cake from multiple angles.

"I went with classic flavors. Chocolate and mint." Picking up a large knife, Austin cut a slice, showing the chocolate inside. "I know green should have been mint, but..." He winked. "Blue is my favorite color, so I broke the mold, so to speak." After nearly dropping the piece, he finally made it to the place, then turned to Aspen. "How about you, Miss Harrison?"

Aspen's eyes twinkled with happiness and Austin knew he would never get tired of the sight. How had he gone so long without her at his side? Being apart in the coming days was going to be absolute torture.

"Thank you, Mr. Edwards," Aspen said sweetly. She then gestured grandly to her own cake. "I also went with chocolate today, but I added a little...something extra." She winked, making Austin grin.

As much as she said she hated the camera, the woman knew how to command an audience.

"I'm a fan of citrus and I used orange emulsion in my cakes with orange zest in the frosting." She cut a slice and expertly placed it on a plate. Holding it up for the camera, she smiled widely. "May the best baker win!"

Jayden cut them off. "Okay, you two have a seat and we'll take these out to the judges, then record the tasting."

"Wait...we don't get to watch that?" Austin asked, dumbfounded. He had thought they would all be together.

"No room for influence," Jayden said easily. He grabbed a plate. "Maeve? You bring the other. Tye, you and I will set up across the room."

They all left, the room suddenly feeling spacious and quiet with them gone. Austin slowly turned to Aspen. "Well, Miss Harrison. What do you suggest we do to pass the time?" He reached out and slowly pulled her into his chest.

Her smile nearly split her face as she allowed herself to be brought closer. "I don't know, but I'm sure between the two of us, we can figure it out."

Austin's head was just dropping when a loud noise came from the front. Both of their heads jerked toward the sound. "That didn't sound good."

"Is someone trying to arm wrestle the judges?" Aspen laughed. She pulled away and walked to the door.

Austin lunged forward to catch up and peered over her shoulder as she pulled it open.

"I want EVERYONE to know!" a voice screamed. "LET GO OF ME!"

"What in the world?" Aspen muttered, pulling the door farther open.

"That stupid boy can't read a lick! Dumbest thing you ever saw!" More scuffling sounds followed the shouting.

Austin stood rooted to the spot as Aspen walked into the front room. He knew that voice...a little too well. How had this happened? Had he done something in a past life to earn this twist of fate? Just as he thought everything was falling into place, Austin's entire life was broken in one fell swoop.

"AUSTIN!" Tye shouted.

Slowly, Austin walked into the front room, the blood draining from his head as he surveyed the damage his mother was causing. Aspen would never forgive him for this. Chairs and tables were upended, cake with blue frosting and Aspen's lovely white frosting were smeared on every visible surface. "Mom," he said softly. Too softly to get her attention. He cleared his throat and tried again. "Mom!"

Her stringy hair flew as she turned his way. "THERE HE IS!" She managed to free her hand. Her eyes were bloodshot and wild, her skin covered in dirt and her fingers shaking.

Austin didn't know what she had taken, but it was clear she wasn't in her right mind. He was also curious as to how she had escaped the rehab center he had put her in. His act of charity was coming back to kick him in the butt. Why couldn't he simply write her off? He wanted to say that next time he would leave her to die on the streets, but he couldn't do it. Aspen had warmed up the hole in his chest and he had discovered there was no going back to being the oblivious person he had been before.

And if he was being honest, he didn't want to.

He turned to Jayden, who was protecting the cameras. Neither was running anymore, as Tye and others, whom Austin assumed were the judges, tried to pin down the mad woman. "How much got on the feed?"

Jayden winced, his eyes darting between the chaos and Austin. "Enough," he admitted.

Loud sobbing broke out and Austin turned to see that his mother had finally given up, collapsing in a heap on the ground and crying uncontrollably.

"Maeve, would you please contact the police?" Austin said softly. "She'll need to be transferred to the closest hospital and then a rehab ward."

Maeve nodded and scurried from the room, looking grateful to have a job away from the chaos.

Austin turned to Aspen and sighed. "I'm sorry. As soon as she's taken away, I have an announcement I'll need to make to the viewers." His stomach clenched. "And then I'll get out of your way."

Aspen's face slowly morphed from shock into anger. "Are you kidding me?" she screeched.

Austin jerked back, caught off guard by her vehemence.

Marching over, Aspen jabbed a finger in his sternum. "If you think for one moment that you having a crazy mother who spills all your secrets to the world is enough to drive me away, you don't know me very well." She began to sniffle. "And you should," she scolded. "I already told you I didn't care if you were dyslexic or if Tye was the writer on your team." Her voice softened, barely heard over his mother's sobbing. "All I care about is the man," she whispered, patting his chest. "But if that man doesn't stop making decisions for me...so help me, I'm gonna smash cake in his face."

Austin gathered her into his chest and squeezed her so tightly she squealed. "I don't deserve you," he whispered into her hair.

"Yeah, well...at least you recognize it," she said through her tears.

"But if you're willing to take all this on, then I'm grateful enough to let you." He pulled back. "I told you she's been an addict since I was a kid. I have no idea how long I'll be dealing with this."

"We'll be dealing with this," she corrected. "You aren't alone anymore."

Austin kissed her forehead, lingering until he was forced to let go. His life was a mess, but in this moment, everything was clear. And as soon as his mother was taken away, he was going to set things right. *All* the way, this time. It was time he came clean to more than just Aspen.

CHAPTER 28

It took just shy of an hour for the shop to calm down. Every minute that they went past their deadline, Aspen was twitching inside. They were supposed to open to the public after the judge's decision was recorded and she knew there was a large crowd outside wondering what was going on.

Especially after the police arrived.

She rubbed her forehead and did her best to calm her angst down. As hard as this was for her, she knew it was even worse for Austin. This wasn't just a disaster of a competition, it was a disaster for his family. And now the few second clip that told one of his deepest secrets was running rampant on the web.

It had been shared more than any of their other videos and in far less time. She knew he had to be hurting in a way that no one else would recognize. Right now, he was stoic, handling things with the police like a pro, as if he'd been through this before.

Aspen stilled. He probably had. He had warned her that his mother was a problem that popped up over and over again in his life. If she stayed with him, this was exactly what she would be dealing with.

Can I handle that?

She had gotten so upset when he'd tried to walk away from her, *again*. And in her anger she had told him exactly what she thought of his martyr performance. But the weight of the commitment she had given him was just now hitting her.

If she and Austin stayed together, she would be taking on his crazy fans, his struggling brother, his learning disabilities and his over the edge mother.

Closing her eyes, Aspen took in a couple of cleansing breaths. Could she do it? She wanted to. She loved Austin and wanted to be strong enough for it all, but it was hard to know if she truly had what it took.

"You look like you're thinking too hard," Harper whispered, sidling next to Aspen.

Aspen opened her eyes and gave her friend a sad smile. "I think the adrenaline is finally coming down enough for me to realize what this will mean for Austin and me."

Harper blinked. "And?"

Aspen shrugged and looked at the ground. "And I'm not sure if I'm strong enough to be what he needs."

Harper waited, then snorted. "You're kidding, right?"

Aspen frowned. "No. I'm not. I want what's best for him and I'm starting to think I'm not it."

Harper glanced at the room, making sure they weren't being listened to before putting her hands on her hips. "The fact that the both of you are so willing to sacrifice yourselves for the good of the other ought to be evidence enough, but tell me, oh Great One, just what is it he needs that you don't have?"

Aspen gave her friend a look. "Harper, come on."

"No. I'm serious." Harper's face softened. "Sweetie, what he needs is someone he can count on. Someone who doesn't hold the struggles in his life against him. Someone who understands that he will give everything of himself in order to help those he loves. Someone who will help refill that bucket that he empties while he helps others." Her voice dropped. "Someone who is willing to give him what he gives to others." She smiled softly. "Any woman would be lucky to have a man willing to give so much. That kind of dedication is hard to come by."

"What if I can't refill his bucket?" Aspen asked, her eyes getting misty. "What if I'm not enough?"

"*He* says you're enough. That's all you need to know." Harper's grin grew devious and she leaned in. "Besides, from what you've shared, all you need to do is feed him cake and he'll be good to go. I think you filled his bucket just fine not too long ago."

Aspen's cheeks heated and she chuckled darkly. "You know, I thought my family's troubles were going to be the obstacle we would have to overcome, but seeing what his life is like..." She shrugged. "It makes my life seem pretty easy."

"No comparing," Harper said easily. "You both have hard things. But if he can survive what he's been through, then I think he'd make a great partner for handling what you're going through."

Aspen nodded and wiped at the corner of her eyes. "Thanks. I needed that."

Harper elbowed Aspen's side. "I know."

Aspen laughed. "So modest."

"Only when I need to be." Harper turned toward the crowd and smiled. "And now that I've done my job, I'll hand you into better hands." She stepped away and Austin took her spot.

He sighed, looking so tired that Aspen had a hard time not insisting he lay down. "Jayden and Tye are going to set up outside and I'm going to give a little...interview, I suppose." He glanced her way. "Will you come stand with me?"

This was it. This was where Aspen declared herself all in or needed to step away. It wasn't really a question, she knew what she wanted. She was simply afraid, the same way she'd been when her father had been diagnosed with a frightening disease. The real question was whether she could overcome the fear.

She slipped her fingers into his. "There's nowhere I'd rather be."

He kissed her temple, the move so sweet and tender that Aspen almost teared up again, then led her out the front door.

A large crowd was waiting for them, and murmurs began as soon as she and Austin stepped outside. Her friends had cleared a small space just in front of the doors, and that's where she and Austin waited.

Shading her eyes, she looked to Jayden, who gave her a thumbs up from behind his camera. The same came from Tye, who stood only a few feet away.

Aspen squeezed Austin's hand and looked up at him, giving him the floor.

"Thank you for joining us today," Austin said, his weariness seeping into his tone, but Aspen was so proud of him for doing this anyway. "As you can see, things didn't exactly go as planned."

An uneasy laughter ran through the group.

"But I'm glad that this all happened, because it gives me the opportunity to do something I should have done ages ago." Straightening his shoulders and sticking his chin in the air, he continued. "My name is Austin Edwards, and I have dyslexia."

FOR A STORY THAT HAD taken a lifetime to create, the telling of it lasted only ten minutes or so. Surprisingly, the crowd was dead silent, other than the occasional noise from a small child.

"I want to offer my personal apology to all my fans and supporters who are hurt by this admission," Austin said. His hold on Aspen's hand was growing tighter. He could see from the crowd that there were mixed feelings about what he was saying. Some people looked sad, some looked angry or disgusted and some looked curious. Only waiting out the online response would tell him for sure what the fallout would be. "I'm sorry that I let my own fears lead my actions, which resulted in my being less than honest with you." He waved a hand toward his brother. "If you've enjoyed any of the writing during my time as a reviewer, then you need to give credit to Tye. He's the fingers and brain behind the words and deserves all the credit for his gift with that."

Austin looked down at Aspen, who was still smiling by his side. "And I want to thank Aspen Harrison for standing by me, no matter what happened. She's been a rock, even after I walked away, feeling less than worthy since I had built my reputation on an untruth." He turned back to the crowd. "I love her and I'm thrilled to say we're back together." He squeezed her hand again. "For good this time, if I have anything to say about it." He took a deep breath. There was one last thing to do. "And finally, I'd like to thank my boss, who helped develop the Eat It Austin persona and gave us a platform to reach so many people. However, as of now, I hereby offer my resignation. Eat It Austin will be retiring."

Austin opened his mouth, then realized there was no more. He'd confessed, apologized, given credit where it was due and now, he had nothing else to offer. Snapping his mouth closed, he looked down at Aspen, raising his eyebrows, silently asking what they should do next.

Without missing a beat, Aspen turned to the crowd. "The competition cakes were ruined, but I've still got a kitchen full of treats. Who's ready to eat?" she shouted.

Almost every person watching them shouted in response, easily distracted with the thought of a good dessert.

"Thank you," Austin whispered as they led everyone back inside.

"I find that treats soften people's attitudes better than almost anything else."

"That's because you're a genius." He held open the kitchen door for her and they slipped into the quiet space.

"Can you help me carry these out?" Aspen pointed to a row of cakes that had been lined up along the back counter.

"Of course." They spent the next ten minutes transferring cakes, cookies and cupcakes from the back to the front, then Aspen forced Austin to stand behind the counter, leaving himself open to speak to people if they wanted.

His heart pounded as people worked their way through the line. He smiled politely, making eye contact, even with those who seemed unsure, but after a while, he was grateful to realize there was no outright hostility.

"Hey!"

Austin blinked and looked around until his eyes landed on a young boy, maybe ten years old. He put his hand on his chest. "Are you talking to me?"

The boy nodded. He glanced at his mom, who smiled, then turned back to Austin. "I'm dyslexic too."

The people in the immediate area quieted down and Austin walked over to the boy, bending over a little so they were closer to the same height. "Wow," Austin said softly. He held out his fist and the boy bumped it. "And how's school going for you?"

The boy shrugged. "It's hard."

Austin nodded. "It is, isn't it. Does your mom help you find ways to make it better?" He glanced up at the woman, who was still smiling.

"Yeah, but I still don't like it. My friends are better readers than me."

"Yeah...it does stink, but you know what?"

The boy shook his head.

"If you keep working hard, it'll get easier. And eventually you'll be stronger than anyone else because you didn't give up."

The boy tilted his head and studied him. "You get to eat food for a job?"

Austin chuckled. "I did. I don't know what I'm going to do now."

"I'd like to eat cake for a job too."

Austin's chuckle turned into a laugh, along with those who were listening to the conversation. "It's been a lot of fun, for sure. But you can set your sights higher than that. Being dyslexic doesn't keep you from any job you want, it just means you have to go about it a little differently."

"I also like making fires. Maybe I'll be a fireman." The boy scrunched his nose.

"Putting fires out might be a better choice than making them," Austin said, still smiling. He reached into his back pocket, pulling out his wallet. His cards were going to be meaningless by the end of the day, but it had his email address on it. "Here. You keep in touch and let me know what you decide. I'd love to hear which way you go."

The mom took the card and put it in her purse. "We'll send a report," she said, raising her eyebrows at the boy. "Right?"

The boy nodded. "Right."

"Perfect." Another fist bump ended their conversation. "Now grab some cake and keep being awesome."

Austin watched the boy, a wide smile staying with him for a good twenty minutes after the conversation. It wasn't until a warm presence slipped to his side that he finally focused on something else.

"That was great," Aspen whispered. "And I think several people were recording it."

Austin sighed. "I wasn't doing it for that."

"I know, but the more people understand why you did what you did and who you really are, the more they'll forgive you."

"You're the only one I want forgiveness from." He wrapped an arm around her shoulders and tugged her in for a quick kiss.

"We need to figure out this whole long distance thing," she said, cuddling contentedly into his side.

"Actually, now that I'm jobless..." Austin teased.

She jerked upright. "Are you serious? Would you really consider coming down here?"

He shrugged. "It would depend on if I could get a job. But I thought I might start looking in this general area." He looked down at her. "Without a job in Portland, there's nothing holding me there."

"What about your mom? Or Tye?"

"My mom will be in and out of rehab for who knows how long, provided she doesn't escape and go hitchhiking again. If I need to travel to take care of her, I will. And Tye would be happy to go where I go." Austin frowned. "It might actually be good to see if I can't get him interested in college. Maybe forcing him out of the nest a little would help him learn to stand on his own two feet."

"I'm sure we can find you something," Aspen said quickly. "I don't know if it would be something you'd enjoy though."

"We'll figure it out," Austin said, feeling confident and assured. The talk with the little boy was just what he'd needed to help lift his spirits from his very public confession. There was going to be a big backlash from this. He knew it. But not everyone was going to hate him, and that helped.

He had no idea what he was going to do next, but he knew one thing. As long as he was close to Aspen, and as long as it didn't involve relying on the public in order to eat, he was going to be okay. And the fact that Stan wouldn't have any more power to hold it all over his head...well, that didn't hurt at all either.

EPILOGUE

Harper pushed a piece of hair out of her face and studied her newest painting. It wasn't quite the type of work she normally did, but this one was special. She had been commissioned to paint a series of pictures that featured The Three Sisters Cafe signature desserts.

She was running a little behind, since Austin was picking them up this morning, but Harper hadn't been able to stop herself from adding just a little more color.

Just as she finished cleaning her brushes, there was a knock at the door. "Perfect timing," she murmured to herself as she went to answer. "Austin! Come on in." Harper opened her door wider. "I've got your pictures back in the studio."

He rubbed his hands together, grinning wildly. "I can't wait to see them."

Harper led the way to the back. It was amazing how well Austin had settled into life here in small town USA. Especially after being such a big name and living the city life for such a long time.

His brother, Tye, had moved down to Seagull Cove and had almost immediately begun to take online college classes. Last she'd heard, Tye was planning to go to college in person next fall. From her chats with Aspen, Harper knew this was a big step for the young man who struggled in large, public settings.

He'd continued his writing, however, and apparently, had been hired for several guest blog gigs, which was doing a lot to boost his confidence after people realized he was the snarky voice behind the Eat It Austin brand name.

As for Austin, he had also found a niche which fit him well. With his experience in building a brand, he had opened an online marketing business, building websites and promoting certain brands. It still required reading and writing, but not so much that he couldn't manage it with a little help.

He was now doing all the marketing for The Three Sisters Cafe, leaving Estelle more time to focus on decoration on the treats and more wedding cake work, which had made her happy as well as giving Austin the start he needed to get his business off the ground. Estelle had gratefully shifted her position after arriving home from Italy. Her father had been on the mend when she'd finally come home and the Harrison women were awaiting word that their parents were ready to come home.

The only downside to the story had been Austin's mom. She had been taken back to the rehab center in Portland, only to once again disappear. This time, however, she hadn't resurfaced. Aspen had confided in Harper that Austin had hired a private investigator to find her, but so far, she was staying out of the limelight.

For all they knew, she could have passed on the street, marked as a Jane Doe, but Harper knew that Austin would keep looking until he had answers.

"Here we are," she announced, opening her studio door and breaking her line of thoughts. The winter had been busy and crazy as everyone had settled into their new roles and their little group of friends had welcomed Austin into their midst. But, Harper was getting anxious for the beauty of spring and the outside art festivals that would help her get into the sunshine and enjoy interacting with the public again.

Being an artist was a solitary life, which she didn't mind most of the time, but the last couple of years, she had found herself growing restless. It more than likely had to do with the fact that she couldn't seem to shake a crush on one stoic and as equally solitary lumberjack.

At least at the festivals, I can watch him do his live carving.

Other than when their friends gathered for game nights or to try one of Aspen's new desserts, she rarely had occasion to see the handsome Mason. But during the spring and summer, their schedules ran very similarly since he did log carving at live demonstrations at many of the celebrations.

No wonder she was looking forward to the coming season. *Even if he doesn't even notice you're there.*

"Harper, they're perfect," Austin said with a smile.

He really had a nice smile. Aspen was so lucky. She was loved and adored by a great guy. Jealousy tried to rear its ugly head, but Harper pushed it back. It was no one's fault that Mason didn't give her the time of day. It wasn't worth being upset at her friend's happiness because of it. Not to mention, it wasn't like Aspen and Austin's road to love had been an easy one.

"Do you have your part ready?" Harper asked.

Austin nodded. "It's in the car." He scrunched his nose. "Tye helped me write it, but it's ready."

"Awesome." She gathered up her canvases. "Let's get going."

It took no time at all for them to arrive at the cafe. Estelle let them inside. It was a Sunday afternoon, which meant they were closed to the public and it was the perfect time to set up a surprise for Aspen.

A half hour later, everything was in place and Austin was calling Aspen. "Hey, babe. Can you come down to the shop for a minute? I have an idea."

Harper held her breath, then relaxed when Austin gave them all the thumbs up.

"We don't have to leave completely, do we?" Estelle asked, raising her shoulders to her ears. "I was hoping to record this for Mom and Dad."

Austin pinched his lips between his teeth. "Do you mind doing it from the back corner, maybe? I'd like to keep her focus out here."

"Of course!" Estelle grabbed Harper's hand and with Maeve trailing behind, the girls made themselves as unobtrusive as possible in the back.

It only took a few minutes for Aspen to arrive. Short commutes was one of the perks of living in a small town and Harper's heart leapt up to her throat. She was so excited for her best friend. They had dreamed of this day since they were little girls and it was wonderful that it was finally happening.

"Austin?" Aspen called as she pushed open the front door. She gasped and came to a halt when she saw the wall. "What's this?"

Austin stood in front of the latest decorations. They had displayed them on the wall around the leopard print sofa, which everyone referred to as the A's Place. He held out his hands and Aspen slowly walked his way, taking in the pictures.

"Did Harper paint those?" Aspen asked. "They're beautiful."

Austin still didn't speak, instead guiding her to sit down. Once Aspen was seated, Austin knelt down on one knee, eliciting another gasp.

Harper clasped Estelle's hand, then forced herself to let go, so she wouldn't ruin the video. This was so exciting!

"Aspen Marguerite Harrison," Austin said carefully. "We both know I'm not much of a reader or writer, but I've spent my life hiding behind other people's words and I wanted to present myself to you with nothing in between us. No fans, no internet, no ghost writers...just you me and a proposal."

Aspen covered her mouth with her hands, tears beginning to trickle down her cheeks. Harper found her own eyes filling with responding emotions.

"I love you," Austin continued. "I love you more than I can express with or without help," he said with a smirk. "You're my rock.

You're the reason I've survived the blowback from my job, you're the reason I have a new job, you're the reason I wake up with a smile on my face and a bounce in my step."

Aspen reached out and cupped his cheek and Harper began to feel like she was intruding on an intimate moment. She glanced at Maeve, who pumped her eyebrows. Apparently, the sisters didn't have any trouble with it.

"I know what it's like to lose that light in my life and I never want to go through it again. I know that everyone refers to this corner as ours and I'm happy to keep going with that, which is why I had Harper paint your cakes. Those cakes are yours. They symbolize everything you are." He reached under the couch and pulled out a framed piece of paper. "And this is so we can put me up there with you."

Aspen took the frame and began to laugh through her tears. "I love you more than peanut butter, marshmallow surprise cake." She giggled and sniffed. "That's our cake," she rasped. "I made it with you in mind."

He nodded and cupped her face. "Which is why I'm going to ask you to keep making peanut butter, marshmallow surprise cake with me forever. Aspen, will you marry me? Will you help keep my days full of joy and my evenings full of sugary sweets?" He nodded to the frame. "Will you hang that on the wall and be my partner for the rest of my life?"

Harper put her clasped hands over her heart. What would it be like to have that kind of adoration aimed at her instead of listening to it spoken to someone else? Harper's heart ached with the desire for Mason to say those things to her. Could she ever be so lucky?

Clapping brought her out of her thoughts and she realized she had missed Aspen saying yes. At least, Harper assumed it was a yes, if the kiss Aspen and Austin were engaged in was anything to go by.

"Woo hoo!" Maeve hollered, followed by a very loud whistle.

Harper jerked to the side. "Whoa."

Maeve grinned. "Yeah. I've been practicing."

"I can't believe you guys were there the whole time!" Aspen said, wiping at her eyes and standing up.

"You were a little preoccupied," Estelle said wryly.

Harper held out her arms and hurried over. "Congrats," she whispered in her best friend's ear. "I'm so happy for you."

They pulled apart and Aspen positively glowed. "Thank you." She gave Harper another squeeze. "And thank you for the paintings. I LOVE them."

Harper smiled. "It was nothing."

"Of course, it wasn't." Aspen rolled her eyes. "Because you're amazing."

Harper just smiled and stepped back, letting everyone else squeal and celebrate the occasion. *If I was that amazing, I wouldn't be looking at another spring spent ogling a lumberjack from afar.* She shook her head. Now was not the time. This was a call to celebrate. Harper's nonexistent love life wasn't important right now. She clapped her hands loudly, getting everyone's attention. "Who wants cake?"

Laughter followed her call and slowly, they all worked their way to the kitchen. Harper was last as she wrestled with herself, but she was determined to stay focused. Aspen, Austin and cake were the subject of the moment. Nothing else. There would be time to sulk later. Right now, she had best friend duties to attend to and they were by far more important.

❦

Don't miss Harper's story next!
"The Sweetest Moment"

CPSIA information can be obtained
at www.ICGtesting.com
Printed in the USA
LVHW050006110322
713213LV00007B/423

9 781956 176223